THE PLOT TWIST

VICTORIA WALTERS

B
Boldwood

First published in Great Britain in 2024 by Boldwood Books Ltd.

Copyright © Victoria Walters, 2024

Cover Design by Alexandra Allden

Cover Photography: Shutterstock

The moral right of Victoria Walters to be identified as the author of this work has been asserted in accordance with the Copyright, Designs and Patents Act 1988.

All rights reserved. No part of this book may be reproduced in any form or by any electronic or mechanical means, including information storage and retrieval systems, without written permission from the author, except for the use of brief quotations in a book review.

This book is a work of fiction and, except in the case of historical fact, any resemblance to actual persons, living or dead, is purely coincidental.

Every effort has been made to obtain the necessary permissions with reference to copyright material, both illustrative and quoted. We apologise for any omissions in this respect and will be pleased to make the appropriate acknowledgements in any future edition.

A CIP catalogue record for this book is available from the British Library.

Paperback ISBN 978-1-83518-960-3

Large Print ISBN 978-1-83518-959-7

Hardback ISBN 978-1-83518-958-0

Ebook ISBN 978-1-83518-961-0

Kindle ISBN 978-1-83518-962-7

Audio CD ISBN 978-1-83518-953-5

MP3 CD ISBN 978-1-83518-954-2

Digital audio download ISBN 978-1-83518-956-6

Boldwood Books Ltd
23 Bowerdean Street
London SW6 3TN
www.boldwoodbooks.com

For all the romance readers

PROLOGUE

It was a rainy night in London and I took cover in a bookshop called Book Nook that I saw was still open. The name suited the shop. It was small and tucked away in a cobbled alley. It was dimly lit, warm and dry, and books lined the walls in a haphazard fashion.

Enjoying the cosiness, I took my time looking around. I noticed there was only one other customer in there with me – a tall, dark-haired man wearing a shirt with his sleeves pushed up, his nose literally stuck in a book. I had to weave past him to get to the romance section, my favourite, when he looked up and saw me.

'Oh, sorry, I always end up lost in my own world in here,' he said.

'I can see why. I can't believe I've never found this place before. It's a real gem.'

'One of my favourites in the city.' He smiled and showed off a dimple in his cheek, and I felt a weird need to make it appear again.

I carried on looking but he had my attention as much as the books. I saw him peeking at me over his book too. Then the owner called out to say he was closing so I picked up the book I'd been looking at – an old romance I'd never seen before in a gorgeous gold hardback edition – and followed dimple man to the till. He had a pile of nine books.

'Let me get yours,' he offered.

I raised an eyebrow. 'Why?'

I'd wrongfooted him. 'Um... why not?'

'I'm an independent woman who can buy her own books,' I said, but I couldn't help but smile at his panicked expression.

'Of course you are, but...' He looked around wildly then met the eyes of the bookshop owner behind the till. 'There's a discount if we buy ten books, right?' He gave the man a pleading look.

The owner laughed. 'Okay, I'll give you guys a ten per cent discount.'

They both looked at me expectantly.

'Unbelievable,' I said, shaking my head, but I handed the book over and got a winning smile from my fellow bookworm, flashing that dimple again.

God, he was cute.

After he'd paid, we left the shop. When we stepped outside, the rain had eased and the glistening pavement reflected the bright full moon above us.

'Thank you for my book,' I said, clutching it to my chest. 'You really didn't need to do that.'

'You're welcome.' There was that dimple again, but then he turned around, and the mystery man walked away before I could say anything else.

I sighed with disappointment and went home alone.

It wasn't until I opened up the book he had bought me that I saw he'd scribbled something on the first page. He must have done it when I'd been waiting for him to pay.

Dinner?

Then he'd written his name, Noah, and his phone number.

Breaking into a wide smile, understanding then why he'd wanted to pay for my book, I realised I'd just had a real life meetcute. In a bookshop! It was what a romance book lover's dreams were made of.

I grabbed my phone and messaged him just one word.

> Yes.

1

SIX YEARS LATER...

I was determined that my first day at Turn the Pages publishing company would be as good as possible.

I had no idea that it would be a spectacular disaster.

Everything started out smoothly enough. I woke up before my alarm as usual and got ready in the outfit I'd bought specially – a striped jumper, black trousers and ballet pumps, which made me feel smart and chic. Grabbing my handbag and my black blazer, I left my flat. I had plenty of time to make the journey from Islington to my new place of work and for once, the London weather was playing ball.

Autumn had wrapped itself over the city like an orange and gold blanket, and I was very relieved I was starting my new job in this season. I hated the stifling heat of summer in London. Autumn with its crisp sunny mornings like this one and the way the city became lit up with colour, the sounds of leaves crunching under my shoes, and the promise of evenings curled up with a book, hot chocolate and scented candle, always made me happy.

As I walked through the park near my flat, I could see in the distance the university that I had, until recently, worked at. My good mood improved further when I saw my best friend Liv waiting at the edge of the park, as we'd arranged last night, waving two take-away coffees at me.

'The nectar of the Gods,' I said gratefully when I reached her and took the iced latte. I didn't know how anyone could function in the morning without one.

'You need it for your first day,' she replied with a smile.

If we were both book characters then Liv looked like Elizabeth Bennet, with her dark hair and hazel eyes, whereas I resembled Alice in Wonderland, with my long blonde hair and blue eyes, and the fact that I always wore some kind of headband to keep it off my face. Today, I wore a pearl one.

'Stevie, you look lovely. Perfect first day outfit.'

Liv was much more of a fashionista than me so that made me smile. 'Why, thank you.'

'So, how are you feeling?'

We walked together towards the university where we had worked together. But for the first time since we met, Liv would be opening up the library and I would be heading in the opposite direction across London to where my new office was.

'Excited but nervous. It feels really strange to not be coming in there with you,' I said, nodding at the historic university building.

Liv grimaced. 'I'm going to miss you like crazy.'

'You won't be here for much longer though,' I said after I had taken a sip of the coffee. Liv had written a fabulous romance novel and had landed a literary agent for it so I was confident she'd have a book deal before long.

'I'm so proud of you for going after your dream,' she said as we paused by the stone steps that would take her into my former place of work.

'Thank you for encouraging me to do it,' I replied. I had been inspired by her writing her novel to finally apply for a job in publishing, something I had wanted pretty much ever since I'd walked into my first library as a child and read *Matilda*. I wanted to help bring new stories into the world, stories that would bring people the same joy they brought me. I checked the time on my phone. 'I better head for the Tube; you never know if there will be delays or not.'

'Okay, good luck – not that you need it,' she said, pulling me in for tight hug. 'It will be fabulous! As soon as you can, let me know how it's going, even if you have to sneak into the loos.'

'Of course. Try not to miss me too much today.'

'I'll have no one to gossip with but I'll try to survive,' she said with a heavy sigh, but she bucked up to give me a cheerful wave. 'Knock 'em dead!'

'I don't want to commit murder on my first day but I will try to channel that energy,' I told her with a laugh.

I watched Liv walk inside and I shook off the momentary urge to run in after her and stay where I was comfortable. I needed to do this – for past Stevie, who'd always dreamed of this day.

Metaphorically pulling up my big-girl pants, I took a deep breath and another sip of coffee, and set off for the Tube to start my new chapter.

* * *

After making my way across the city, I soon stood in front of my new place of employment. It was opposite The Shard in a sleek, glass building which, after the cosy library, was a little bit intimidating. Thankfully, the Tube had run smoothly and I had arrived much earlier than I needed to. It had been just over a month since I interviewed, but finally, my first day was here.

I walked around the block three times and then it was close enough to the time my new manager Annie had told me to come in for so I went through the revolving doors and up to the reception desk. I was directed to the tenth floor so I climbed into the lift and did that automatic thing of turning to look at myself in the mirror. I was never sure why lifts had to have mirrors because the lighting was always terrible and you always left them worried your make-up looked clown-like. My cheeks were definitely flushed but hopefully that was just down to the autumn breeze and not too much blusher.

Stepping out of the lift, I found myself across from the Turn the Pages reception. Through double doors to the side of the reception desk was the office, which was open-plan with big glass windows, and those grey carpet tiles that offices always seemed to have. But what had thrilled me when I first walked in for my interview, and what made me smile all over again today, was the floor-to-ceiling bookshelves packed with all the titles they published here.

Gazing up at the titles, my eyes instantly went to the ones I had read or wanted to read. Mostly romances. Anything with a pastel cover was right up my street. I couldn't wait to be able to read the new ones before anyone else.

As I was looking at the shelves in awe, I wasn't paying attention to the group of people hurrying past me, but when I decided I better stop gawking at books and go over to the desk, there didn't seem to be anyone manning reception. I leaned against it, wondering whether to just go on through to the office and find Annie myself, when a loud, urgent voice rang out.

'Mind!'

I quickly pulled my arms into my body as a man in a suit barged past carrying a cardboard box filled to the brim with books.

More people filed past me.

'Unbelievable – can we go to a tribunal, do you think?' a woman asked the group of people following her towards the lifts. 'After all our hard work...'

'The Shark was worse in person than his reputation...'

'He loves the power; you could see it on his face...'

'Can we sue?'

I was starting to get a bad feeling in the pit of my stomach. Then, relief shot through me as someone familiar came out from the main office floor.

'Annie!' I called, waving to the tall, grey-haired woman who had interviewed me. I straightened up and threw on what I hoped was my most competent smile. 'I'm so excited to...'

I trailed off as she stopped suddenly, her mouth falling open in horror at the sight of me. That was not a good sign.

'Oh God, Stevie, I'm so sorry,' she said, shaking her head.

'What's wrong?' I asked, nervous at the sad look on her face.

Annie gestured to another group of people stalking out of the double doors behind her. 'We've just all heard... the company has been bought by an American firm and they're restructuring. We've all been made redundant. Me included.'

I swallowed the huge lump that had appeared in my throat with difficulty. 'You're... leaving?'

'I just can't believe they've done this.' She started to walk towards the lifts again. 'I'm sorry. You should go in and see what they want to do with you.'

'What? But Annie, you hired me and you ran the department and...'

She shrugged bitterly as she joined the queue for the lift. 'That evidently means nothing. Good luck, Stevie.'

'You'll need it,' a man added darkly.

I turned to the double doors, unsure whether I wanted to even go in and see what my fate was to be. I couldn't be fired on my first day, could I? Would the library take me back if I was? I looked back and saw Annie getting into the lift with her colleagues, all wearing expressions varying from devastated to pissed off.

As I summoned up the courage to find out what this new

company wanted to do with me, I pushed open the double doors and surveyed an office in utter chaos. People were putting belongings into boxes, phones were ringing incessantly, doors to offices slammed and reopened, someone was crying in the corner, and outside, I could see it had started to pour with rain.

This had to be the worst first day of all time.

I didn't know in that moment it was about to get even worse.

2

'Excuse me,' I said loudly over the noise in the office to a woman leaning against a desk sipping a coffee. She didn't look upset or furious so maybe she hadn't been made redundant. 'I'm supposed to be starting today and I have no idea what's going on.'

She grimaced. 'Bloody hell, talk about the worst day to join us, eh?' She came over and held out her hand and gave mine a firm shake. 'I'm Gita. I'm editorial director here. You're joining us in publicity?'

I nodded. 'Annie Leon hired me. I'm Stevie.'

She clucked her tongue. 'Poor Annie, she's been here years. They're joining up marketing, sales and publicity so I think they want some new blood on board. Until they sort everything out, the new boss is running everything and...' She leaned in close. 'His nickname in the industry is The Shark so we're all pretty shaken up.'

'The Shark?' I gulped. That did not sound at all promising.

Gita nodded towards a door at the end of the open-plan office. 'He's been calling us in one by one. I made the cut, thank God, but I can't believe how many haven't. If you can handle it, I'd go in there straight away so you know where you stand.' Someone called her name. 'Good luck,' she said and headed off to talk to a group of her colleagues.

I turned towards the ominous office door ahead of me. I was half inclined to make myself a cup of coffee and wait a few hours but I knew that was a bad idea. If I was going to be told to leave, it was better to know straight away and save myself a nervous wait. Like most things in life, ripping off the plaster was usually the best option so I walked across the floor towards The Shark's office, singing the *Jaws* theme in my head, which actually diffused the tension in my body a little bit.

The door burst open as I approached and I stopped as a woman rushed out, her mascara smudged from tears. God. This really was awful. Did I even want to work here any more? The woman hurried off and left The Shark's office door open so I supposed I had no excuse not to find out my fate.

I exhaled and started walking again up to the door. Even though it was open, I knocked anyway and heard a gruff 'enter'.

As I rounded the door, I saw a tall figure with his back to me staring out of the window at the rain. The office was bare expect for a desk, chair and an empty bookcase. It looked like it had been stripped for him to take it over. I wondered who had had to vacate it for him, and whether The Shark felt guilty at all about it.

When he still didn't turn around straight away, I cleared my throat.

'Hi, this is my first day here and I'm wondering whether I should just turn around and go home or not?' I asked in my boldest tone, because I had a sense that someone called The Shark didn't do BS. 'Oh, and I'm Stephanie Phillips but everyone calls me—'

'Stevie,' he supplied for me.

I frowned, wondering how he knew that. Then he turned around.

It was like it was happening in slow motion. But not like a sexy slow-motion music video featuring a shirtless man drizzled in oil, but in a this is so huge, it has to happen in an excruciatingly slow way so you know that everything in your life is about to change, way.

Finally, the turn was complete and my mouth fell open.

'Oh my God,' I said as I recognised The Shark. And not because of his so-called fearsome reputation in the industry. This recognition was personal. Very personal.

He met my gaze. 'Hi, Stevie,' he said calmly.

'Hi, Stevie?' I repeated, not at all calmly. 'This... can't be happening?' I asked, addressing the universe as much as him.

He sighed. 'It is. I joined this morning. I am your new boss.'

A *dun dun dunnnnnn* sound rang out in my head as my eyes flicked to the name on the desk which I hadn't noticed when I came in. Noah Anderson. I looked back at the man in front of me as he waited patiently for me to get my head around this situation. But I doubted that I ever would.

Realising I couldn't yet speak, Noah shifted on his feet and put a hand in his pocket then took it out again. 'I know this is a shock...'

'That's an understatement,' I was able to cough out. My pulse was speeding up by the second. I wondered if there was any part of my body that hadn't turned red or sweaty. I doubted it.

He nodded. 'I know. It all happened so quickly and I didn't even know you'd been hired until I got here this morning. HR here has been dealing with everything directly with HR in New York.' He cleared his throat. 'You're not on the redundancy list. The plan is to get a sense of what is needed here so in the meantime, you will need to step up and take over publicity. It would be great for your career, of course, but you need to think about it. Because obviously, I will now be your manager. So, I understand if...' His coolly delivered speech faltered ever-so slightly. '...you'd rather not.'

My eyebrows shot up. If I'd rather not? I wanted to scream at him, *Hell no, I would very much rather not!* and turn and run out of this office, leaving a cartoon character-shaped hole in the wall. But this was my dream job. And here he was telling me that I almost had a promotion straight away. I couldn't believe this was happening.

'I don't know what to say,' I admitted.

'Think it over tonight. Go home now and come and see me in the morning with your decision.' He turned around to look out at the rain again, signalling that our conversation was over.

I was able to really look at him then, now his eyes were no longer on me. Noah with his tall and slim frame, his short jet-black hair, his dark-rimmed glasses that shielded eyes the colour of chocolate, that dimple in his right cheek when he smiled, the sleeves of his shirt that were always rolled up, the line of stubble around his chin – he looked the same. A tiny bit older and rougher around the edges, and he'd always been clean shaven when I had known him, but annoyingly, the stubble... it looked good. He looked good. He even smelled good. It was a new scent. Deeper. Muskier. Sexier...

Without warning, my body reminded me of the nights I'd been in his arms. How his body had felt next to mine. The way his touch made me...

Quickly, I shook my head to clear it of those kinds of thoughts. Noah might have been the best sex of my life. We might have been that close once but we sure as hell were not now.

And this sexy appearance of his was all a lie. He was goodlooking on the outside but not on the inside. I knew the space in the centre of his chest was empty where his heart should have been.

Because he might be The Shark to everyone in this office, but to me he was the man who had broken my heart.

I swallowed and turned to go, shook to my very core that I was seeing my ex-boyfriend again. After all this time. And that he was now my boss. The universe really did have a sick sense of humour.

I walked out and closed the door behind me, and then I kept on walking. Out of the office and through reception, into the lift, like I was in some kind of trance, my legs moving of their own accord. I walked out of the main revolving doors into the rain and I kept on walking. My mind wouldn't focus on anything. I had honestly never been so shaken by something before in my life.

No, that was a lie. It had happened once before.

The day Noah walked away from me.

And now, five years later, he was suddenly back again.

Fuck my life.

3

When I realised where I had walked to, I pushed open the doors and leaned against the wall, taking a breath. I had trekked all across London back to the place where I felt most like myself. Probably because seeing Noah again had made me feel suddenly lost.

I walked down the university corridor and through the double doors of the library and breathed in the smell of old books. There was nothing I loved more. I'd worked in libraries since I left university and took this job two years ago. I had really enjoyed working here but now finally, I had made the move I'd always wanted to, into publishing, and it had so far gone completely wrong. Was I cursed or something?

'Stevie, what are you doing here?' Liv poked her head around a stack of books as I walked in. 'You're soaked. Are you okay?'

'Not really, no. Don't suppose you're due a break? I need a coffee with about four extra shots in it,' I said hopefully. I brushed my fingers across the shelf and spines of the books that I knew better than the back of my hand.

'Definitely,' Liv said. She went over to the desk to tell Jamal she was taking a break then she hooked an arm through mine and steered me towards the university cafeteria. Instructing me to find a seat, Liv went off to the coffee stand. I walked to the corner table, hoping no other ex-colleagues would spot us and try to join, and waited for her to return. She came back with two ice coffees and when I took a sip of mine, I gratefully tasted the extra shots she'd added.

After I had taken another sip, I could face speaking. 'I walked in and the office was in chaos. The company has been taken over and they're restructuring so loads of people have been made redundant including Annie, the woman who hired me and who I thought was going to be my boss.'

Liv grimaced. 'That's awful. Have they let you go?'

'They told me to think about whether I want to come back and to tell them tomorrow. Tell him, I mean. My new boss.' I looked at Liv across the table. 'Who also happens to be my ex-boyfriend.'

She gasped. 'What? No! Which one?'

'You remember me telling you about the boyfriend I had before I started working here, the one who took a job in New York and who I never heard from again? Noah Anderson. Who, I might add, is nicknamed The Shark in publishing. Which is pretty damn perfect, if you ask me.'

'I can't believe it. Oh, Stevie, I'm sorry. That is... shit.'

I nodded. 'Shit is right. He just stood there saying they wanted me to stay, to think it over, no apology, no explanation, nothing, waltzing right back into my life like nothing happened. Like he hadn't broken my heart!' I cried.

Now the shock of Noah standing in front of me in that office was wearing off, anger was taking its place. He had hurt me so much. We'd been together for just over a year after meeting in a bookshop. I had thought it was the perfect romantic meeting. And not only did he love books, but he worked in publishing too. I thought I'd finally found the man of my dreams. Turned out, he'd been a nightmare instead.

'So, what, am I supposed to just be cold and professional like him? Act like we didn't know everything about each other once upon a time?'

'I can't believe he didn't say anything about the past.'

'No apology, just said he understood if I'd rather not work there with him. Rather not!' I took a gulp of coffee. 'I would rather stab myself with hot pokers! But...'

'But this is your dream job,' Liv supplied. She knew how much getting this job had meant to me. Like me, she'd always had a dream; hers was to write a book. And so, I knew she understood.

'It was like we had meant nothing,' I said, my voice smaller than I wanted it to be.

'No way,' she said firmly. 'He loved you once. There was no way he couldn't have.'

I smiled. 'Well, that's very sweet but even if he didn't lie for the whole year we were together, he left me in the end so he didn't love me any more then.' I sighed. 'This summer, I decided that I was going to focus on my career. I deleted my dating apps, I decided against any more shit dates that didn't go anywhere, or the ones who slept with me only to ghost me straight after. How has that decision turned into working with my ex-boyfriend?'

'No, you're right,' Liv said. 'You should stick to the plan. Focus on your career. Screw Noah. You're better off without him and I bet he regretted leaving you. You're the winner here.'

'I don't think so but I appreciate the pep talk.' I sat up straighter. 'You're right about one thing though. Why should I let Noah chase me away from the job I've wanted since I was a kid? This is young bookworm Stevie's moment. And Noah is not going to put me off.'

Liv beamed at me. 'So, you'll go back?'

'It took me years to land a job in publishing. And Noah said that

I will be practically running publicity for now. So that will get me some great experience for my CV. I will treat Noah as my boss, and my boss only. I will act like we didn't know each other before. I won't mention our relationship at all,' I said emphatically.

'And you could always look for another job in six months,' Liv said.

I tried to think about the idea of working with Noah for even six months and it made my confidence shake a little bit. I tried to not remember how upset I had been watching him walk away from me the day he told me he was going to New York, but it was imprinted on my heart. Time heals wounds, sure, but it doesn't make you forget. And Noah hadn't been forgotten no matter how hard I tried. It was not going to be easy to work together and act like I hadn't been hurt by him. But what was the alternative?

'You're right. I can use this to get experience under my belt then move on as soon as I can.' Six months was nothing when you thought about the fact I'd survived five years without him. I nodded. 'This was a real shock but I can do this, can't I?'

'Yes, you can,' Liv agreed firmly. 'This job is what you've always wanted. It doesn't matter that Noah's there; you'll probably hardly see him if he's the boss anyway – he'll be busy all the time, under pressure as it's all new... and he'll steer clear of you too, surely?'

'Let's hope so.'

We finished our coffees and Liv had to go back to work. I went outside and thankfully saw the rain had eased, so I walked back to my flat and when I let myself in and I was alone again, my bravado wavered a little bit. I leaned against the wall and tried to slow my heartbeat down.

The sight of my flat helped a little bit. I'd moved in here soon after Noah had left. Before that, I'd shared with two other girls. Once I started seeing Noah, I'd spent more time at his place than at home. So it had been healing to have a space all to myself to try to get over him. I had to make a new life for myself, and I had done it. Even if this flat did resemble a shoe-box. I rented it from a family friend who let me pay well below the average rent in Islington because they wanted someone they knew and trusted.

The flat was just one main room with a tiny kitchen and lounge area with room for just one sofa and a TV then my bedroom with bathroom attached. I liked to think of it as cosy but that really was being kind. Still, it was all mine and it allowed me to live in Islington, which I loved.

I peeled off my work clothes, pulled on a comfy loungewear set and headed into the kitchen area to make something to eat. Before I left this morning, I'd been too hyped up for my first day to eat and now I was starving. I made a bacon sandwich then curled up on the sofa to eat it. I pulled my phone onto my lap and, knowing it was better to be armed with as much information as I could find before I faced work again, I googled the takeover of Turn the Pages, and specifically Noah Anderson, our new CEO.

> Noah rapidly rose through the ranks of US publishing giant Matthews & Wood Publishing from editor to publisher and then deputy CEO. Recent acquisition Turn the Pages is the UK's third most successful publishing company and the takeover will net Matthews & Wood Publishing shareholders millions. Anderson has been given the job of CEO, moving back to London to take over the company, and having earned a ruthless reputation for getting results. Industry insiders predict he will take the publishing company all the way to the top.

I winced at the mention of Noah's American career, knowing that it started when he left me in London. And then I felt angry. The article called him Noah Anderson and there was no mention of the reason he worked for Matthews & Wood Publishing. Despite trying not to, our relationship flashed through my mind.

After we'd met in the bookshop, Noah had swept me up in romance and I'd fallen fast. It had been a whirlwind of dinners and drinks, book shopping and walks by the river on a Sunday, and sleeping over at his flat. His flat had a river view and he worked at a small publishing company as an editorial assistant – a job I could only dream of. He had felt like everything I wanted.

The only thing I had wondered about was, despite the fact Noah had regularly met my family and got on with them brilliantly, I'd never met his. He told me they weren't close but I was worried he didn't think I was good enough to introduce to them.

So when he told me that he was leaving for New York to start working at his father's publishing firm over there, it all clicked into place. Why he had such a lovely flat working in a junior role in publishing, why he'd not told me anything about his parents. His father was rich and powerful and Matthews & Wood Publishing, the company he left me for, was owned by him. Because Noah Anderson used his mother's maiden name at work to avoid accusations of nepotism. But he was, in fact, Noah Matthews.

I shook off my bitterness about Noah's lie and scrolled to the next article in the Google search results.

> Staff at Turn the Pages had a huge shock this morning when the takeover by Matthews & Wood Publishing was suddenly announced. Everyone outside of the board of directors was unaware the company was even in takeover discussions, and many were handed redundancies as the company looks to restructure and bring over employees from America to make changes and grow the business.

A shock was an understatement, I thought. I felt so sorry for everyone who had been given their marching orders so abruptly. Including Annie. She had seemed like someone I could learn so much from. Now, I had no idea what working there would look like.

I looked at one more article.

> Noah Anderson, New York's most eligible bachelor, is moving to London to take over as CEO of publishing company Turn the Pages.

I threw my phone down. I did not want to know about his personal life, although it did help a little bit to know he hadn't got married since he left me. And I hadn't either. My heart – left pretty fragile by him, I'm not going to lie – hadn't found anyone to fall for. I had used dating apps, said yes to party invites, gone to London's hottest bars and clubs, but despite going on my fair share of dates, there had been no one I'd really clicked with – certainly no one that I'd fallen in love with. So I had decided to concentrate on my career, and it looked like he had too.

I decided to give myself one nostalgic trip down memory lane before waking up tomorrow as a cool cucumber who would treat Noah as her boss, and her boss alone. I scrolled back on my phone to the photos of our time together which I had not been able to bring myself to delete.

Pausing when I reached one of my favourites, I stared at the screen. A selfie Noah had snapped of us looked back at me. We'd been in bed together in his dreamy London flat. It was the morning after the first time we'd slept together.

God, I remember that night so vividly, even now. Noah had taken me by surprise in the bedroom, telling me what to do in a way that turned me on so much, I had had the best orgasm of my life.

I want you on top of me so I can watch you riding me. I'm going to fuck you so good, you'll never want to be with anyone else.

It had been so hot. No man had ever been like that with me and I'd loved it. We had barely slept. We couldn't get enough of one another. When we finally did sleep, we woke up snuggled together and that's when he took that picture. In it, we're smiling at one another as if we're each other's whole world.

When had he decided that was no longer the case?

Clicking my phone to the lock screen, I decided that whatever sick joke the universe was playing on me, I was not going to let it ruin my new career. I just had to get through six months of pretending Noah meant nothing to me and then I could find a new job.

I could do this.

I *had* to do this.

Because there was no way I was letting him know how much I'd missed him these past five years. Or how much I had loved him, pretty much as soon as we'd met in that bloody bookshop. I'd spent a lifetime reading romances and finally, I'd met my leading man. I thought I was about to get my happy ending. But real life wasn't like books. And Noah had decided I wasn't the one.

He'd walked away from me, but this time, I would walk away from him.

4

My parents FaceTimed me on the way to work the following morning, wanting to know how my first day had gone. I was due to have dinner with them Friday night so for now, I fudged the details, only telling them about the shock of redundancies at Turn the Pages and having to work under a new boss. I left out the part that my new boss was my ex-boyfriend.

The thing was, Liv had never met Noah. She hadn't known us together – I wasn't friends with her back then – but my parents had. Like me, they remembered it all. They knew how much happiness meeting Noah had brought me and how I'd been heartbroken when he moved away. They wouldn't be so quick to support me going back to work under him as Liv had been, I knew, so for now I lied by omission and decided I'd wait to speak to them about it face-to-face at the end of the week.

If I could keep my nerve and stay at my new job until then.

At least today I was prepared for what I was going to face. I walked in through the doors to the open-plan office and took in the atmosphere. People who hadn't lost their jobs yesterday had evidentially decided that coming in early was the best plan, so everyone was at their desks and the room resembled a tomb. Nothing like the office had been when I came for my interview – it had been buzzy and seemed fun then.

It was clear that Noah still had the power to put a pin in happiness.

I went to the coffee station and made myself a strong one, taking a long gulp before I marched through the office towards Noah's closed office door, not giving myself a chance to chicken out of this. Eyes followed my walk and I knew everyone was wondering what I was doing.

When I knocked on his door, I heard a muffled 'enter' so I went in and saw Noah was sat behind his desk. The woman I'd met yesterday, Gita, was standing by the door.

Noah's eyes moved to me then back to her. His face remained expressionless so I set my mouth in a hard line, determined to be as emotionless at seeing him as he was with me. He was wearing a suit and tie today and it looked good on him. I was pleased I'd put on my pleated dress and my favourite headband for extra confidence.

Noah continued talking to Gita as if I wasn't there though, which was annoying.

'I understand that everyone feels unsettled but I need people to get on board. We don't have time to keep going over what happened yesterday. I want everyone at a staff meeting in the boardroom now, and I want no complaints. We have a job to get on with,' he told her. 'Thank you,' he added in a dismissive tone.

Gita's eyes slid to me. 'I'll tell everyone,' she said, her voice making it clear she'd rather do anything but. She mouthed 'Jesus' to me as she slipped out and closed the door, a little bit more firmly than was needed. I didn't blame her.

I stared in disbelief as Noah typed something on his laptop, clearly feeling like I could wait until he was ready. He was certainly living up to his The Shark reputation. A reputation completely at odds with the man I had fallen in love with.

'Are you serious?' I burst out after thirty seconds of him ignoring me.

Noah finally looked up and raised an eyebrow. 'Excuse me?'

'You're just going to act like I'm not here?'

'I have a lot going on...'

'I don't care,' I snapped. 'You don't have to be this rude to everyone. We all had a big shock yesterday and people lost their jobs. A little bit of empathy wouldn't go amiss, would it?' I folded my arms across my chest. 'I'm staying. This is my dream job and I'm not going to let you ruin it for me. But I'm also not going to stay silent when you're acting like a...' I trailed off, my bravado faltering at the hard stare he was giving me.

'Oh, don't stop now, Stevie. Tell me what I'm acting like. I'm all ears,' he said, his dark eyes behind those glasses boring into mine. Even his voice sounded different. He had been born in London but I knew his mother was American, and living and working in New York these past few years had given him a slight New York lilt to his accent. His tone sounded deeper and harsher too.

I looked back at him defiantly. I didn't enjoy confrontation but I had longed for the chance to tell Noah Anderson exactly what I thought of him.

'A dick,' I replied.

Noah spluttered a little bit.

'I'll see you in the meeting,' I said as haughtily as I could manage, and with a nod I walked out, shutting the door behind me, Noah's shocked face the last thing I saw. I couldn't help but feel a bit pleased at wrong-footing him like that. I knew that I'd planned to act like he meant nothing to me but really, was there a need to treat everyone so badly? Nope. I was probably skating on thin ice now but I wasn't sorry I had told him what I thought.

The Plot Twist

Gita was waiting for me. 'Have you ever met someone both so gorgeous and so unbelievably grumpy?'

There was no way on earth I was going to admit to even knowing Noah, let alone having been in a relationship with him. No one here would want to be friends with me once they knew that. I wasn't sure I would have any respect for me either based on how he was acting now.

'It's very unfair,' I agreed. 'So, where do I sit?'

'There's a free spot behind me,' she said, pulling me along with her. Then she told everyone about the boardroom meeting. There were murmurs of dissent but they all got up and followed her.

My new desk was by the window, which cheered me up a bit. After leaving my things on my chair, I trailed after the others as we walked towards the boardroom, all of us pretty fearful of what the new boss was going to say.

I walked in to find the twenty-five members of staff left were either sitting around the long table or lined up around the walls. I joined a group against the wall.

'Why does this feel like I'm back at school?' a woman with gorgeous red hair leaned over to ask.

'Like we've been called to see the headmaster,' a man next to me agreed.

I wasn't really able to relate as I had never been in trouble at school but I knew what they meant. The energy in the room was like we were about to be told off. I leaned against the wall and hoped we could escape soon.

Noah swept in then. All conversations ceased as he walked to the front of the room by the only empty chair left. He didn't sit down, but looked around at us. He'd taken off his jacket and pushed back his sleeves once again, like he always used to. I hated that the fact he did that showed he hadn't completely changed from the man I had known. I'd rather believed he had.

'Thank you for coming,' Noah said, clearing his throat. 'I understand that it has come as a shock to you – the takeover and me becoming CEO,' he said, his voice clear and strong in the silent room. 'But this is a crucial time. We have to prove ourselves. I know there are a lot of rumours and I can confirm this company was in trouble before Matthews & Wood Publishing bought it. The board of directors are keen to turn this into a successful arm of the business, and I am determined that we can do that. I hope you feel the same way. If not, then you should leave.'

There were mutterings at that but Noah ignored them and continued.

'I'm not trying to be harsh or mean or act like a dick,' he continued, his eyes finding mine. His gaze sent a jolt of electricity through me, which I did not want. I looked away quickly. 'But all our jobs are on the line. I'm not someone who sugar-coats anything. What's the point? We have six months to show enough improvement or we will be shut down.'

5

People broke out into conversations then, everyone talking over one another in shock. So, I had to put up with Noah and then I might lose my job in six months anyway! Bloody fantastic. And talk about pressure for us all! It did explain Noah's no-nonsense attitude a little bit more. He had to prove himself here. His job was on the line as well as ours. I reluctantly returned my eyes to him. He ran a hand through his hair. Maybe I was the only one who saw it shake slightly. I didn't feel sympathy but it made a little more sense out of everything that had happened in the past twenty-four hours.

Noah held up a hand. 'Okay, I know it's a shock to hear that but like I said, we don't have time to whinge about it. We need to get on with saving the company. I will be meeting next with each team to talk about what projects take priority and what we can start doing to turn things around. I've emailed the meeting times to you all. For now, I'll be head of sales, marketing and publicity so I will lead that meeting next. If you are part of those teams, stay in the boardroom please. Thank you.' He sat down and waited for everyone to sort themselves.

With much grumbling and shuffling, people filed out of the room and my colleagues in sales, marketing and publicity stayed with me. I sat down opposite Noah and wondered whether he cared that everyone in the room hated him or whether he saw this as just all business, not personal. I was sure old Noah would have hated upsetting everyone but maybe five years in New York had changed him. That thought made it easier to see him now as just my boss.

'I better redo my CV tonight,' the redhaired women muttered as she sat down next to me.

'Okay,' Noah said then, looking at the six people left in the room. 'As you can see, we lost a few people yesterday including Annie Leon who's been running this department. It was felt that things needed particularly shaking up in this area so we can increase our profits. Let's start with names and jobs and then what projects should be taking priority.'

He waited expectantly.

The woman beside me spoke up first. 'I'm Emily. I'm the marketing executive.' She seemed about ten years older than me and her red hair fell thickly over her shoulders.

'Paul, sales manager,' said a man in his late forties, the only one other than Noah wearing a suit. He had an accent that would make the King proud. I tried not to feel intimidated by that.

'Lewis, sales executive,' a younger guy with spikey hair said quickly.

'Aaliyah – marketing assistant,' the youngest in the room said. She wore a dress with books on – I'd have to ask her where she got it because I needed it.

Everyone looked at me expectantly. 'Stevie, publicity executive,' I said.

'Stevie is the only member of the publicity team for now. Until it's decided what we are going to do with the team, I will take on the role of publicity manager,' Noah said, avoiding my gaze. So, he wasn't going to be a hands-off boss like Liv and I had hoped for; I would be working in publicity with him? I wavered in my decision to stay. 'Okay, what are your priorities at the moment?'

'Well, the next title to come out is Deborah Day's new book, *Bitten*, and that's slotted in Halloween week,' Emily said. She sighed and the others looked down at the table. 'She's not been very happy with how things are going,' she added, shifting uncomfortably in her seat.

'Deborah Day?' Noah's eyes drifted to mine. I knew he knew she was one of my all-time favourite authors. I tried not to react to his gaze.

'She writes romance,' Emily said.

'Brilliant romance,' I said without thinking.

Paul looked across at me. 'You're a fan?' The way he spoke made it sound like he was suggesting I had poor taste.

'She was my gateway romance book.'

He raised an eyebrow. 'Gateway?'

All eyes were on me now and I wished I'd kept my mouth shut but I ploughed on. 'The first romance book I read,' I explained. 'My mum loved her. *Loves* her. Her books are classics in the genre.'

Noah nodded. 'I've read a couple.' There were a few shocked looks at that, me included. I didn't remember Noah ever reading romance when we were together. 'She's a big name so why isn't she happy?'

'She *was* a big name,' Paul corrected. 'Her latest books haven't been doing that well. She has some dedicated fans but that's it. She keeps saying she should be on the bestseller list but her books aren't seen as fresh.'

'And she's quite... demanding,' Emily said carefully. 'Wanting a huge budget for publicity and advertising but her sales just aren't good enough to warrant it. So, at her last meeting with us...' She trailed off.

'She got quite angry,' Aaliyah said. 'Her agent too. They kind of stormed out.'

'That's not good,' Noah said sharply. 'We don't want her to create negative publicity for us, especially after all the news about the takeover.'

'I don't understand why her books aren't doing well,' I said. 'They are classics. Everyone who reads romance has read one. We always had them stocked in the libraries I worked in. I used to love her books.'

'When was the last time you bought one though?' Emily asked me gently.

I thought that over. I had seen some of the classic ones in the university library, although they weren't taken out much, just sometimes for English Literature when they did a romance module, and my mum had some at home, but Emily was right – I hadn't paid much attention to her newer books actually.

'Oh, I can't even remember,' I admitted. 'I suppose I call her one of my favourite authors but then don't keep up to date with what she's writing now.'

Emily nodded. 'Exactly. You're not alone in that. She's not seen as fashionable now. There are newer, fresher authors in the market that younger readers especially prefer. Her books would never be talked about on TikTok, for example. We can't change minds. She's just not trendy now.' Emily shrugged. 'She won't accept it though and is threatening to leave us if the book doesn't hit the bestseller list. Which I really don't think it will.'

'We've kind of run out of ideas,' Aaliyah admitted.

'What a shame,' I said, feeling bad for Deborah and all the romance readers who had fallen in love with her books years ago. 'What's her new book about?'

'It's a vampire romance,' Emily said. 'Like I said. Not trendy.'

'But I love a vampire romance,' I said. All eyes turned to me again. I didn't think I was particularity endearing myself to my new colleagues but I was confused. 'And we haven't had a big one for ages.'

'Because there isn't any demand,' Paul told me shortly.

'*Twilight* fans are now my age or older,' I said. 'We deserve a new one.' Paul glared at me but I wasn't going to let a man stop me giving my opinion. I shrugged. 'I'm just saying, I would buy a new one if I saw it in a bookshop.'

'It's hard with romance,' Emily said. 'We don't get much help in the press because they prefer other genres so we rely on social media and building a buzz with romance readers and they just don't see Deborah Day as someone they would want to read.'

'Ugh,' I said, shaking my head. 'Romance is never respected like it should be.'

Paul sighed. 'I think we should focus on our other books,' he said to Noah, ignoring me.

This made me think about one of my other exes. He thought my reading taste was inferior to his because I exclusively read love stories. I hated the way the genre could be looked down on sometimes.

'I'll do it,' I said, before Noah could speak.

'Do what?' Noah enquired with an edge to his tone.

I got the sense the table were pissed off by me but I didn't care. I had loved romance my whole life and no one was going to make me feel guilty or ashamed about it. And poor Deborah Day clearly was at the end of her tether too.

'I'll take over all the publicity for it, and I'll make the book a hit,' I declared.

I swore I heard Paul snort.

'I'm not sure...' Emily began.

Noah turned to me. 'You can handle that, Stevie?'

'Of course,' I said, flinging him my fiercest look.

'Okay.' He tapped his pen against the table. 'It sounds like Deborah is dissatisfied with how we are handling her books and you guys aren't sure what to do with them,' he said, giving the group a piercing look. 'But Stevie thinks she knows what will work. So, I'm moving you all off the campaign. Stevie will take over Deborah Day with my assistance and we will create a new publicity plan for the book. Everyone else, write a list of what you're currently working on and email it to me by the end of the day please and I'll get back to you as to what to focus on. Thank you.'

Noah got up without waiting for a response from us and swept out of the boardroom.

I watched him go, suddenly wondering what my big mouth had got me into. I'd be taking over the book and he'd be working with me on it? Oh, hell.

'I'll be working on it with Noah?' I said out loud.

Paul sniggered. 'That didn't go the way you planned, did it?'

'You better join me in rewriting your CV,' Emily said.

I scooped up my things and trailed after the team but instead of joining them in the office, I detoured to Noah's room again. The door was open this time so I edged in. Noah was facing the window, seemingly lost in thought. I cleared my throat. 'Uh, did you mean what you said about us working on Deborah's book campaign together?' I asked hesitantly.

Noah turned around. 'Yes. I didn't say anything in there but Matthews & Wood Publishing need a big result and fast. If you think Day is our best shot then let's go for it. But Stevie, this has to work.'

I swallowed. 'Okay. Well, I think we can do it.'

Noah shook his head. 'No thinking. We *have* to do it. So, are you okay with working with me on this even if you do think I'm a dick?'

His mouth twitched slightly and I got a glimpse of the dimple in his cheek. It was still cute, damn it.

'If you're fine with it then I am,' I replied as breezily as I could manage.

'Why wouldn't I be?' he said dismissively.

Was he baiting me? My eyes narrowed.

'No reason at all,' I said slowly.

I couldn't believe he was acting like nothing had happened between us but there was no way I was going to break first. If this was a game Noah wanted to play then I was going to win it.

'Just let me know when you want to start. Boss,' I said, adding the word with as much sarcasm as my voice could carry, then I left his office again. Honestly, I was exhausted and it was only just heading for lunch time. I wasn't sure if I'd make it through six months doing this dance with Noah.

'Stevie, do you want to read over the current publicity plan for Deborah Day?' Emily called as I approached my desk. She sat in front of me.

'Great idea,' I said, grateful for anything to take my mind off Noah and us now working together on this project. 'Also, can I read *Bitten*?'

'Sure. Noah's asked for a copy too. He wants it printed out.' She rolled her eyes.

'I'll do it,' I said, happy to have tasks to fill the day. I supposed it didn't bother Noah as he was more than over me but the thought of having to work in close proximity to him was making my heart beat hard in my chest. Not because I was attracted to his new demanding and curt persona but because the memories of that year we spent together were always close to bubbling up, and seeing him again meant it was impossible to push them back down as I was usually able to. It was annoying, especially when I was determined my focus should be on my job. And now I'd given myself this huge project, I had to make sure Noah didn't distract me.

The problem was, we were now working on a romance book together.

I really should have thought that through.

6

When I looked up later, I was surprised to see the office floor around me was empty. Most of my colleagues had gone home while I was reading. Getting lost in a good book was the best feeling though. I'd started reading *Bitten*, and I was completely hooked already. This was definitely the vampire romance that had been missing from my life.

Seeing I better head home, I reluctantly stopped reading then remembered I needed to give Noah a copy of the book before I left. So I grabbed my jacket and slung it over my arm with my bag, the manuscript and publicity plan I'd printed out for Noah, and knocked on his office door.

I went in and he looked up with a start, checking his watch.

'Oh, it's six thirty already,' he said.

Another jolt from the past. He was the only man my age that always wore and checked his watch for the time, and not his phone.

'Here's the manuscript and publicity plan. I started reading *Bitten*, and OMG, they are all crazy for not wanting to push this book. It's brilliant and it should be a success. Every romance lover I know would want this. And the vampire love interest, I only have one word,' I said, getting carried away without meaning to. 'And that is SWOON.'

Noah's mouth twitched again. 'Swoon. I haven't heard that as an adjective before.'

I walked over to his desk and held out the stack of paper for him. 'You'll know what I mean if you read it. Well, not that a male vampire will make you swoon but you'll see why I'm already in love with him.'

'I remember you had a lot of book boyfriends,' Noah said.

'Fictional men can't let you down,' I replied.

Noah eyed me and started to say something, but I pushed the manuscript into his hands. He looked down at my bare wrist. He gently held it to stop me pulling it back. I let out a little gasp at the sudden contact. Noah heard and dropped my wrist immediately.

'You got a tattoo,' he said, so softly I only just heard him.

My heart had sped up at his touch and I hated it. I lifted my wrist to show him, making sure I didn't touch him again. I could still feel his skin against mine. Muscle memory had crept in and I remembered how his touch had the power to make me melt. It had been a long time since I'd been with anyone who could make my knees tremble just by touching my wrist. I was furious at my traitorous body for the way it had reacted.

Noah looked at the tattoo. It was of a book with flowers coming out of the pages.

'Of course it's of a book. When did you get it?' he asked, keeping his eyes on the tattoo, which I was relieved about because I was certain eye contact right now would cause my pulse to speed up even more.

'A week after you left,' I said, forcing the words out because part of me didn't want to admit it. But he'd remembered I hadn't had a

The Plot Twist

tattoo when we were together. At last, we were acknowledging we had known each other once.

Noah slowly looked up at me and I drew my wrist into my body.

'I see,' he said.

I stared at him. What did he see, exactly?

'Well.' Noah put the paperwork on his desk and turned away from me. 'Thank you for this. I'll read it tonight and then maybe we can meet and make a plan for what we can do to make this book a hit. Good evening, Stevie.'

'Goodnight, Noah,' I echoed, trying to sound as calm as he'd been even if inside I was freaking out, then I spun around and rushed out, not caring if he noticed because I needed to get away from him. And fast.

I left the office and frantically hit the call button for the lift. The doors opened quickly, thank God, so I slunk in, hit the ground floor button and leaned against the mirror with a sigh. How could my body betray me like that?

But then again, it always had when it came to Noah. From the first night we'd met right up until the last when I'd thought the heart he had jump-started might break down forever.

The memory of Noah saying goodbye five years ago slipped into my mind even though I really didn't want it to.

'I am moving to New York.' He had said this out-of-the-blue sentence as we sat on a park bench together. 'My family need me.'

I'd stared at him in disbelief. 'But I need you,' I said. I had thought our future was together.

'I'm sorry but I can't do this any more. I have to go,' Noah said, not looking at me.

'So, that's it?' I asked.

He looked at me once more. 'This is it. Goodbye, Stevie.'

I had stared at him, stunned that the man I'd fallen in love with had just told me he was not only breaking up with me but also moving to another country.

I watched helplessly as he got up and walked away from the bench. People passing by me were oblivious to the fact my world had just been turned upside down. I thought for a moment about running after Noah. Begging him to change his mind. But I knew it was pointless. I couldn't make him want to stay with me. He clearly didn't feel the same way about me as I did about him if he could leave me so easily. And move so far away too.

Itching to do something other than chase after him, I had picked up my phone.

The screen was blurry through my tears but I scrolled to Noah's number and I selected 'block'. Then I had gone on all my social media accounts, unfollowed, unfriended and blocked him there too. It had felt cathartic. A small victory for a moment. But afterwards, I felt even worse.

Conscious that I was in public and my mascara had run, making me resemble a panda, I got up and numbly walked home, unable to believe that I'd never see him again.

Now though, five years later, I had.

The lift opened and I stepped out and left the building, walking into the dark London evening, glad of the fresh air and distance from my ex. I rubbed my wrist before I pulled my jacket on, remembering Noah's surprise at seeing a tattoo there. After Noah had left, I had tried really hard to do what I wanted even if it scared me, because nothing could ever be as bad as Noah leaving me, making me wonder what my future was going to look like. Like getting the tattoo I'd always wanted but been too chicken to get. Or moving out of my flatshare into my Islington flat to live alone for the first time in my life.

I knew I'd got too comfortable working in the university library though and meeting Liv had cemented that feeling. So I'd got this job. The one I'd always wanted in publishing. I had finally created the future I wanted.

But now it felt like I was being punished for trying to make my dreams come true, the universe flinging Noah right smack into the middle of it all.

7

Annie Leon had let me start work on a Wednesday so now I only had Friday to get through before two glorious days off where I wouldn't have to see Noah. I would also try not to think about him but I wasn't sure how well I would do at that. I had a meal with my family tonight then I was due to spend tomorrow with Liv, so I was in a better mood.

I decided I'd walk in to work to start the day off as best I could.

It was a glorious crisp and sunny autumn morning and I picked up an iced coffee from Starbucks to romanticise the start of the day as much as I possibly could. I was also excited because I was going to be working on Deborah Day's new book and I'd stayed up late to finish it, and I thought it was bloody brilliant. I was absolutely invested in helping make it a bestseller even if my colleagues had warned me she was a diva. I often thought women who knew what they wanted were labelled as such so I wasn't too worried. I bet she was frustrated her books weren't being found like they used to be. And rightly so if this one was anything to go by. I'd downloaded the rest of her books I hadn't read to my Kindle and I was looking forward to spending my Sunday reading as much as I could.

The Plot Twist

When I arrived, Gita was leaning against Emily's desk talking to her.

'I had to work at home all evening to send everything Noah asked for,' Gita said with a sigh. 'And all I got was a curt thank you email this morning.'

'Ugh,' Emily said with a grimace. 'But at least you're still running the editorial department. I can't believe they got rid of Annie, and now The Shark is running our team.'

'You definitely have it worse.'

'Stevie, poor thing, will have to work closely with him.' They both looked at me as I sat down at my desk. 'I don't know how you'll get through it,' Emily added.

'Why does he have such poor people skills, that's what I want to know,' Gita said. 'Woman troubles?'

'Did you see that article about him being an eligible bachelor?' Emily asked. I nodded along with Gita. 'He's fit, don't get me wrong, but I doubt he ever cracks a smile. And the barking of instructions. Although actually maybe I'd like that in the bedroom.'

Gita snorted.

My cheeks flamed instantly because my mind went to being in bed with Noah. He'd been extremely good at telling me what to do in there, and I'd loved every minute of it. He'd never been bossy outside of it though.

I blamed Noah for my weakness over alpha males in romance books. Every instruction from them had me remembering the way he used to take control with me. And God, I missed it. Every sexual encounter after Noah had felt vanilla in comparison. I made myself cough then to cover the fact I must have had a trance-like expression on my face. Bloody hell. I needed to stop thinking about sex at work. And with my boss too!

'Well, if it's not woman troubles, maybe it's just because our jobs are on the line,' Emily continued, unaware of my inappropriate thoughts.

'I think he has a lot to prove to his family too,' I mused as I shrugged off my blazer.

'Why?' Gita asked.

'Well, his dad is his boss. That dynamic is never easy and if we think Noah is a bad boss, I heard that Mr Matthews...'

'Wait,' Gita said. 'Are you saying Noah's dad is Mr Matthews?'

'As in Matthews & Wood Publishing?' Emily asked. 'The vultures who took us over?'

I swallowed. It seemed like no one had worked out the Anderson/Matthews connection. I assumed that would have been rumbled already.

'That's right,' I said, wondering whether to feel bad. But Noah had lied to me for a year about that, so why should I let him carry that lie on now? 'He worked for his father in New York and now he's running things for him here.'

'Nepotism.' Gita tutted. 'You'd think he'd be more grateful then instead of grumpy.'

'I heard Mr Matthews is terrifying so maybe you're right,' Emily said to me. 'He has to prove himself to his father.'

The doors opened and we fell silent, turning to watch as Noah walked in. He looked over and I knew he knew we'd been talking about him.

'Stevie, shall we have that meeting about Deborah Day?' he called over, his expression unchanged. 'Say half an hour, okay?'

'Sure,' I said back, hoping I sounded just as chill. He continued the walk to his office and I leaned back in my office chair with a sigh. 'I hope he isn't too demanding in this meeting.'

'Take him one of those,' Emily suggested, pointing to my coffee. 'Paul said he was inhaling caffeine in their meeting.'

I nodded. 'Yeah, we always joked that we'd both like to be

hooked up to a coffee IV someday,' I said as I logged on to my computer. Gita and Emily stared at me. I realised what I'd said. Shit. 'I mean, we joked yesterday.'

'Noah jokes?' Emily asked, her eyebrows raised so high they disappeared into her hair.

I stared at her, unsure what to say.

Gita crossed her arms. 'You know more than you're letting on, Stevie, and we will find it out, I warn you now. There's nothing that happens here that me and Emily don't find out about.'

I tried not to panic. 'Um...'

'Gita, where are the edits for James Archer?' Noah barked out then, peering around his office door, making the three of us jump. Gita hurried over and I let out a sigh of relief that Noah had inadvertently saved me from a grilling. I had a sinking feeling though that they weren't going to let it go.

* * *

I nipped out of the office and went across the road to Starbucks and picked up two coffees. I went full autumn and got two pumpkin spice lattes, with cream on top, of course.

As I walked back across the open-plan floor, Gita gave me a thumbs-up and Emily did a slit-throat mime, which made me snort, earning me a few curious glances.

Noah's door was open so I went in and kicked it closed behind me.

'Okay, I have the fuel so let's do this,' I said, waving the coffees in the tray.

Noah's eyes widened. 'What are they?'

'The autumn drink of dreams, and if you don't drink it all, I'll never bring you a coffee again,' I said, sitting down in the chair behind his desk. I slid his coffee over to him and waited while he took a tentative sip through the straw.

'Could this be any sweeter?' he asked, wincing.

'You need all the sweetness you can get,' I replied and took a long gulp of mine. I sighed contently. 'One of the best bits about the best season. Yes, I am a basic bitch about autumn and I don't care.'

'Well, it will certainly keep me alert today. I'll be bouncing off the walls after it,' Noah said, putting his coffee down, ignoring my comment about him needing more sweetness. He pushed back the sleeves of his shirt. 'So, I finished Deborah's book. Did you?'

I reached into my bag and pulled out my Kindle and a notebook. 'Of course. I made some notes last night but basically, I loved it. I think it's...' I realised Noah was staring at my Kindle. 'What's wrong?'

'I just never thought I'd see you reading on one of those,' Noah said. 'You said you were always hardbacks until you die.'

We looked at one another. It was the second time he was bringing up knowing me after noticing my tattoo. And yes, I was probably going to count every time he did it. It proved that I hadn't imagined the whole year I'd spent with him, which sometimes after he'd gone I'd felt like I had.

I was the one to look away first.

'Well, my flat has no room for my book collection. They're all at my parents' house. Until I have enough space, my reading is all done on here.' I tapped my Kindle.

'Oh, I see. Where is your flat?'

'Islington. Do you still have yours by the river?' I had assumed when Noah left for New York he'd got rid of his flat, but his concierge phoned me once to say a parcel for me had arrived there by mistake a few weeks after and had kindly sent it on to me, but I had no idea if Noah had kept it after that.

'I'm back living there,' he confirmed. We looked at one another.

I couldn't help but wonder if he ever thought about the nights we had stayed there together.

Noah cleared his throat. 'So, you liked *Bitten*?'

I was relieved we were getting back to business. 'I did and I was surprised how current it felt. Like I said, I haven't picked up a new book of Deborah's for a long time. I've been missing out so I think many of her readers have been missing out too.'

'I agree. It felt very on trend despite what the team said about her being outdated. It made me wonder if they had really read it or just gone with the brief from editorial. I know people are busy and we can't read every book but it's a shame. I feel like you do – that romance readers would love this. We just have to make sure they know about it.'

'You think it's on trend?' I asked, wondering how Noah knew what was popular in romantic fiction. Just by keeping an eye on the bestseller list, I assumed, and information gleaned from what people who worked for him told him.

'It reminded me of these.' Noah reached behind him and put a stack of books on his desk for me to see. 'I think readers of these would love it and they are who we should target. But what do you think? No one knows the genre better than you.' He said it matter-of-factly like he said everything, but I couldn't help it – I glowed at his praise.

'Hang on,' I said, looking at the books then at Noah. He was right. They were exactly the books I would sit *Bitten* alongside. 'You've read these?' They weren't Matthews & Wood Publishing books.

'Yes,' he said, oblivious to my widened eyes. He gestured to the publicity plan in front of him. 'And these are the readers we need to target. We can't just rely on her existing fanbase. Looking at the current publicity plan, they are promoting her books the same way they always have and so not reaching younger readers.'

'I agree,' I said, still taken aback he'd read all those romance books. He had been mainly a thriller and non-fiction reader when we'd been together. Business motivation and murder were his go-to's, not pink-covered love stories. What had changed? 'It's such a shame she's been overlooked. I feel bad because I haven't read her books for years. Although that could be because they are just not visible enough. If we can get the word out, I think it could really sell.'

'This is why I thought we'd make a good team on this. We can do something different. And not get stuck in the "let's do what we always do" mentality that I feel the team here have been in.'

I tried not to dwell on the words 'good team' too much.

'Well, they are missing an effective social media strategy, for sure, and they haven't been targeting fans of authors like these books you have here. They also seem to be missing the author herself.'

'What do you mean?'

I waved my hand over the plan. 'There's no promotion involving Deborah, like an event, a signing, a talk, a reading. Why?'

Noah leaned back in his chair. 'The team did say they thought she was difficult.'

'Ugh, probably because she's a woman who knows what she wants.'

His mouth twitched again. 'Well, perhaps. I'm guessing they didn't want to have to do an event as they don't get on with her. Which is a poor excuse. It doesn't matter if personality-wise it's not a match; if it sells her book, we should do it. I think we need to meet Ms Day and see what she thinks about it all.'

'You think you can cope with her?' I said, my lips curving into a smile. I hoped Ms Day would be difficult for Noah to deal with.

'If not, we have you to diffuse any tension. You were always good at that. Who can be bad tempered with you in the room?'

The Plot Twist

Noah began to shuffle papers then seemed to realise what he'd said and froze, lifting his eyes cautiously to meet mine.

I stared at him, unsure how to respond to that. Noah was complimenting me. Reminding me why we'd made such a good team in the past. Telling me he'd read some of my favourite books. Supporting me in trying to promote a romance book when everyone else had dismissed it. I needed to remind myself that he hadn't thought that much of me when he moved to New York, and quickly.

'Stevie...' Noah said so softly that I held my breath to hear what he was about to say.

The phone on his desk rang out shrilly, making us both jump.

I scrambled to my feet. 'Well, I'll set up a meeting with the author and I'll email you some ideas that we could suggest to her,' I said as I grabbed my things. When I had everything, I finally looked at Noah.

He was watching me with an unreadable expression.

He waited a moment before nodding. 'Thank you,' he finally said then he answered his phone.

I left in a hurry, but I knew my mind would replay Noah's words over and over for days.

8

I didn't see Noah for the rest of the day, which flew by. I spent my time coming up with publicity ideas for *Bitten* and I emailed Deborah Day's agent, Ed Thomas, to ask if she would meet us to discuss the publicity for her book.

> After how badly the last one went?

His blunt reply didn't really bode well but I was hopeful that two fresh faces ready to help the book would win both him and his author over. I told him that Noah and I loved the book and we were committed to doing all we could in the month left until publication day, which admittedly wasn't long but it was the perfect Halloween book. I told him that if they still wanted *Bitten* to be a success then this was their chance to make it happen. And I ended the email with an 'x' because everyone in publishing seemed to.

His reply came a minute later.

> You're enthusiastic, I'll give you that. Debs is in London Monday. We'll come by your office at 9 a.m. You have fifteen minutes.

The Plot Twist

Okay, not everyone used a kiss or an exclamation mark then. I booked the meeting in our calendars and crossed my fingers that it would go better than our email exchange.

'Hot date tonight?' Emily said as I slipped on my jacket at home time.

'Nope. I have officially given up dating.'

She raised an eyebrow. 'Seriously?'

'When you've had as many bad dates as I have... I'm concentrating on my career. Which, you know, seemed like a good idea before all of this.' I gestured to the room.

'I get it,' Emily said as she got up from her desk to walk out with me. 'I had some horrific experiences with dating apps. I met my boyfriend at a wedding. So, no hot dates for me either. We've been together three years.' She smiled though and I knew she was happy with him. 'We should have work drinks next week with Gita; we can share dating horror stories.'

I smiled as we walked to the lifts and I pressed the call button.

'I'm in,' I said. 'Having workmates will make this experience much more bearable.'

'Tell me about it. I think I would have lost it if they'd let Gita go. We need all the solidarity we can get. I have a feeling The Shark is only going to—'

'Hold please.'

The deep voice made us both jump. We turned to see Noah hurrying to catch the lift, and I saw Emily bite her lip as she realised he must have heard some of our conversation. The three us got into the lift and Emily pressed the ground floor button, the doors sliding closed as a tense silence descended inside.

I turned to Emily, not daring to look at Noah. 'I'm actually having dinner with my parents this evening. My mum is trying a new recipe.' I found myself having to say something. 'Which is terrifying because she always makes changes to every recipe, and they are never good.'

Emily forced out a laugh. 'Thank God my boyfriend is a chef otherwise I'd have got scurvy by now with my cooking skills. Do you take after your mother?'

I shook my head. 'I had to learn how to cook at a young age so we'd have something edible to eat at every meal. I would tell her it was just a side dish but I'd make it big enough to feed my mum, dad and me just in case. I've got a lasagne I made yesterday to bring with me tonight.'

The lift doors opened and we stepped out.

'Well, have a good weekend,' Emily said, giving an awkward wave and hurrying off.

I watched her go, my stomach sinking. Finally, I glanced at Noah and saw he was looking at me, a wistful expression on his face. I started walking and he fell into step beside me. 'Remember when your mum made a curry but she put in sugar instead of salt and we secretly rung the local Indian and ordered—'

'Noah,' I cut in as we reached the building doors. 'I can't do that.'

'Do what?' he asked, frowning.

We stepped out into the evening together. Workers hurried past us, eager to get away from work for the week. We stopped on the pavement, forcing people to weave around us.

'Exchange funny moments, share memories...' I said, frustrated. I was all for acting like Noah was my boss and only my boss but not when he kept bringing up our past. It was too confusing. 'When I walked in on Wednesday, you didn't even acknowledge we'd been together, and now you're talking about my mum! You either talk about what happened with us or we don't mention it at all. To use your words, think about it over the weekend and let me know.'

Before Noah could answer, I slung my handbag over my shoulder and disappeared into the crowd.

* * *

My parents lived in Surrey in the same house I grew up in. It was an hour's train ride out of London and the house was right by the station so it was super easy to get there. As soon as I left the city, I felt some of the tension in my shoulders slide away. I'd been on edge ever since I walked into the chaos at Turn the Pages two days ago, and it was a relief to get away from the office, and my ex-boyfriend. And breathe freely for the weekend.

'There she is, publishing boss queen,' my dad called out as he opened the front door while I walked up the path, clearly having been watching at the window for me.

I did a curtsey then bounded up the steps to give him a bear hug. 'It's been a hell of a week, Dad, and I only started on Wednesday.'

'I've already opened a bottle of wine.' He leaned in to whisper then. 'Please tell me you brought food; your mother is making chilli and I swear I saw her put apples in it.'

Snorting, I pointed to my bag. 'I have lasagne, don't worry.'

'This is why you're my favourite child.'

'I'm your only child,' I replied as he closed the door and I walked on through to the kitchen to find my mum. I always tried to come home as much as I could but it wasn't because of only-child guilt. My parents were both parent and couple goals. 'Something smells good,' I said, going over to my mum at the cooker and giving her a kiss. This room always smelled of the vine tomato candle Mum burned when she cooked. The lights were on as darkness had settled over the village and I instantly felt more relaxed and comfortable being home. 'I made too much lasagne for myself so thought I might as well bring it,' I lied, taking the container out of my bag.

My mum, whose similar blonde hair to mine had a few grey streaks in now, wore a blue apron and a frazzled expression.

'That was a good idea; we hate food going to waste, don't we?'

'Wine?' Dad said as he went over to the kitchen table, dropping me a wink when Mum turned back to her cooking.

'Definitely. It's been a stressful couple of days,' I said, joining him.

'How is it going? We were so shocked about the takeover,' Mum said, looking over her shoulder at me.

Dad poured me a glass of rosé, our favourite, and I took a long sip of the delicious cold drink.

'Mmm, I needed that. Well, I have been given an exciting project to work on, which has helped amidst all the chaos. I'm going to be working on the publicity campaign for Deborah Day's new book.'

'Oh, I used to love her work!' Mum cried.

'I know. Weirdly, I hadn't kept up with her books but this one is fabulous. I really want to make this a success. And the pressure is on; our new boss said we have six months to make improvements otherwise the company that took us over might just dissolve the whole thing.' I winced as I said the words 'new boss'.

'I looked up Matthews & Wood Publishing,' Dad said as he sat down at the table. 'Because I thought it sounded familiar.'

I sank into the chair opposite him, knowing I'd been rumbled. My parents knew Noah's real surname.

'I had to let the news sink in.'

Dad nodded. 'How do you feel, love? You don't have to see him much, do you?'

'Well, I have to work on the Deborah Day project... with him.'

'With Noah?' Mum screeched then abandoned the cooking to

join us at the table. She took a gulp from her glass of wine. 'Oh, darling, is it really worth it? Maybe you should leave. That...'

She trailed off, struggling for the word.

'Dick?' I said. 'I told him he was one to his face.' They both snorted at that. 'He told me to think over whether I wanted to stay knowing he was my boss but he didn't acknowledge anything that happened with us. So, I thought fine, let's do that. I can stay six months, treat him just as my boss then find another publishing job. But then he started to say things.' I sighed. 'About the past. Noticing things new with me. So, I told him, either he talks about what happened or we just keep on pretending not to have known each other before. So, we shall see.'

Dad whistled. 'Well done, love. He should get down on his hands and knees and grovel for leaving you like he did.'

I smiled. Dad had taken it as a personal affront to him when Noah left. Both he and Mum had really liked him.

'He's so different at work,' I said. 'Demanding, gruff with people, has a no-nonsense attitude, and lacked any empathy when he let all those people go. I think working for his dad in New York has rubbed off in a serious, and bad, way.'

'Well, at least you can count yourself better off,' Mum said, patting my arm. 'You don't want to be with a man like that. It happened for a reason.'

'Definitely,' Dad agreed. 'You're doing the right thing. Stay six months for the experience and for your CV then you can walk away from Noah and never see him again.'

'That's the plan,' I said, but there was a pang in my chest at the thought, which I really didn't want to feel. I should want to leave in six months and be free of my ex, right? I decided it was best to change the subject. 'So, I really need to make Deborah Day's new book a hit.'

'You will,' Dad said. 'Let's hear your ideas over dinner.'

'We better microwave your lasagne, Stevie; I think my chilli has burnt,' Mum admitted then. 'Ridiculous! I followed the recipe to the letter.'

I couldn't look at my dad because otherwise I'd never have stopped laughing.

9

I stayed over at my parents' but I left late morning to head back to London as I'd promised I'd spend the day with Liv and her boyfriend. Aiden had got us tickets to a concert in Hyde Park. He was a film professor and he'd heard that an orchestra were playing songs from movie soundtracks. It sounded like a fun day out so we'd agreed to come with him.

It was a sunny but crisp day so I wore jeans, a striped cardigan and sneakers with a cross-body bag and I added a black headband to keep my hair off my face.

'I'm so relieved it's not raining.' Liv greeted me with a hug. As usual, she looked stunning in a knit dress, boots and a beret and Aiden was in trousers and a shirt. They did make a gorgeous couple. 'I haven't eaten breakfast so I can try all the food vans.'

'And the coffee ones,' I agreed.

'We better get started then,' Aiden said with a grin.

We walked through the gates, showing our tickets and getting wrists bands. The park was packed with people, lined with food and drink vans and a stage had been set up with deckchairs dotted around.

'Ooh look,' I said, pointing to a pink van. 'Isn't that the company Dan saw on TikTok?' I asked. Liv's brother was a social media influencer and always found good things to try in the city.

'Yes!' Liv cried, taking Aiden's hand and pulling him that way. 'Apparently the coffee is chef's kiss.'

'And they do cupcakes,' I added, spotting the menu.

'This van couldn't be more you two,' Aiden laughed as he trailed after us.

We joined the queue behind a tall, dark-haired man wearing jeans and a t-shirt.

'I didn't tell Aiden anything about your new job as I thought we would have a big debrief today,' Liv said, turning to me.

'I have even more to tell you,' I replied, thinking about having to work with Noah on the Deborah Day campaign.

'Sounds like we better buy a box of cakes,' Aiden said.

Liv leaned against him. 'I knew I was with you for a reason.'

Laughing, I turned to look at the menu and the man in front looked over his shoulder at us. Our eyes locked and I stopped laughing.

'Oh,' I said, when I realised who it was.

Noah turned around to face us fully. 'I knew I recognised that laugh,' he said, smiling enough to flash his dimple.

'What are you doing here?' I blurted out in shock, wishing my eyes hadn't just shot to that dimple. Why was it still so adorable?

His smile wavered a little bit. 'Well, I love classical music, you might not remember, so when I heard about this, I thought it sounded fun. And I don't really know anyone after being away for so long so I thought it would get me out of my flat.'

I was stumped as to what to say. Of course I remembered he loved classical music, but I couldn't let myself admit how much I did remember. Or how I had compared every man I met to him.

'Where have you moved from?' Aiden asked as Liv gave me a

subtle nudge in the side. 'I'm Aiden, by the way,' he said, glancing at me, no doubt wondering why my mouth was hanging open.

I shook myself. 'Sorry. This is Noah, my new manager at Turn the Pages. This is Liv, and her boyfriend Aiden. We all worked at the university together. Well, until I... uh, left,' I said, coughing at the end to cover my discomfort.

'A pleasure,' Noah said, shaking hands with Aiden then Liv. 'I moved recently from New York. I'd been there for five years but my company asked me to run their new acquisition so I came back.'

It was Liv's turn to stare at him, stunned now she realised who he was. I nudged her this time.

'Well, how... lovely,' she said, looking at me with wide eyes.

'If you're here alone, why don't you join us?' Aiden asked.

I spluttered. 'Oh, I'm sure Noah doesn't want us disturbing his peace,' I said quickly, trying to ignore Liv giving Aiden an annoyed look.

Noah kept his eyes on Aiden. 'Actually, I'd love to, thank you. Why don't I get the drinks and cakes and you guys find us deckchairs? What do you want?'

'Oh, we couldn't,' Liv said, letting go of Aiden's arm to clutch mine. I was glad of the support.

Aiden looked at us, confused at why we were acting so strangely. 'Are you sure, mate?'

'I insist. It's been a tough couple of days at work and I couldn't have got through it without Stevie. What will you have?'

Aiden looked at us but Liv and I had been rendered speechless. He realised then this was serious so he replied to Noah. 'Iced lattes for Stevie and Liv, I'd love a mocha and how about a cupcake selection so we can try them all? Come on, let's get a good spot.' Aiden moved in between the two of us and deftly steered us away from the van as Noah reached the front.

'Okay, what is going on?' Aiden asked as we moved away.

'That's Stevie's ex-boyfriend!' Liv cried.

'Wait? What? I thought you said he was your new manager?'

'He's her new boss and her ex! He broke her heart five years ago,' Liv hissed. 'And now he's back.'

'Olivia, why didn't you tell me?'

'The one time I wait to tell you gossip!' Liv shook her head. 'I thought we'd discuss it today.'

'Oh, shit, Stevie, I feel terrible,' Aiden said, looking at me in horror.

Now I was away from Noah, I could breathe again.

'It's okay,' I reassured him as we reached the deckchair area. 'You didn't know. And I can't believe he agreed to it.' I sighed. 'I have to get used to being around him, I guess. Now he's my bloody boss.'

'Quick, tell me everything I need to know,' Aiden insisted as he looked at Noah waiting for our order. 'I don't want to put my foot in it again.'

'I can't believe you asked him to join us.' Liv tutted as I told Aiden briefly the story of how Noah had dumped me and how I was now having to work for him.

Aiden whistled when I finished. 'I admire you, Stevie. I couldn't work under Olivia if we spilt up.'

'Well, you better not mess this up then,' she told him with a mischievous grin. These two loved to banter.

I rolled my eyes. 'Just help me, you two; don't leave me alone with him.'

'Pinkie swear,' Liv said, holding out her little finger to me. Aiden did the same.

'You two are nuts but I'm glad you're here,' I said, giving their little fingers a shake. 'Anyway, shall we sit here?' I said, seeing Noah was coming over. We found a group of four chairs to the side of the stage and claimed them.

'Okay,' Noah said. 'Here are the coffees and I got two selection boxes – the pink cupcake selection and the brownie selection.' He handed around the coffees and then sat down on the spare deckchair beside me. He passed me the cakes. 'I haven't eaten cake in about a year.'

I raised an eyebrow. 'That sounds like a tragedy. Here.' I passed him a cupcake. 'No one can feel sad eating this.' I took one out and gave the boxes to Aiden and Liv. 'Picture?' I asked as Liv selected her cupcake.

'Of course.' Liv pulled out her phone and I took out mine. 'Get closer,' she instructed.

I held out my cupcake and she held hers next to mine. 'Ooh, let's tap them together like a cheers.'

'A cupcake cheers, that's going to be my caption,' Liv agreed excitedly. We filmed us on our phones tapping the cupcakes together. 'Right, taste test.'

I took a bite at the same time as her then I noticed Noah staring at me.

Aiden leaned forward around us to talk to him. 'Yes, they are always like this.'

'Oh God, that's better than sex,' I moaned at the deliciousness of the cupcake, ignoring Aiden.

'Don't you dare agree,' Aiden joked to Liv.

'Just wait till you've tried some. I think you might agree,' Liv replied as she began to feed him some.

I turned to look at Noah. 'Well?'

He bit into his and met my gaze. 'Better than I remember,' he replied once he'd swallowed.

Well, fuck.

I looked away, heat rising at the back of my neck. There was no way that wasn't a double entendre. My mind had already strayed into dangerous territory remembering my sex life with Noah and now it was right back there again. I was half-pleased he remembered how good it had been and half-annoyed because, like watching someone eating a cupcake when you were on a diet, I now craved something that was definitely bad for me.

10

The orchestra started up after we'd had coffee and cake so the pressure was off to talk. The music was incredible and Aiden enthusiastically shouted out the films the music came from as soon as the first note of each sounded.

I tried to listen and watch the musicians and not be aware of Noah on the deckchair next to me, but it was difficult. And I was sure a couple of times he was looking over at me even as I made sure I faced the front.

In the break, Noah turned to us. 'They are amazing, aren't they? I haven't watched a live orchestra for so long. There's nothing like it.'

'I had goosebumps after the last one,' Liv said, touching her arm. 'So, you didn't go out in New York much, Noah?'

I looked at her, wondering why she was asking him that.

Noah shook his head. 'Too busy working, I guess. I'm afraid I became a bit of a workaholic. And it's likely to be the same thing here. We have a lot to do to get the company in shape. But Stevie and I are going to be working on a campaign that I think will help.'

'Oh?' Liv turned to me, eyebrow raised so high it almost disappeared into her hair.

'I didn't get a chance to tell you,' I said. 'Noah has asked me to help with the campaign for Deborah Day's new book. And it's brilliant, Liv. We've been missing out on her books recently. It's a vampire romance.'

'Oh, swoon.'

I gave Noah a look that said, *See?* after she used the same word as I did.

'When can I read it?' Liv asked eagerly.

'Stevie can give you an advance copy as long as you don't tell anyone,' Noah said. He smiled at me, the dimple back. 'Although I'm still shocked she read it on a Kindle.'

I was taken aback at his good humour. 'Oh, well, yes, it's a hardship but...' I looked away from Noah back to Liv and tried to get the conversation back on track after he'd surprised me. 'One day we'll have the library of our dreams, right, Liv?' I said.

She nodded. 'We will. So, how did Deborah Day end up writing about vampires? And are they sexy?'

'It's a really sexy book,' I said. 'You will love it. I loved it. I was so surprised that was what she's writing now. It should be huge.'

Liv frowned. 'It is a shame she's not as popular now. She was one of my gateway romance books.'

I nodded. 'Me too. I think they perhaps relied on her faithful readers too much.'

'I agree,' Noah said. 'They kept doing what they'd always done but we need to attract younger readers and new fans.'

'I get the feeling Deborah Day is just as frustrated.' I turned to Noah. 'Maybe we shouldn't do a glossy presentation but just ask her what she thinks? Make it clear we want to make this a hit, and give her the chance to have input.'

Noah smiled. I hated how handsome he still was. Even his glasses looked sexy on him. Ugh.

'Completely agree. The staff have labelled her as a diva but I think she's just fed up with staying stuck in the midlist. There's no reason this book couldn't be a bestseller if we create an effective campaign.'

'You're actually agreeing with me?'

'Don't get too used to it,' he joked back.

We looked at one another and I got a jolt of the past sparks I used to feel when we talked. How we'd been on the same page on so many things. I couldn't let myself get confused though. That was then. This was now.

Noah went to say something else but then his phone started ringing. He glanced at the screen and sighed.

'Excuse me.'

He walked away to answer it.

'Oh my God, Stevie, is this terrible for you?' Liv asked when he'd gone. 'Although he's not as grumpy as you said he's been? Right, Aiden?'

Aiden saw my face and held a hand up. 'I don't think my opinion is valid here.'

I had to smile at that. 'Well, he's being friendlier than at work. Everyone calls him The Shark there. He really had no sympathy for the people he made redundant. It was cruel how he told them to just go. Basically, everyone left there hates him now and...'

I stopped abruptly as Noah reappeared so suddenly, I didn't see him. I looked up and I couldn't deny the look of hurt on his face. I had no idea what to say. There was no point pretending that I hadn't been talking about him.

Noah cleared his throat. 'Um, so, I have to go.' He shifted on his feet. 'I have to do some work to send back to New York,' he said shortly. He looked at Liv and Aiden. 'It really was a pleasure to meet you. Thank you for today. I hope you enjoy the second half. Stevie, I'll see you in the office on Monday.' He didn't look in my direction when he said that.

Without waiting for us to say anything, he started to walk away.

I felt too guilty to leave things like that so I jumped up and hurried after him.

'Noah, wait,' I called out.

He stopped. 'Yes?'

So cold. Back in manager mode.

I put my hands on my hips. 'You're leaving just because I said what you must already know. You're called The Shark, for God's sake!'

'I know what people at work say about me, Stevie. But hearing it from you...' He trailed off and went to push his sleeves up but then must have remembered he had a t-shirt on so he raked a hand through his hair instead. 'But they don't understand. How difficult my job is. Dealing with everything going on above me. It's hard. You have no idea what the past five years have been like.'

I narrowed my eyes. 'Am I meant to feel sorry for you? You think it was easy for me when you left?'

We stared at one another.

'It wasn't?' Noah asked.

Was it my imagination or was there hope in his eyes?

I hesitated because I really didn't want to admit how much he had broken my heart when I was sure he hadn't thought about me since.

Noah looked away with a sigh. 'There's no point in talking about us. We should just pretend we only met for the first time on Wednesday. I think it'll be better for me, and it's definitely better for you. We need to focus on work. The past will just complicate things.' He briefly glanced at me to give me a nod. An actual nod! 'Until Monday.'

Frustrated, I watched him walk out of the park. Noah had never been this reserved with me. He was cold, shut down, business-like. A million miles away from the man who had held me in his arms and told me I'd changed his life.

Stevie, I swear my life was like grey clouds until you walked into it, and then it was like the sun came out.

I shivered as I remembered those words he'd said to me the first time we told each other we loved one another. No man had ever said anything like that to me before or since. That's why him leaving had been such a shock. Had he lied to me for a year? Was my Noah a figment of my imagination? Was the man who just stomped off through the park the real him?

My head was spinning. But I thought about what my mum had said the night before. That maybe it was a good thing when Noah was cold and reserved and grumpy and stand-offish. Because if he was nothing like the Noah I had known then my feelings were safe.

The problem was today had given me a glimpse of what he'd been like five years ago. A glimpse that suggested maybe, just maybe, that man was still there underneath.

And that didn't feel safe at all.

11

I'd never been someone who suffered with the Sunday Scaries, that feeling when you're dreading the start of the working week, because I'd always worked with books and books brighten any day. But I really was dreading seeing Noah again as I had no idea if he'd be just my bad-tempered boss or whether, like I had on Saturday, I'd see another glimpse of the Noah I'd known and loved. But most of all, I wasn't sure which one I was actually hoping for.

I tried the usual self-care activities that always made me feel better. I went for an early walk to my favourite park and took photos of the gorgeous autumn colours to post on Instagram. Then I came home and had brunch followed by a bubble bath with my Kindle. I started to read a new book but I quickly realised it was a second-chance romance and I did not need that messing with my heart, so I swapped it for one of Deborah Day's books that I hadn't read and was relieved that this was enemies-to-lovers with a supernatural twist. After my bath, I put on a loungewear set and curled up with tea and a Netflix series I was in the middle of.

But if I was honest, nothing could completely erase Noah from my brain. It was still so crazy that he was back here in London.

When he left me, I'd had to come to terms with the fact that I'd never see or speak to him again. And when you've been so in love, it's not like you can turn it off like a tap. I had still loved him even though he'd stopped feeling anything for me. And my heart. My body. They remembered Noah far too well.

It didn't help matters that I'd sworn off dating so it had been longer than I cared to admit since I'd spent the night with anyone. And getting flashes of my nights with Noah coupled with no one to help me forget them was making me crave them all over again.

I sighed, switched off Netflix and picked up the book again, but I was getting close to a sex scene and that didn't seem like a good idea. So I grabbed my phone and went to the app store. My fingers hovered over the dating app I'd used in the past. But I knew I was only considering it because Noah was back, not because I actually wanted to go through all that again. I'd made a plan to focus on my publishing career and I didn't want him to derail that.

Noah was my past. I had to focus on my future. I had to forget how he was with me on Saturday and tell myself he was just my grumpy boss. And dating your boss? Surely that was an even worse idea than going back to an ex. So, there we had it. Noah was off limits with a capital O and a capital L.

Throwing my phone down, I got up and decided pasta and wine were in order and then an early night so I'd be on the ball for our meeting with Deborah Day tomorrow.

I had no idea I was right to be feeling the Sunday Scaries because my first meeting with Deborah Day was not something I'd forget in a hurry.

* * *

I got to work early on Monday to get things ready for our meeting. I wanted to make a good impression on the author and her agent and prove that I was meant to work in publishing. This felt like my first test at Turn the Pages, and I wanted it to be a success.

'Oh, you're here.' Noah stopped short in the doorway of the boardroom as I was putting out a bottle of water and glasses for four on the long table.

He was in a crisp suit but his hair was ruffled and his stubble was ever so slightly unkempt. And were those bags under his eyes?

I frowned. 'You look tired.'

'And I'm the one that lacks people skills?' He sighed as he put his leather-bound notebook and pen next to my things on the table. 'It's been a working weekend. The phone call I took at the park was my father and I had to send things over to him yesterday.' He raised an eyebrow. 'Then he wanted to know how suddenly everyone here seemed to know I was his son.'

I stopped putting out biscuits onto a plate.

'Oh.' I straightened up and allowed myself to meet his gaze. 'That was me.'

'So I assumed,' he said dryly.

I put my hands on my hips. 'Well, I didn't want anyone else to almost have a heart attack when they realised you lie about your name and who you're related to. And why hide it? If you don't think your father got you this job, it shouldn't matter what anyone thinks.'

Noah stared back at me. 'I don't think that,' he said coldly. 'But, naturally, it's made my father even more demanding that we get results and quickly to stop anyone crying nepotism. And maybe I had a plan as to when and how I was going to tell everyone. You didn't give me the chance.'

'Fool me once, shame on me, fool me twice...' I muttered.

'Excuse me?'

'What does it matter? The cat is out of the bag and we just have to make this a success, same as we had to before I told anyone.'

Noah sighed. 'I forgot how black and white you see the world.'

I finished piling the plate with biscuits. 'And you still like to play in the grey it seems but after what happened last time, you can count me out of joining in,' I replied, trying not to let him get to me, but it wasn't easy.

'Last time?'

This was not how I wanted to start the working week. After telling myself to label Noah as my boss and my boss only, he was suddenly becoming all chatty about the past.

I threw my hands up. 'You lied to me for a whole year about your real name and who your father was. Why should I keep your secret now?'

The anger I'd been trying to reign in was spilling out. I could blame nerves for this meeting but mostly it was the calm way Noah was watching and talking to me. Like he didn't have a clue about how much he had lied. How it had been all part of a game that I hadn't known I was playing. He could say I saw the world in black and white but it was definitely preferable when people were genuine and gave it to you straight. Why pretend you loved someone when you always had one eye on the door?

He pushed the sleeves of his shirt up. 'I didn't lie because…' He trailed off. 'I didn't want you to think…' He looked as if he was struggling with what to say.

I crossed my hands over my chest. 'You lied. About everything.'

Noah looked flummoxed, which was a relief as Emily appeared in the doorway then. 'They are here,' she said. 'I'll make them coffees and bring them in, if you're ready, Stevie?'

I smiled. 'We are, thank you, Emily, that would be great.'

She nodded and disappeared again.

'I get no say then,' Noah said under his breath. 'We need to talk, Stevie,' he said, more firmly.

'What else is there to say?' I asked him.

Taking a breath, I focused on smiling at the door, ready to greet our visitors, and hoped I could ignore the waves of resentment rolling off Noah beside me. I had no idea why he was annoyed with me when it clearly should be the other way around.

'You said it yourself on Saturday. We should just focus on work, right?' I said through gritted teeth.

'Fine,' he snapped.

12

A couple of minutes later, Emily showed in Deborah Day and her literary agent, Ed Thomas. Deborah was in her sixties now with a neat grey bob and she wore a stylish suit. Her agent appeared to be about twenty years younger, relaxed in jeans and a jumper, with vivid blue eyes. They both shook hands with us firmly and then we all sat down with coffees provided by Emily who shut the door and gave me a thumbs up behind the glass.

'Well, it's a pleasure...' Noah began, but Ed held up a hand.

'We don't want any bullshit. We've told Deborah's editor this is our last book with Turn the Pages. Sales have been declining each year and we are constantly told things will change yet nothing happens. The last meeting we had here was the final straw. It is clear the team don't care about Deborah's books any more.'

'They suggested that I was a has-been,' Deborah added. 'That my books were something they were forced to publish as I had such a long contract. Well, that's up after this book and I can't wait to leave. I want a team behind my books who actually enjoy them. I have the distinct feeling half the team hadn't even bothered to read

Bitten, and my budget for marketing is non-existent. So I don't really know why you even called this meeting.'

'We hear you,' Noah said. 'I promise you we both have read *Bitten* and we loved it. I understand why you'd want to leave. I'd do the same if I was you.'

Ed and Deborah looked at one another in surprise.

'But we are a new team. And we are hoping we can change things, and get this book in the hands of readers who we know would love it. Stevie is exactly the type of reader we need to be talking to about your new book, Ms Day.'

He looked at me and gave me a nod.

I was nervous. Both Deborah and her agent were fixing us with steely looks that would make the most courageous of lions want to turn and flee in the other direction, but Noah giving me a reassuring nod gave me the confidence I needed.

'I grew up reading and loving your books; they were part of the reason I fell in love with romance books,' I said. 'But I haven't read one in years.'

'This is supposed to be making us want to stay?' Ed said with a sigh.

'I haven't finished,' I told him sternly. He put both hands up and I swore that Noah chuckled under his breath. 'But reading *Bitten* has made me so cross with myself for not reading your more recent books. I loved it. And I think *Bitten* is even better than your classics and I know so many readers who would be captivated by it. I mean, Marcus is the book boyfriend we all want.'

Deborah smiled slightly at that. 'It's refreshing to hear that you think my book has relevance today as I don't think your colleagues have felt that way in years. I know your team call me difficult, but it's only because I have been treated like I know nothing.' She shook her head and leaned forward in her chair. 'I have suggested so many ideas but they've all been rebuffed even though your publicity plans haven't done anything to help my books. And frankly, it's insulting – this attitude that I can't have any say as the lowly author. Who pays the wages here?' Deborah pointed towards her chest. 'The authors. And yet you all know better than me.' She arched an eyebrow. 'If my book isn't number one on the bestseller list, you'll never publish one of my books again.'

Number one?

I exchanged a look with Noah. That would be a tall order. I swallowed hard.

'That's a big goal,' I said slowly.

'We'd love to get you there,' Noah added. 'Why don't we talk about publicity ideas...'

'No,' Ed said, cutting him off firmly. 'You won't be getting any help from us. As Deb said, we've been here before and we're tired of it. You come up with a campaign that gets *Bitten* to number one. And we will wait to see what happens.' He turned to me. 'Maybe some new blood will help.'

'It will,' I replied fiercely.

Ed stood up. 'Stevie, why don't you show us out?'

'Oh, yes, sure.' I scrambled up, as did Noah, but Ed and Deborah merely gave him a nod before sweeping out. I hurried after them and showed them out to the lifts. 'I promise to do everything I can,' I said as I pressed the call button.

Deborah looked at me. 'You know what? I think I believe you but I'm not sure it'll be enough.'

I hated to see such a talented author look so defeated. 'I really believe in this book and Noah does too.'

'I'm shocked that The Shark wants to help push a romance book,' Ed said, eyebrow raised. 'Matthews & Wood Publishing have been slowly cutting romance titles for years.'

'They have?' I was surprised after Noah revealed how many romances he'd been reading since he'd been in New York. Unless he had kept his love for romance away from Matthews & Wood Publishing. I wondered why.

'Romance doesn't always get the same respect as other genres,' Deborah said.

I nodded. I knew that and hated it.

Ed handed me his card then. 'My mobile is on there in case you want to chat about *Bitten* more. If you can somehow pull off making this book a bestseller, I will be headhunting you for a job with me.' He glanced around. 'Even if you can help *Bitten*, I'm not sure you can save Turn the Pages.'

His scepticism only made me more determined. 'I'll email over my plan ASAP!' I called out as they got into the lift. Just before the doors closed, I thought I saw them roll their eyes.

I walked back to the boardroom where Noah was sipping his coffee. 'That could have gone better,' I said.

'What's that?' He nodded at the card in my hands.

'Ed's business card,' I said, putting it in my pocket. I might need to rally him and Deborah to help me with my plans and I hadn't missed Ed's suggestion about headhunting me. With everything going on here, I wasn't in the position to not keep his card. It might come in handy soon.

Noah's eyes narrowed. 'Why did he give you that? He wasn't chatting you up, was he?'

'Why would you care if he was?' I asked, taken aback that he might be jealous.

'I don't,' he said quickly, shutting down my thought in two words. 'I just heard he can be a bit sleazy, that's all.'

I hadn't got that impression. I shrugged. 'Actually, he gave me this in case I needed to talk to him about the book. And said if I can pull off making it a bestseller, he might offer me a job,' I replied. 'Besides, I decided a few months ago I was done with dating. I am sick of bad dates. I'm focusing on my career, starting with making this book a success.'

Noah looked flummoxed again. 'Okay. Well, that's probably a good idea.' He stood and scooped up his paperwork hastily. 'I have a meeting. Do you want to write up the ideas you had and email them to me and I'll get back to you?'

Without waiting for me to respond, he strode out.

I stared after him. Noah thought me giving up dating was a good idea? Great. My ex thought I was so terrible, I should avoid trying to find anyone. My heart sunk, even though I told myself not to care what he thought. Still, it smarted that he was so over me.

Emily came in then.

'How did it go?' she asked. She saw the look on my face. 'Okay, drinks with me and Gita after work, no arguments.'

I shook my head. 'No arguments here.'

13

I spent the day looking into Deborah Day. I stumbled on an old interview from a nineties TV show that had been uploaded to YouTube. Her biting wit was fun to watch. She won everyone over and came across as someone you could have a good bitch and moan and gossip over coffee with. It sparked an idea and I emailed my thoughts to Noah just as the end of office hours rolled in. He'd been shut in his office all day so I wasn't expecting a quick reply.

Gita and Emily were starting to collect their things so I pulled on my blazer and reapplied my lip gloss. I brushed my hair and spritzed myself with perfume.

'We know a really cute bar nearby,' Emily said when I stood up. 'It's been the scene of the end of many a bad day here.'

I glanced behind them as we left the office together and saw Noah coming out of his office. He watched us walk out. I guessed he didn't go to many work drinks. A far cry from the sociable guy he'd been when we'd dated. As we got into the lift, I checked my phone. Liv has messaged to thank me for sending a copy of *Bitten* to her and there was a new email on my work account from Noah.

Thank you for your ideas, Stevie. How about we discuss how to present to Deborah tomorrow? I could do a coffee meeting at 9 a.m. Meet me in the Starbucks opposite the office. Noah.

'Everything okay?' Gita asked as I quickly put my phone into my bag.

'Sure. I just have an early meeting with Noah,' I said.

A coffee meeting. In Starbucks. For some reason, this made me feel a bit nervous. In the office, there was a strict boundary with him as my boss but outside work was completely different. Saturday had proven the lines could get wobbly. And I did not want to deal with any more wobbly lines when it came to Noah.

'You're becoming teacher's pet,' Emily teased. She saw me bite my lip. 'I'm only joking. I know it's an important project you're working on.'

'Just make sure you tell us anything he might let slip that we can use against him later on,' Gita added with a laugh.

We climbed out of the lifts and set off for the bar nearby. 'Now he knows I told everyone about his dad, he's not going to tell me any more secrets,' I said, trying not to feel guilty for the weary look on his face when he came into the boardroom this morning. I'd got the feeling years ago that things with his father weren't easy and it seemed like maybe they'd only got harder since then.

The bar wasn't too busy as it was a Monday night and we found a corner table and got a bottle of rosé to share. Emily and Gita said they had worked together for years and had hit it off from day one. They reminded me of me and Liv, who I told them I missed working with already.

'She's a big romance book fan too and Noah said I could give her a copy of *Bitten* so it'll be interesting to see if she loves it as much as I did.'

'You make me feel bad for not reading it,' Emily said. 'I just assumed her books weren't my sort of thing and with so many books coming out, I mainly just read the brief the editor gives.'

'I was just relieved I made it through the editorial process with her,' Gita said. 'Deborah Day is someone who argues about every editorial note she's given.'

'She certainly doesn't take any prisoners,' I said. 'But, seriously, her book would sit alongside all the ones going viral on social media right now. I think we can make her popular again.'

'It's nice to see someone not jaded by the whole industry,' Emily said, giving me a fond look. 'Although a few months working for The Shark is likely to change all that.'

'Okay, now we have got you alone and plied with wine,' Gita began, 'how did you know that he works for his father? How did you know he's really Noah Matthews?'

'I used to know him when he lived in London before moving to New York,' I said. 'He was very different in those days.'

Emily whistled. 'By your blush, I'm guessing he was just as gorgeous back then too. But less intimidating.'

I was relieved they didn't seem to think we'd had any romantic involvement. I guessed we seemed like a very unlikely couple. Maybe we had been then as well but I just hadn't seen it clearly. 'I keep wondering if the old Noah is underneath still or not,' I admitted.

'I doubt it,' Gita said. 'Five years in New York working for his father has probably stamped out any nice qualities. Well, we might only have to put up with him for six months before we're all out on our ears.'

'Can we not depress ourselves tonight?' Emily pleaded. 'We need to welcome Stevie to the company and hope that she doesn't get scared easily because she's keeping Noah away from hassling us too much.' She grinned. 'What a team player!'

They laughed and raised a toast to me and I played along but inside, I was hoping that working with Noah wouldn't last too much longer because we were skirting around our past and it felt like at any moment, we'd fall right bang into the middle of it.

And I wasn't sure if I could handle it.

* * *

'I need an extra shot, please, and extra syrup,' I asked the Starbucks barista the next morning. My head pounded, my eyes stung and my throat scratched with every word I spoke.

'Rough night?' he asked with sympathy as he made my drink.

'Never go out on a weeknight,' I advised him, and I turned around, spotting Noah at a table in the back of the coffee shop. He looked up and did a little wave to me. I really hoped he was in a better mood today otherwise my hangover was about to feel even worse.

'Hope this helps,' the barista said, handing me my drink.

Before I moved, I took a long gulp even though it was hot and prayed for the caffeine to hit me fast. Then I made my way to where Noah was, hoping I didn't look as bad as I felt.

'Did you get any sleep last night?' he asked in lieu of greeting.

I sank into the chair opposite him. 'Gee, thanks for the compliment. Good morning to you too. And no, Gita and Emily are animals.' I shook my head. '*Animals.*'

Noah chuckled, stopping when I shot him a glare. 'Sorry, but I think you're right – they were in the office when I left and they looked pretty chipper.'

'Fantastic,' I muttered, and I took another gulp of coffee. I hadn't drunk that much on a Monday since university and if that was a typical night for them, I might have to say no to their next invitation. Still, it had been fun and it was nice to make friends at work; I needed all the support I could get for the next six months.

'So, I read through your email,' Noah said, immediately back to business. 'And I love the idea of getting Deborah to be more visible on social media and in the press again. You're right, she is dynamic and will be entertaining. I think a Q&A with her core reader base is a great idea and we can film that. And getting Deborah to do some bookshop events would be good publicity too. I also think sending copies to the big social media bloggers and book accounts on TikTok is a great idea. We can also send to popular authors to see if they will endorse it. And if we move some of the budgets around, I think we could stretch to some Tube and online adverts too.'

'I'm not sure the team will agree to giving Deborah more of the budget,' I said, thinking about how they had wanted to get this publication over and done with then move on to other books. 'And Ed said your father's company has been slowing down publishing romance books?'

'Ed?'

'Deborah Day's agent,' I said with a frown.

'I didn't realise you were on such friendly terms, that's all.'

His tone had an edge to it that confused me further. 'I'm too hungover to understand you. If you can get us some more budget then great. Anything else?'

'Have you been thinking about his job offer?' Noah asked, as if I hadn't spoken.

Suddenly, I snapped. 'So what if I have? Joining Turn the Pages hasn't exactly been what I hoped for.'

'I thought you wanted *Bitten* to do well like I do.'

'Yes, but this isn't easy for me,' I said, gesturing between the two of us.

'Why do you think it's easy for me?'

My eyes widened. Was he completely clueless? I leaned in so the people around us wouldn't hear. Lord knows I'd been humiliated enough by this man for one lifetime.

'What do you want me to say? You get off on hearing that you broke my heart when you left? That I was gutted you broke up with me? That seeing you again makes me remember not only being with you and how happy I was, but also how upset I was when it was all over? How I still loved you even though you'd turned off your feelings, if you'd had any for me in the first place?'

I was furious. The hangover coupled with lack of sleep and Noah looking at me like I was talking crazy had made me finally see red. I was saying what I'd wanted to say since he left me.

'You haven't even acknowledged what you did. Or said sorry. But you expect me to be happy that we now have to work together? Jesus, Noah. I know you're called The Shark now but I didn't think you could be so cruel.'

Once the words poured out, I felt annoyed I'd let him get to me and allowed myself to tell him all of that. I stood abruptly and bolted out of the door before he could say anything.

Outside, I walked to the rail that overlooked the river and leaned against it wearily. I breathed in the fresh air, letting it cool my cheeks and the anger inside me.

'Stevie.' Noah appeared beside me and leaned on the rail too. I went to move but he put his hand over mine. I raised my eyes to meet his. 'Stevie, don't go,' he said urgently. 'Please, will you let me say something?'

He gave me a pleading look and gently squeezed my hand underneath his. I moved my hand from the railing, but nodded that I'd stay.

Noah exhaled loudly. 'Of course I don't get off on hearing that. How could you think that badly of me? I've been trying not to think about the past, about us, because I didn't think I had the right to talk to you about it. I thought that we should just kept things professional. I knew I'd hurt you but... I didn't know it was that much.'

My eyes narrowed. 'You knew I loved you.'

'I hoped you had feelings for me, but I wasn't in a good place when I left. I had a lot going on that I kept from you. And it made me feel like maybe you didn't... that you shouldn't. That you *couldn't* love me.' Noah sighed. 'When I saw you again, you looked so...' He trailed off and looked frustrated. 'I thought you were completely over it all. That's why I was so... well, why you thought I was acting like a dick.'

'I am over it,' I said, not wanting him to think I was still pining for the crumbs of his heart. 'But it was a shit time for me. Back then. And you're acting like you're confused that I'm angry with you.'

He made a move for my hand again but saw me flinch so dropped his hand to his side. 'I'm sorry, Stevie, so sorry for hurting you like I did. I know it won't mean much but it has haunted me for years. I know you think I've changed and maybe I have, but that hasn't changed. I really do regret the way I ended things.'

I took that in. He regretted *how* he broke up with me but not for breaking up with me in general. That was what I'd expected.

I nodded. 'I don't really recognise you any more but it's kind of a relief. It took a long time to fall out of love with you but now I can see it was for the best. We are clearly not compatible. I'm just kind of sad, you know? That it didn't work out like I once thought it might.'

'Shit. I really am that different?' Noah asked, hurt crossing his face. He seemed shocked and upset by that.

'You let all those people go like they just didn't matter.'

'I had no choice. I didn't enjoy it, but if I showed weakness...'

'Empathy is not weakness,' I interrupted. 'And nor is saying sorry. I'm glad you have. Now, we can keep things professional like you want.'

Noah looked frustrated again. 'That's not what I meant... Do you know how hard it is for me to keep things professional with you?'

I didn't move in time and he touched me again. He brushed his fingertips against mine. I shivered and knew I couldn't blame the autumn breeze swirling around us.

'That first day, you walked into my office and I thought, *Oh God, she's even more beautiful now*.'

Sucking in a breath, I stood back, breaking our contact because it felt like he had burnt me. 'You can't say things like that.'

'Why not?'

I looked into those dark-brown eyes of his and part of me wanted to surrender. To sink right back into them and into him. Him calling me beautiful was both the last thing and the only thing I wanted to hear.

'You left me,' I said. 'It was so hard for me to get over you. It was your decision to break up. You left me,' I repeated, anger returning. He wasn't the one who had been left with a broken heart.

We looked at one another, the air thick with tension. Noah opened his mouth to say something but his phone suddenly started ringing in his pocket, making us both jump. He pulled it out and sighed when he looked at the screen. 'It's my father. Stevie, I want to talk about this more.'

I was relieved we'd been interrupted. I almost believed he was going to say he made a mistake in breaking up with me. But I knew that wasn't the case. I couldn't let myself feel things for Noah ever again.

I shook my head. 'No, Noah. I just wanted you to acknowledge that we had been something once, and that you hurt me. Thank you for apologising. That's all we need to say. Let's just move on and focus on work, okay? It wasn't meant to be.'

'If that's what you think,' Noah said quietly, his phone still ringing.

'Take the call; I'll see you back at the office.'

I spun around and walked away. My eyes started to burn but I really didn't want to cry. I could stay angry at Noah or stay sad that we didn't work out or I could continue what I'd done for the past five years and focus on me and my dreams and building the life I wanted.

And I was determined to do just that.

14

Over the next couple of days, I didn't see much of Noah. I threw myself into work. I sent out hundreds of press releases about *Bitten* and contacted every social media influencer that reviewed books to see if they wanted a reading copy. I also asked Deborah to film a few videos for social media for the lead up to the release. And Emily designed some new graphics for the book.

So, it was full steam ahead trying to build a bigger buzz for *Bitten* than the team had so far, but I didn't want to admit to myself how many times Noah's words by the river echoed through my mind.

Especially alone in bed at night.

Do you know how hard it is for me to keep things professional with you?

That sentence haunted me. I was confused why he'd said it when he was the one who had decided we were over. I didn't know how I'd feel seeing him again so it was a relief that he rarely came into the office and when he did, he just walked straight through into his space and closed the door.

But then an email came through from him telling everyone who was working on Deborah Day's book to come in for a team meeting in the boardroom. I immediately felt nervous about facing him. I had no idea how he would act around me. I'd put an end to us discussing our past and whatever else Noah had wanted to say. Was he relieved I'd walked away? Disappointed? Angry?

So, that Thursday morning, I walked into the boardroom apprehensively.

'Okay, thanks for coming in, everyone,' Noah said when we sat down. It was a chilly day and he had on a brown jumper that matched his glasses over his work trousers. The look was the most casual I'd seen him in save for our weekend meeting in the park. His gaze went straight to me and his brown eyes looked even deeper than usual, and when he smiled at me, I got the full dimple treatment. Not angry then. He looked pleased to see me. I willed my body not to react but the more he reminded me of the Noah I had loved, the harder that was proving to be.

In the boardroom were me and Noah, Emily and Gita, along with Paul, who headed up sales, and Aaliyah.

'I have been talking to the team in New York the past couple of days and have found us more budget to work on the campaign for Deborah Day's book. We met with the author and she is on board with our new publicity plan, albeit sceptical about whether we can deliver better sales for her. I think this book has really big potential for us and we only have three weeks to get it on the bestseller list.'

A few looks were exchanged around the table.

Paul coughed. 'Do you really think that's possible based on her previous sales? And the short time we have to increase advertising and promotion? Not to mention the fact retailers will have made buying decisions a long time ago. It won't be in enough shops to be that visible.'

'I think Ms Day has slipped under the radar here. She was once this company's biggest author but after relying for too long on her backlist and fan base, you have lost the potential for new readers and bigger sales,' Noah said. 'There is no reason *Bitten* shouldn't be a must-buy for romance readers. I want us to try. As I said before to you all, New York are watching. We have six months to make some increases in profits. My father is talking about bringing some of the team here and I want to make sure that's to add to our numbers, not replace.' There were nervous looks around the table. Noah put his hands up. 'That's not a threat. I just want you all to be clear on the situation here. And what we need to do. If *Bitten* unexpectedly sells more copies than you planned then that helps us get where we need to be, right?'

'There are so many better titles we could be pushing though,' Paul said, shaking his head.

'Because this is a romance?' I cut in. 'You don't think it's worth getting behind?' I looked over at him, annoyed again at his dismissive tone when it came to talking about this book.

'I'm just giving my opinion,' he said, leaning back in his chair.

'It does seem like a tall order,' Emily said, shooting me an apologetic look. 'No matter the book, three weeks is a very short time to promote it.'

'Well then, we will all have to work extra hard on it, won't we?' Noah raised an eyebrow. 'I'll email you what I need you to do. Stevie, stay behind please. I have an idea I want to run past you. That's all.'

I saw Paul roll his eyes at Emily as they got up. Gita smiled at me but she looked worried as she followed them out. I sighed as the room emptied and the door closed behind them.

'I think they hate me for wanting to push this book,' I said.

'Do you really care what they think?'

'I care a bit,' I said. 'I want to get on with my colleagues. We're supposed to be a team. But now they resent me for changing their plans.'

'So, you just have to prove to them you were right.' Noah looked across the table at me, a challenge in his eyes.

'Be more shark?' I asked, trying not to laugh.

'I can be a bit too tough as a boss. I suppose when I started in New York, I didn't want people to think I was there as a favour from my father, that I was going to take it easy and rest on my laurels, you know? I wanted to show them I meant business.' He shrugged. 'I get why they call me that. I wanted to prove myself, and I did. And it got people's backs up. But I got results, Stevie, and my father demanded a lot from me. I had to prove that he'd made the right choice in hiring me. And I have to do that here too.'

'That's a lot of pressure to put on yourself.'

'And you're not putting pressure on yourself? You're not thinking this is your first campaign and the author wants it to be a bestseller so you're worried about what happens if it doesn't sell enough?'

I sighed. How did he know what I was thinking?

'If it doesn't, they're all going to say they told me so.'

'We've always learnt a lot from each other,' Noah said, his tone softening as I admitted my fear. 'Maybe I could be more empathetic sometimes but maybe you could care less what people think.'

There it was again. A reminder of our past. Noah was killing me.

'But you care a lot about what your father thinks?' I asked, wanting to know more about their seemingly complicated relationship.

'He expects the best,' Noah said simply.

'He made you CEO here though. He must have done that because you are the best.'

'I like the way you see the good in people, Stevie. Maybe he did it so he could watch me fail.'

'Bloody hell, Noah.' I was shocked that he thought his father capable of that, but another question was burning inside of me. 'If your father is really that hard on you, why did you go to work for him in New York in the first place? Why join the family business?' I knew it was close to asking him why he left me but I was confused. His father didn't sound like the kind of guy you'd want to work for, so why was Noah still trying to prove himself to him?

Noah looked down at his watch. 'As much as I love discussing my father,' he said, his New York lilt heavy as his sentence dripped with sarcasm, 'we need to head off now or we'll be late.'

'For what?'

'My publicity idea for *Bitten*. Come on, I think you'll love this.' He jumped up and I had no choice but to gather my things and follow him out, no closer to understanding why he'd run off to New York five years ago. But maybe it was better not to know. It wouldn't change the outcome, would it?

I went to my desk and grabbed my coat and bag. Eyes watched curiously as Noah pulled his coat on and we walked out together. I knew everyone still pitied me for having to work so closely with him, even though they seemed to be warming to him gradually: I'd noticed fewer people rolling their eyes after leaving his office.

I wondered what the hell they would think if they knew he was my ex-boyfriend.

15

'So, where are we going?' I asked Noah in the lift on the way down.

'A bookshop that I think would work really well for the idea I had, but I need your opinion.' He looked across at me. The lift was a small space and he was only a foot away.

I smiled and saw his eyes flick to my lips. 'I doubt there's a bookshop in the world I wouldn't like.'

Noah chuckled. 'Me neither. You would have loved the bookshops in New York. I remember going to one and thinking, *Stevie would think she's died and gone to heaven if she was here*,' he said, his expression turning wistful.

My pulse sped up as he looked down at me. Had he stepped closer as well?

I breathed in the fresh shower smell he always had. My heart hurt to think about Noah going to bookshops over there and thinking about me.

Noah stepped closer again. I sucked in a breath and quickly turned to face the lift doors. He was too close. This space was too small. Lines were blurring again and I didn't want that.

Thankfully, the doors opened then and I darted out.

The Plot Twist

I tried to wave off his words. 'Probably for the best. I would have never fit all the books I wanted into a suitcase. So, are we getting the Tube?'

I couldn't look at him so I had no idea what he was thinking but he seemed to accept my change of subject.

'It's not far if you're happy to walk?'

'Sure,' I said, preferring wide-open space and fresh air right now.

We set off around the city together. Now that Noah had mentioned it, I couldn't help but imagine what it might have been like if I had gone to New York with him. And not just for a holiday. I imagined strolls like this around the city, coffees in hand, yellow taxis passing us, Sundays spent having lazy brunches and browsing in bookshops and... I shook off the fantasy. Even if he had thought about me, Noah hadn't wanted me to come with him. And that was that.

'It's just around the corner,' Noah said, breaking into my thoughts.

I looked around as we stepped off the main road. I recognised this quiet area, the cobbled alleyway lined with old-fashioned-looking shops with painted signs and gold lettering. Hanging baskets made the alley pop with colour. It was quieter here as if this was a secret part of London that not many people knew about. I realised I'd been here once before.

No, no, no!

'Noah...' I said, alarmed as he walked towards a shop right in the middle of the alleyway. I stopped as I looked up at the all-too familiar bookshop. 'But this is...' I whispered as I saw the sign.

Book Nook.

'Isn't it the best?' Noah said, looking at the bookshop and not seeing the horror on my face. 'I loved it when I used to live here. In fact, I'm not sure if you remember but—' He turned to me then.

'Let's go in,' I said, cutting him off. I did not want him asking me if I remembered this bookshop. Of course I bloody remembered it!

'Okay.' Noah opened the door and let me walk in first, following close behind. With a deep breath, I stepped over the threshold and looked around.

It was exactly the same as it had been on that rainy night six years ago. The bookshop was still filled to the brim with titles, shelves placed in a haphazard fashion, and the smell of books mixed with the sweet pumpkin candle that burned on the till desk. But instead of the older man that had been there that night and given Noah a discount for our books, there was a woman with long black hair.

Noah greeted her warmly with a wave but he stayed by my side, watching me as I took the shop in. I spun around, the memory of us meeting in here flooding back as if I'd opened the page of one of the books to find chapter one of our story written in it.

'It's still my favourite bookshop,' Noah said softly. 'Stevie, you must visit it a lot?'

I stepped over to a shelf and ran a finger across the spines, a habit I'd picked up in the library when I needed comfort. Books never let you down, after all.

'I never came back here,' I told him. It had been too hard. I'd walked past a few times but hadn't been able to go inside and then I'd avoided this area completely. This was where we had met. Why would I want to relive that?

Noah seemed oblivious to the fact this was a painful memory. He walked over to the woman behind the till.

'This is Georgina. The previous owner's daughter,' Noah said, introducing us. 'This is Stevie. We, uh, work together.'

'Lovely to meet you, Stevie,' she said, smiling at me. 'Do you guys want to come back and see the event room?'

'Definitely. Stevie?'

All I could do was nod, still stunned I was back in this bookshop. And Noah was with me.

Georgina led Noah through a small opening in the bookshelves and I followed, ducking a little bit to get under the archway. We were then in the back room. There were more bookshelves but these were against the wall and in the middle were chairs lined up and some cosy bean bags and a platform at one end that could work as a kind of stage.

'I was thinking we could hold a launch party for the book here?'

It was a cosy and intimate space, and it had a feel of being out of a different time, which would work brilliantly for a vampire romance.

'It's perfect,' I said. 'We could have an exclusive invitation list. We could send invites out on real stationery, use lots of candles and maybe heavy drapes over there too, make it feel like the library of the vampire's home. And wine in goblets, and oh my God, we could do it on Halloween night, the week the book comes out. It's perfect and...' I stopped, noticing Georgina and Noah both staring at me. I bit my lip. 'Sorry, did I get carried away?'

Noah's dimpled appeared. 'I love watching you get carried away.'

My heart stuttered inside my chest.

'I love all those ideas. Can we have it here, Georgina? I don't think Stevie will survive if you say no.'

'Well, of course,' she said.

They beamed at one another.

I tried to not to feel a pinch of jealousy. 'Can I take some photos? Show the author and help to plan the night?'

'Go ahead. Noah, let's book it in...' Georgina led Noah back into the bookshop and I took some photos, knowing this place would work brilliantly for the book and people would be so excited about it after attending a party here.

'My dad was so excited when I told him you were here,' Georgina was saying to Noah when I re-joined them. They stood close together by the desk. I watched them, irrationally hoping that there wasn't anything going on between them. 'You were always his favourite customer,' she continued. 'And when you stepped in and bought the place...'

I did a double take and even though I shouldn't have been eavesdropping, I blurted out my thoughts anyway.

'Wait, what?'

Noah slowly turned around as Georgina gave him an apologetic look, as if she had just let something slip she shouldn't have.

'I bought the bookshop,' Noah said after clearing his throat. 'I'm, uh, the owner.'

'How?' I wasn't sure I was breathing properly.

'Just before I went to New York, Georgina's father told me the shop was struggling and we exchanged email addresses. We shared ideas and talked about books we liked. And then he told me a couple of years later he needed to sell so he could retire and so I offered to buy it. And keep Georgina on as manager.'

I didn't know what to say.

'We've worked hard to bring sales up,' Georgina said. 'Noah's been a lifesaver and now we're in the same city, we won't have to Zoom all the time.' She laughed and again, I felt a weird pinch in my stomach. 'I can't wait for this event. It sounds fun. Do you want my email, Stevie, and we can plan it together? I'm sure Noah is busy enough with his new job.'

'Uh, sure,' I said, still shocked by the news that Noah owned this place.

We swapped details and I said I'd be in touch after clearing the party with Deborah.

'So, I really need a coffee and it's lunch time so shall we stop off somewhere before we go back to the office?' Noah was saying as we

The Plot Twist

stepped outside. I couldn't answer. I felt like I was still in a trance. My mind was racing. We walked towards the end of the alley. 'Stevie, yes to lunch?'

'Wait.' I stopped by the wall and leaned against it. 'I need a minute.'

Noah stopped too and stood in front of me. 'What's wrong? Are you okay?'

'No,' I admitted. I looked at him. 'This is crazy.'

'What do you mean?'

'I feel like my head hasn't stopped spinning since I walked into your office and saw... you.' I took a breath. 'You bought our bookshop?'

It was a question because I still wasn't sure it was real. I wasn't sure what was real any more. For a minute, I wondered if I had imagined our year together, but now I'd been back to the place where we met, I knew it had happened and it'd been real.

'Yes.' Noah moved closer. 'I had to buy it. It was going to disappear otherwise. And then it would have really been like...' He trailed off but I knew what he'd been about to say.

'We never happened?'

There was a short silence as we both looked at one another. I longed to know what he was thinking and I could bet he felt the same.

'When I saw your name on the list of staff at Turn the Pages the first day...' Noah broke our silence then, speaking urgently. 'I couldn't believe it. That you were being thrown in my path after all these years, after all this time. I never forgot about you. Of course I didn't. Stevie, I was happy to see you again.'

I raised an eyebrow. 'I'm not sure if I can say the same.'

He sighed. 'No, I know. I don't blame you either.'

'You dumped me like the year we spent together meant nothing and—' I started, my eyes blazing at him.

Noah moved forward and leaned an arm against the wall above my head, stopping me in my tracks. 'It didn't mean nothing to me. It meant *everything*.'

I didn't dare blink as we looked at one another. I was even more confused but my heart was pounding at his words. At his closeness. He was close enough to...

'Why did you buy the bookshop?' I asked him, my voice so faint it seemed to disappear on the breeze.

'Because it led me to you.'

God. I didn't know what I was thinking. Well, I wasn't. I was feeling a lot. Too much. But Noah telling me he had bought our bookshop so it wouldn't disappear, because it had brought us together, snapped something in me. It was like he'd flicked on a switch and even though it was a terrible idea, I couldn't stop myself. I reached out and pulled his coat lapels, drawing him towards me. I caught a glimpse of his dimple before our lips met and I closed my eyes, letting my body sink into his.

Our lips met in a frenzy. I seemed to remember our kisses before being sweet and moreish like a cupcake, but this kiss was hungry and dangerous and decadent. It was like a deliciously rich dark chocolate cake covered in smooth buttercream that after one taste you could happily gauge on and finish the whole thing in one sitting.

Noah kept one arm above me on the wall and the other hand moved to my waist, gripping me tightly as I moved my hands around his neck, and then into his hair. When our tongues met, I murmured and Noah moved his hand from my hip to my leg, lifting it and wrapping it around him, melting us closer together. He devoured me with his mouth yet it wasn't enough.

'Closer,' I said between kisses, desperately. I needed more. I needed everything.

Noah brought his other hand down and picked me up. I

wrapped both legs around him and he pressed me up against the wall. My hands hooked around his neck again as our lips reconnected. Noah's tongue danced in my mouth. I groaned when I felt what this kiss was doing to him. I moved against him and I felt him tremble.

'Stevie,' Noah grunted, pulling away from my mouth. He dropped kisses down my neck and onto my collarbone. And this time, I was the one who trembled. 'I want you so badly,' he said, whispering in my ear before pulling my lobe into his mouth and sucking it.

I could feel how much he wanted me. Even with our trousers separating us. And I felt the same need right between my legs. My nipples were straining against my top too. My body remembered every kiss, every touch, and it craved it all again.

'Noah, tell me...' I started to say, thinking about how he'd driven me crazy in bed telling me what to do.

But then a siren sounded out. It was sudden and loud and piercing and it was like someone had thrown a bottle of water over us.

I froze. I looked over Noah's shoulder and saw a police car zoom past on the main road. We were in an alleyway just a few feet away from the hubbub of London. In broad daylight. And my legs were around his waist. We had lost all sense of where we were.

Seeing the horror on my face, Noah pulled back. 'Shit,' he said.

He put me down slowly. Gently.

My feet found the floor but I stumbled. Noah quickly wrapped an arm around my waist and held me upright. My breathing was ragged. My legs felt shaky. I looked up at him, unable to believe what had just happened.

'Shit is right,' I said.

Noah let go of my waist and took a big step backwards. His chest was rising and falling rapidly and I could see he was still straining against his trousers. He pushed his tousled hair back as he watched me, cautiously.

I sucked in air, trying to slow my pulse. I leaned back against the wall, needing it to take my weight in case I slid down onto the floor. I reached up to touch my fingertip to my swollen lips. Every part of my body wanted to pull Noah back and continue that electric kiss. But my head had been switched on by that siren. We were in public. And this was not only my ex, but also my boss. The moment had gone and now panic washed over me.

'Are you okay?' Noah asked finally, as if he couldn't take my silence any longer. He made to step closer again.

I put a hand up and he froze. All I could think about was how this man had hurt me once. And he would do it again.

'I can't do this,' I said.

Noah flinched. 'Stevie...'

I shook my head and pushed myself off the wall, walking away from Noah and out of the alley.

And he watched me go just like I had watched him on the day he left me.

16

'IKISSEDNOAH.'

'Sorry, what?' Liv asked down the phone.

Admittedly, it had come out rather hysterically. I tried again. 'I kissed Noah.'

I was walking aimlessly around the city. The October sunshine filtered through the gap in the coloured leaves above me. People walked past oblivious to the monumental thing that had just happened. It was crazy that London could continue to beat just as it had before that kiss because I felt completely different.

'Or *he* kissed *me*. No, I think it was me, Liv. It was me. I made THE MOVE.'

'Bloody hell,' Liv said. 'Are you okay?'

'Nope, not even a little bit.' I pushed my hair out of my eyes and looked around. I was a mile or so away from the office. I spotted a bench and sank down onto it knowing I couldn't face going back there just yet. I had no idea where Noah was but I really didn't want to see him right now.

'Okay. Breathe. And tell me what happened exactly,' Liv said soothingly. Thankfully, she wasn't at the library, she was writing in her flat, so my panicked phone call had been picked up immediately.

So, I told her. About Noah apologising for how things ended between us, saying he regretted it, him telling me it was hard to stay professional, that I was more beautiful now... and then the big hitters – him buying the bookshop we'd met in and him saying that our year together had meant everything to him.

'Then we were in an alleyway, I was against a wall, there was no one around and he looked at me... You know when they give you *that look*?'

'Oh, yeah, you didn't stand a chance,' Liv agreed.

'So, I just grabbed him and pulled him in for a kiss.'

She whistled. 'Okay, that's hot. I mean, he bought a bookshop for you. Talk about a grand gesture.'

'I can't even think straight. Why did he say our year together meant so much to him when he was the one who left me? Why have I not heard from him for five years? Why is he saying all these things when I am over him?'

I wasn't sure if the last part was a lie or not. I'd been over Noah, hadn't I? I mean, I thought he was never coming back and I had moved on. But completely over him? I suppose if I had been, that kiss wouldn't have felt so good. Shit.

'All I do know is he dumped me five years ago and that I don't want my heart broken all over again.'

'Of course not. That's completely understandable. He left you and now he's acting like it was a big mistake. That's so confusing.'

'So confusing,' I agreed.

'I have one question though – what was the kiss like?'

I leaned back against the bench and sighed. 'It was perfect.'

'Oh, man. You're in trouble.'

'I really am. I need to go back to work. What do I do, Liv?'

'How did you leave it?'

'I told him I can't do this and I just walked away.'

'Wow. That's main character energy right there,' Liv said approvingly. She, like me, had read one too many romances but I liked her way of putting it. 'The ball's in his court then. He needs to apologise, tell you why he left and what he wants now if he really does have feelings for you again. Or still has them. It's not up to you. I think you walk on into your office, head up high, and act like nothing happened. He won't say anything to you at work.'

'True. He is my boss.' Another reason to add to the list of why that kiss was a crazy thing to have happened. 'What about at the end of work though?' I asked, not sure I could deal with another conversation with Noah today.

'Walk out with other people and face the music another day. If you don't know how you feel about things then you don't need to say anything or do anything,' Liv said firmly.

'That's true. I have no idea what to feel right now. I loved him but that was a long time ago and he's different now. I'm different now. And one swoon-worthy kiss doesn't change the fact he broke my heart. Okay, I'm going back and I will be an ice queen. I will not let on that kiss has shaken me up at all.'

'I'm waving imaginary pom poms,' Liv said.

'Thanks, Liv. Speak to you later.'

I ended the call and stood up. I wouldn't bring up the kiss. That was on him to do. And with Liv's pep talk echoing in my ears, I went back to the office, marching straight to my desk without glancing in Noah's office direction.

'Oh, Stevie,' Gita called over from her desk. 'Noah said to tell you he's out for the rest of the day so if you need to chat about the Deborah Day event, just email him.'

Talk about an anti-climax.

'Thanks,' I called back, shaking my head. Of course I would flip out at our kiss and Noah would not be affected by it at all.

Email him! Not likely. The ball was firmly in his court for our next interaction. And for someone who always preferred to have the last word, that was not an easy decision for me to make but I knew it was the right one.

I opened up a document and started to write an email to Deborah Day and her agent about our idea for a launch party at the bookshop that had started all of this mess. All the while, I tried very hard not to think about the kiss with Noah.

* * *

Ever get a feeling someone is avoiding you?

Noah didn't come back on Thursday, and on Friday he rushed into his office and holed himself up in there for most of the day. We didn't even have any email contact. I wasn't sure whether to feel relieved or disappointed. I'd spent the night tossing and turning and replaying our kiss outside the bookshop way too many times to not call myself obsessed. That kiss had been unlike anything I'd had the past five years. Every man I'd been with since Noah now seemed like they'd been in black and white whereas Noah was vibrant colour.

But what was I supposed to do?

Yes, Noah had said some things that suggested he was feeling the same pull towards me that I was towards him, and he'd kissed me very enthusiastically, but he hadn't said anything about wanting me back. And until he did, he was still the man who had broken my heart. I had to be careful. I had to be cautious. I couldn't risk being hurt by him again. Because I had got over him once. But twice? I wasn't sure that would be possible.

I stared at my computer screen feeling that Friday feeling. I really just wanted to go home. I was tired. And I was annoyed that Noah was avoiding me. It was all very well channelling ice queen energy but if the person you were trying to ice was never around, it was a moot point. I just wanted to be alone and get into my pjs and maybe eat a lot of ice cream.

I focused on working with Georgina at the bookshop to create the perfect Halloween launch event for *Bitten*. I sent a brief to Emily who started to design invitations and posters, and I created a list of people to invite. I sent over everything we'd decided so far to Deborah Day and got a smiley face emoji back, so I took that as the closest thing to praise I was likely to get from her.

After lunch, the final copies of *Bitten* arrived in the office and the whole team helped me pile them in the boardroom with press releases and envelopes. Then I started to pack them all and put on address labels. The afternoon wore on and I was starting to get RSI from the job. The whole time, I was keeping one eye on the clock, waiting for the moment I could escape for the weekend.

But suddenly, Noah marched out of his office and shouted at everyone on the floor to come into the boardroom for an emergency meeting. I sat there with the books and looked up in surprise as everyone filed in.

Noah followed everyone in and stopped short when he saw me and the table covered in books, envelopes and paperwork.

'What the hell is all this?'

All eyes turned to me and I tried to stay calm. 'I'm posting out copies of *Bitten* – to reviewers, authors, retailers, everyone we can think of like we planned,' I said, trying to stay cheerful. 'Do you like the envelopes?' I showed him the black envelopes I'd found and managed to get at a discount price. We were going full Halloween with the campaign now and the address labels had tiny pumpkins and bats on courtesy of Emily's design skills.

Noah looked non-plussed for a moment then gave a dismissive wave of his hand and moved to the front of the room.

'Anyway,' he said. 'I just heard that my father is flying in on

Monday. That's Mr Matthews of Matthews & Wood Publishing, so I want you stop and spend the rest of today making sure you are on top of the priorities we agreed you should be working on and are ready to answer any questions that he asks you. Because he will ask you questions. And I want everyone in the office by 8 a.m. He believes that's when the day starts. And he'll expect to see us here too. If anyone is running late, don't bother coming in at all.' Noah looked around the room. 'Go on then,' he barked, and everyone scattered.

My mouth fell open. 'Jesus,' I muttered, and went back to my envelopes.

'Something to say, Stevie?' Noah snapped at me.

I looked up. We were alone again. For the first time since our kiss. I wondered if Noah was as aware of that fact as I was. Probably not.

I shrugged. 'No, boss,' I replied, sarcasm heavy.

Noah stormed to the door but then he paused and looked back. 'This has to go well,' he said quietly.

'You got it, boss,' I replied, carrying on with what I was doing.

'Stevie,' he said with an exasperated sigh. 'Can you not call me that?'

'What else should I call you?'

He let go of the door handle, spun around and leaned on the desk opposite me. My breath hitched as I looked at the fire in his eyes.

'You said you couldn't do this again,' he hissed.

'Do you blame me?' I challenged.

Noah sighed. 'No. You're right. It was a mistake.' His words pierced my gut like a knife. 'I am just your boss.' Bitterness tinged his words but I wasn't sure if that was because he regretted that fact or just wasn't happy about having to work with me. 'I have to focus on work. My father is not coming to see the good things here, he's looking for a reason to get rid of everyone and replace them with a team from New York. Do you want that to happen?'

'Of course not,' I snapped back.

We stared at one another for a few seconds before I had to look away. I heard Noah exhale.

'Good. We are on the same page,' he said finally.

I started back up stuffing envelopes, needing to do something with my hands to stop them trying to reach for him. 'We haven't been on the same page for five years,' I replied.

'Stevie,' Noah said then, all anger gone from his voice. He said my name like it was a wistful sigh. It made my hands still.

I held my breath for what he was going to say.

But then there was a knock on the door, and Emily edged into the boardroom cautiously, her eyes darting back and forth between us. I knew she couldn't miss the tension in the room. 'New York are on the phone, Noah. Do you—'

'I'll take it,' he said, cutting her off and sweeping out.

I let out a puff of air.

'What did I just walk into?' Emily asked, her eyebrows disappearing up into her forehead.

'Nothing,' I mumbled, but I knew my voice didn't sound at all steady.

She looked at me for a moment. 'Look, I've been wanting to tell you that I'm sorry. I should have backed you up about *Bitten* straight away. Especially when Paul was criticising romance books. I hate it when he treats love stories like they're beneath him, I always have. I guess Deborah got all our backs up. I hadn't had the time or inclination to read it but I started it yesterday, and you're right; it is really good. I'm glad you joined us here, Stevie. We can learn a lot from you.'

'Thanks, Emily.' I sighed. 'That is if I can keep working with Noah though.'

Right now, leaving seemed like the more attractive option but then I thought about not seeing him again and I couldn't imagine it.

'I'm kind of in a mess,' I admitted then, both to Emily and to myself.

'Oh, hon,' she said. 'I know you think me and Gita are gossips but we'd never tell a secret. I won't make you tell me but I think you should think about sharing what's going on with us. I can see you're upset and I know it has something to do with Noah. Yeah, he's pissed us all off but with you, it seems different.'

When someone is nice to you when you're upset, it's really hard not to cry.

I nodded. 'Thank you.'

I knew Noah wouldn't really want people here to know about our past but it was becoming harder each day to hide it. And it did feel like Emily and Gita would have my back.

'Can we talk about it later?'

Emil's face lit up. 'Drinks?'

I was exhausted but I also didn't want to go home alone. 'Yes, please.'

17

'Woah,' Gita said after I had spilled my guts to her and Emily. It was after work and we were at the bar opposite the office again. We'd all stayed late to make sure all our work was finished then headed here for wine. It was much busier as it was Friday night but we'd found a corner table by the window, and I had told them how I really knew Noah. I couldn't bring myself to admit to the kiss outside the bookshop though. We had both agreed it had been a mistake so I had to try to forget all about it, no matter how hard that might prove to be.

'You can't tell anyone though,' I begged.

'Well, of course not,' Emily said, waving her hand. 'I knew there was something in the air between you two. Sexual tension.'

I snorted. 'Just tension more like.'

'So, when you walked in that first day...'

I nodded. 'I had no idea my new boss was my ex-boyfriend. And it's so hard to focus on this new job working with him.'

'Well, he's more of a dick than I first thought if he dumped you,' Emily said.

'Yes,' Gita agreed. 'You were the best thing that happened to him.'

'How do you know that?' I asked with an appreciative laugh.

Gita waved her hand. 'It's obvious. I see the way he looks at you; it's like he knows it too.'

'I don't think so,' I said, wishing she was right about that. 'But he has said some things... and the bookshop where we met? He bought it. He said he didn't want it to disappear.'

'Oh, that's romantic,' Emily said dreamily. 'Who knew our big bad boss had such a sweet, sentimental side to him?'

'You're supposed to be giving me a pep talk to forget him,' I reminded her. It was such a beautiful gesture though. Damn it. I buried my head in my hands. 'I can't believe the universe has done this to me.'

'What will you do?' Gita asked.

'I keep telling myself I only have to stay for six months and get this experience on my CV then I can look for another publishing job.'

'Solid plan,' Emily said, nodding along. 'And we will be joining you if things don't get better. I'm sorry, Stevie. It must suck working with your ex.'

'It really does suck,' I agreed, draining the remainder of my wine glass.

'But everyone in the office loves you and hates him so everyone is on your side even though they don't know it,' Gita said. 'And I bet Noah regrets running off to New York. Seeing you again must have made him see what a mistake he made.'

I smiled. 'You're too sweet. I'd be lying if I said I didn't hope that was the case, but I don't think it is. Noah is so stressed at work that I doubt he's even thinking about me.'

I didn't like how annoyed that made me feel. I wanted him to be thinking about me as much as I was about him, I couldn't lie.

'He seems pretty worried about his father coming over,' Gita observed.

'I never met him,' I said. 'I don't understand why Noah wants to work with him if he's that bad though.'

Emily shrugged. 'Family pressure maybe. I guess we have to help and make it go well but after hearing your story, I kind of want to sabotage it,' she said with a mischievous grin.

'We'd only be sabotaging ourselves though,' Gita pointed out.

'I suppose so,' Emily huffed.

'Let's hope we make it out the other side,' I said. I smiled at them. 'I'm glad I told you both. I thought that I should keep it a secret but it's really hard working with him every day.'

'Of course it is,' Emily said. 'I'd hate to even see any of my exes, let alone have them as my bloody boss! You are a braver woman than me, Stevie, and we are now a team, okay? We will get through this together and in six months, we'll find amazing new jobs and stick both fingers up at Noah on our way out.'

We clinked glasses to that but I knew it would be far easier said than done.

* * *

Monday morning arrived and I woke up an hour before my alarm after a restless night, nerves high for the morning ahead. It felt important to impress Mr Matthews. And I got the distinct feeling he was not an easy man to impress. At least he knew nothing about mine and Noah's past. We'd never met before. I was nothing to him but a member of staff. And I knew I could do this job. I needed to be confident and get through this.

I put on the dress that made me feel the most capable and the headband my parents got me for Christmas for good luck. And I stopped off for an iced latte on the way in for a caffeine kickstart.

> Good luck! You've got this! I'm still cheering you on! xxx

I smiled at the message from Liv. I'd told her what was happening today when we had coffee at the weekend, and she reminded me that however nervous I was, Noah would be feeling much worse, and that was true; he had everything riding on this. I knew we had to put our situation to one side, and that was actually a relief.

When I walked in, Emily rushed out of the office floor and met me in reception. She looked frantic. Not a great start to the morning.

'Have you heard anything from Noah?'

'No, why?' I checked the time. It was ten to eight. We were all supposed to be in by 8 a.m. I would have thought Noah would have been the first one in.

'He's not here,' she hissed. 'But his father is. And we thought Noah was bad tempered...' She shook her head. 'Anyway, where the hell is he?'

'Has anyone called him?'

'No, we didn't think of that!' Emily tutted. 'Of course we have, and emailed, but nothing. His father is waiting in his office and looks pissed.'

I leaned past her and saw everyone in the office standing around nervously.

I really didn't want to say what I was about to, but I sighed. 'I could check his flat, I suppose.'

'Are you sure?' she asked. 'Will it be too awkward?'

'I'm not sure we have any choice,' I said reluctantly.

'It makes no sense him not being here.'

'No, it doesn't.' I bit my lip, wondering if I should be worried.

'Okay, tell Mr Matthews that we think there's been a mix up and Noah went to the airport to pick him up,' I said, turning back to the lift.

'Good thinking! Text me as soon as you find him!'

I stepped into the lift. 'I will.'

Emily gave me a wave as the door shut.

I was confused. Noah had been so stressed about his father coming to the office, so where the hell was he? I walked out of the building and flagged down a taxi. On my salary, I would usually either walk or take the Tube but this was an emergency. I gave the driver Noah's address that I still knew off by heart, and we set off towards the river.

Noah's flat was in a plush, modern building overlooking the Thames, and yes, he lived in the penthouse. I don't know why I hadn't twigged there was more to his family than he'd told me as soon as I went there but I guess the cliché is true – love really is blind.

Walking into the lobby, I saw with relief that the concierge I knew was still there. I had practically lived here once and seen this man a lot, and he had rung me about a parcel, but that had been five years go so I wasn't sure if he would still recognise my face.

'I don't know if you remember me—'

'Stevie!' He beamed. 'Of course I remember you. Are you here to see Mr Matthews? You must be so happy he's back.'

I forced on a smile. 'Yes, is it okay to go up?'

'You're always on the green list,' he said cheerfully. 'Go on up, and it's good to see you!'

I thanked him and headed to the lift. My heart was pounding in my chest as I rode up to the penthouse. My mind flashed back to all the times I'd stayed in this flat. I had actually thought Noah was going to ask me to move in when he'd said he had something important to talk about. But then he'd told me he was moving to New York without me.

The doors opened then, and I was in front of his door. I couldn't believe I was having to do this but I thought about all my colleagues and knew they needed Noah there.

I took a breath and rapped on his front door.

18

'Noah? It's Stevie. Why aren't you at work?' I called through his front door when there was no response to my knock. 'Your father is there! And everyone is freaking out so I came to find you...'

I heard a weak noise followed by a cough.

'Noah?' I said through the door. I heard another cough. He was definitely in there but clearly not coming to the door. So I turned the handle and it opened up, thankfully. I walked in and called his name. I heard a weak sound again so I turned and headed for his bedroom.

I stopped in the doorway. Noah was in bed, the bedding all messy around him like he'd had a restless night. The curtains were drawn, shutting out all light. He was on his back, his top half uncovered, flashing his bare chest. His eyes were shut. On the bedside table were piles of tissues and on the floor was a smashed glass. 'Noah?' I said.

He opened one eye and groaned. 'Why is it so loud in here?' His voice was weak and hoarse.

'Um, it's completely silent.'

'No, roadworks,' he said, lifting one hand to his head. 'Pound, pound, pound. And there is no water.'

'I think you dropped it,' I said, looking at the broken glass. 'Does your head hurt?'

Noah coughed and rolled over onto his side. He pulled the covers up and opened his eyes fully. 'Everything hurts. Have I fallen?'

'No, I think you have the flu.'

His eyes widened as he looked at me in the doorway. 'Stevie?' Then he shook his head. 'I'm dreaming again. You are in the bookshop and I bought you a book.'

'Oh, shit,' I said. He really was out of it. 'Close your eyes again, rest; I'm coming back.'

'That's what you always say then I wake up,' Noah mumbled, rolling onto his back again and coughing.

I left his room and walked into the open-plan kitchen area. My whole flat could fit into just this part. It was a dream kitchen. I tried not to think about how I once saw myself living here. There was no point in thinking about that now. Onwards and upwards. I grabbed a glass and filled it with water then looked in a couple of cupboards until I found a dustpan and brush. I hurried back into his room. 'Noah, you need to drink this. Sit up,' I said, walking to the bed.

'Can't,' he moaned.

'You can. Here.' I reached behind him to pull up a pillow. Noah groaned but managed to prop his elbow on it and lift his head up. I handed him the water as he opened his eyes and looked at me but I wasn't sure if he had grasped whether I was really here or not. 'And these.' I passed him two paracetamol tablets I'd had in my bag and watched as he dutifully swallowed with the water. It made him cough but he did it then he flopped back down with a heavy sigh.

I cleared up the broken glass then went back out into the

kitchen to throw it away, then I remembered everyone at the office was panicking so I put my phone on speaker and called Emily.

'Stevie, please tell me you found him?' Emily hissed into the phone.

'Yes, and he's ill. Looks like the flu. He can't come in. He's half-delirious with it.'

'You are fucking kidding me!'

'Afraid not. Put me through to speak to Mr Matthews and the rest of you carry on with work,' I instructed as I went to look in Noah's fridge. It was empty save for some fruit and vegetables, and two bottles of wine. But I spotted lemon and ginger so I grabbed those and put the kettle on.

'I love you,' she said as she put my call through to Noah's office.

His father gruffly picked up the phone. 'Matthews.'

'Hi, Mr Matthews, my name is Stephanie Phillips. I work with your son,' I said in my politest voice as I made Noah's hot drink.

'Yes?'

'I'm at Noah's flat. He's caught the flu and can't get out of bed.'

Mr Matthews tutted. 'Are you serious?'

'Deadly. But I'm sure you'll find everyone at the office really helpful if you need anything, or did you want to come and see Noah?'

'I don't want to catch it,' he replied. 'Tell him to call me tonight and I expect to see him tomorrow before I fly back.'

He hung up.

'The apple doesn't fall far from the tree then,' I muttered as I fixed Noah a hot lemon and ginger drink. I added a drop of honey to it too then carried the mug into Noah's bedroom. 'Noah?' I said softly as his eyes were closed again.

He opened his eyes. 'Stevie, am I dreaming again?'

'No, I'm really here. I made you another drink. You sound so hoarse.'

'I dropped my water,' he said weakly.

'It's okay, I cleared it up.' It sounded like he hadn't been able to get up for more water so no wonder his voice sounded so bad. He needed fluids. 'Drink this, okay? Can you try sitting again?'

I lifted Noah's pillows up and helped him to sit up. The duvet slipped again and his bare chest was on show. This was definitely not the time to notice those ripped abs I remembered but I was only human. 'Here you go,' I said, averting my eyes and passing him the hot drink.

He took a sip. 'I can't believe you're really here. How?'

'Well, you didn't turn up to work to see your father so everyone was worried. I came to find you,' I replied.

His eyes widened. 'Oh my God. My father,' he croaked.

'I've sorted it, don't worry. Just rest. And drink all of that, okay?' I turned to go.

'Stevie,' he said, sounding pained.

I glanced back. 'Don't talk, save your throat.'

'But I don't want...' He coughed and had more of the tea. 'I don't want you to go,' he managed to finish, leaning back against the pillows.

'It's okay, I won't,' I found myself promising. I couldn't not. He seemed so helpless and had clearly struggled on his own being so poorly. 'But you have nothing in so let me pop out and bring you some things to help. I won't be long.'

'What a dream,' I heard him murmur as I left the bedroom. I hoped the paracetamol and fluids would help soon as he still sounded like he couldn't grasp me actually being there. Although, it did feel somewhat surreal to me too.

I left the flat and went to the supermarket over the road. I messaged Emily to tell her what I'd told his father and that I'd be in soon once Noah seemed okay to be left.

> Stay there. His father is on the warpath! Just come in tomorrow with Noah. And don't catch it!

Then she sent loads of crossed finger emojis.

I wasn't worried about catching it; I had a good immune system like my dad. My mum would constantly have colds but we seemed to avoid them so hopefully I'd be fine. And it was a relief Emily suggested I stay because I didn't want to leave him alone just yet. He had nothing in the flat, no one to help, and I knew he'd be worried about not seeing his father. I had twenty-four hours to help him feel better.

Rushing around the shop, I grabbed everything I thought would help Noah feel better then headed back up to his flat. I peeped in and he'd fallen back asleep but he had drunk all of the hot lemon and ginger drink I'd made so that was good news.

I unpacked the shopping then started to make a homemade chicken and vegetable soup. Noah's flat was hooked up to everything so I just needed to ask for some background music and some soft jazz started to play. I even found a spare pair of slippers in the bathroom so I put them on as the kitchen floor was cold.

I pulled my hair into a messy bun and hummed along to the music as I cooked. I hadn't made soup from scratch for ages and there was nothing cosier. Cooking had always been relaxing to me and I soon forgot to worry about being in my ex's flat and just enjoyed the moment.

The kitchen soon smelt amazing and my stomach rumbled. Outside, the day had turned grey and cloudy and eventually, it started raining.

While I let the soup simmer, I wandered around Noah's flat. My eyes were soon drawn to his bookcase in the living room and I couldn't stop myself from snooping at the books he had on it. When we were together, he'd been a crime junkie and loved non-fiction but now those books were mingled in with some very familiar titles.

I looked at the pastel-coloured spines of some of my favourite romance novels past and present, a few that were my all-time favourites, ones I'd definitely talked to him about or ones that I'd read in the year we were together. The sight of them gave my heart a jolt. He had hinted he read romance now but I hadn't realised he read quite so much.

My heart whispered that maybe they'd reminded him of me but my head told it to shut up. Noah had always been a book lover and now he worked in publishing, he had to read all genres. It didn't mean it had anything to do with me.

I hated the hope I felt that maybe it did.

Turning away from the books, I went back to the soup, which was ready, so I ladled some out into two portions and cut up some crusty bread. I picked up one of the bowls and before taking it in to Noah, held it by the window and snapped a photo with the rain behind.

Peak cosy vibes

I captured my photo and posted it on Instagram. Then I carried the tray into the bedroom.

'Lunch time,' I said as he stirred at my entrance.

'You came back,' Noah said in wonder. His eyes seemed to be focusing properly now.

'I did, I'm here,' I said. 'And I made soup to help you feel better. Can you manage some?'

He managed to sit himself up and watched as I balanced the tray on his lap. 'You made this?' he croaked.

'Yes, and it's delicious so eat it all. It'll help. I'll come back in a bit but shout if you need me.'

'Eat with me,' Noah said as I turned to go.

I looked back and saw his hopeful expression. 'Okay.' I went back into the kitchen and put my bowl of soup on a tray and took it into his room. I sat down in the boucle chair by Noah's bed. Noah kept stealing glances at me as he ate as if he still couldn't believe I was really there. It was making me uncomfortable so I cleared my throat and started talking, my go-to to diffuse tension.

I waved my phone. 'I took a picture of my soup with the rain behind it, and Instagram is loving it. I don't know what it is about autumn and everything cosy but I can't get enough. I just love this time of year. Although I'm guessing you don't as it's made you ill,' I added with a sympathetic look. 'But look at how many likes the photo is getting. Your flat is definitely more aesthetic than mine.'

I showed him the picture.

Noah leaned over with a groan to see it. 'You post things like that?'

'Yeah, and books, of course.' I scrolled through some of my recent photos so he could see, and I smiled at one of me and Liv in a bookshop. 'Aiden took that after complaining we'd been in there for two hours,' I explained. 'Anyway, you don't want to look at my Instagram.'

I put my phone down.

'I do. I haven't been able to,' Noah said as he looked down at his food.

'What do you mean?'

'You blocked me,' he whispered, still looking at his food. 'Everywhere.'

'Oh. Yeah.' I remembered sitting on that bench and cutting him out of my online life. 'I needed to. Otherwise I probably would have stalked you for years,' I said, trying to joke, but it sounded hollow. 'I didn't want to see how happy you were in New York,' I admitted, my cheeks turning pink.

Noah was still staring at his soup. I wondered for a moment if he'd heard me or not.

'This is delicious,' he said as he took the final mouthful.

I should have known he wouldn't want to talk about him dumping me again. I needed to remember that we were supposed to keep things professional now. I tried not to let hurt seep into my voice.

'Good. It's the perfect autumn recipe. Do you want more?'

'I'm starving. Oh, I haven't eaten all weekend,' he said, as if suddenly realising that.

'God, Noah, you have to look after yourself. There is such a thing as Deliveroo, you know!' Tutting, I got up and re-filled his bowl with the rest of the soup and sliced up more bread and took it back to him. 'Okay, eat that. You need to build your strength back up. You should have called me and told me you were ill. You know I would have come over.'

'But I've been so mean to you,' he croaked as he ate, keeping one eye on me.

'True,' I said. 'But you can always ask me for help.'

Noah shook his head but didn't say anything else. I realised as I watched him eat that he really was all alone here. He didn't have anyone to reach out to. And that made me feel sad for him. And for what could have been. I didn't say anything else but took the tray into the kitchen to clear up.

When I'd finished, I messaged Emily to see how things were at work. She replied:

> Mr Matthews is what nightmares are made of.

Oh dear.

I logged on to my work emails and sorted a few more things for *Bitten* then I peeked in to see Noah was stirring after another nap.

'You're still here,' he said.

'Yeah,' I said, amused he was still struggling to believe I was there.

'Sit with me,' he said, his eyes pleading.

'Okay. I'll get us another hot drink.'

I went to the kitchen and made myself a coffee with Noah's fancy machine and made him another lemon and ginger drink. Then I went back in to see Noah had sat up. He definitely looked less pale now.

'How are you feeling?' I handed him his drink then I sat in the chair and nursed mine.

'Slightly more human but still weak,' he said before taking a sip. 'This is gross.'

I nodded. 'Yup, but it will help. You really should have drunk and eaten more this weekend. No wonder you feel weak.'

'I was so out of it,' Noah said, shaking his head.

'Do you want to sleep more?'

'No, I'm more awake now. Will you still stay?' He looked worried I was going to go.

'I suppose I could stay until this evening, make sure you're okay,' I said slowly, unsure if this was a good idea, but I would feel really bad if I left him when he was only just starting to recover.

'Please,' he begged me.

'Okay, I guess we could watch a film?' I said, knowing that would be easier than talking. It felt strange to suggest it though. Like we'd slipped back in time. I had to firmly remind myself that we hadn't. I was just helping someone who needed me. 'Then I can make us something nutritious for dinner.'

'Thank you,' he said softly. He was staring at me and it was unnerving.

'So, an easy watch for sure, something cosy?' I asked as I grabbed his remote and looked at the huge TV that hung on his wall, preferable to looking into those eyes of his that were tracking every single move I made. 'Ooh, a murder mystery,' I said, finding something that looked like a comforting watch. 'Perfect for sick day, right?' I was babbling but I couldn't help it. I was in Noah's bedroom and I couldn't stop thinking about how before I would have been beside him on that comfy bed of his, snuggled into his strong and sexy chest. I fidgeted on the chair as I started the film before Noah had even agreed to it.

I really tried to concentrate on it but after fifteen minutes, I didn't know who any of the characters were.

Noah coughed then and weakly said my name. 'Stevie.'

'Are you okay?' I asked, looking over in concern.

'You blocked me and changed your email so I couldn't contact you,' he said.

'What?' I said, trying to work out what he was saying. 'Do you have a fever again?' I reached over to feel his forehead. He flinched at my touch but I kept my hand there. 'You don't feel too hot.'

'No. I...' He spoke more firmly then. 'Can I please have your email address now? Your personal one, not the work one.' He coughed. 'Please?'

I let go of his forehead. He looked so desperate and it confused me. 'Why? You can email me at work.'

'No, I can't. Not... this. Stevie, please.'

'Okay. If you want it. I'll text it to your work phone.'

I did and he checked, smiling when he saw it and visibly relaxing. I frowned, hoping he wasn't still delirious. He leaned back and turned his eyes towards the TV so I did the same, but I really had no idea what was going on in the film. I hated being so close to Noah but so far away.

I knew though that that was the way it had to be.

19

Noah fell asleep before the end of the film so as I hadn't concentrated on it, I slipped out before finding out who the murderer was to make us dinner. Liv messaged me to ask how things were going with Noah's father so I sent her a voice note as I chopped vegetables.

'Noah didn't turn up for work this morning so I came to his flat to see what was up and he's been ill all weekend. Something like the flu. He looked like shit when I got here, no food in and I don't think he's really eaten or drunk enough. I've stayed with him to try to get him to feel better. His father didn't seem very sympathetic when I told him, said he expected to see him tomorrow whatever. So, we have a clue as to why Noah is so often in a bad mood. What a douchebag.'

I made a chicken and vegetable pasta bake for dinner to try to get all the food groups in and when I put it in the oven, my eyes fell on an open bottle of red wine on the counter so I poured myself a glass. Because if there was a day that required wine, this was it. I checked Instagram and then opened my personal emails. I didn't ever get many. Just book deals or shops tempting me with autumn decor or cosy cardigans or memes from my parents.

But I saw I had one from Noah.

Email from noahmatthews1 to Steviebookworm.
Stevie,
I am in my apartment in New York and all I can think about is you. And the look on your face when I walked away from you that day in the park. I don't think I'll ever forget it. If telling you I was moving and we were over didn't break my heart, that look shattered it into a million tiny pieces.

I looked up from my phone, my heart thumping inside my chest. It was dated a couple of months after Noah broke up with me. I looked again. It had originally been addressed to my old email. The one I'd deleted after I blocked him everywhere else. I had wanted no way to contact him or look at his new life and torture myself, but I'd cut him off too. He'd tried to email me. I'd never got it. But he'd sent it to me now so I'd read it.

But did I want to?

My phone beeped with a voice note reply from Liv. In a trance from seeing that email, I pressed play and her voice rang out in Noah's kitchen.

'That explains your picture of soup on Instagram,' Liv said. 'Noah's flat looks fabulous. You're so sweet to look after him. I bloody hope he appreciates it. And is nicer to you! You'll look after yourself, won't you? I don't want him to hurt you. You're the sweetest; he doesn't deserve you.'

'She's right.'

I spun around to see Noah in a dressing gown, shuffling out of his bedroom into the open-plan living area. I stared at him, my cheeks flushed, my heart still aching.

'You shouldn't be out of bed,' I said.

'I sent you something,' he said, nodding to my phone.

'I saw it but...' I trailed off then gestured weakly to the oven. 'I'm making dinner. It's almost ready, go back and rest.'

'I think it will do me good to be up for a bit,' Noah said. 'I'll sit though.'

He walked to the leather sofa and sunk into it. Then he waved me over.

With some trepidation, I sat down next to him and took a long sip of the wine.

'Oh, was this okay?' I asked, gesturing to the glass.

Noah smiled. 'After today, you can have anything.' Then he coughed and groaned.

'Best not to talk. Dinner should be ready now.'

I jumped up and went back into the kitchen, feeling awkward as hell. My phone burned in my pocket with Noah's email. I looked over to see he was looking out of his window at the rain, so I quickly opened up his email and carried on reading.

> I don't know if it will make you feel any better to hear that I regretted it as soon as I left you. I knew I'd made the biggest mistake of my life. But things are so complicated. I wasn't thinking straight. I'm not thinking straight.
>
> I have no idea if you even want to hear from me. You must hate me. And you should. I hate myself for leaving you. I am trying to do the right thing for everyone. But this isn't the right thing for me. I know that.
>
> Stevie, can we talk please? There are things I should have told you. That I want to tell you. If you'll give me your time. If you can bear to listen.
>
> But I understand if you can't. If you don't ever want to talk to

me again. I wouldn't blame you. I can barely look at myself in the mirror.

I'm thousands of miles away from you but you're still the first thing I think about when I wake up, and the last before I go to sleep.

Please let me explain.

All my love,

Always,

Noah.

My eyes blurred with tears as I put my phone down in disbelief. I turned back to see Noah was now watching me. He looked like he was about to get up but I shook my head.

I walked to his bathroom and closed the door before grabbing a tissue to dab at my eyes. Noah's words had broken me. He had really written that in New York? I had no idea.

A moment later, there was a soft knock on the door. 'Did you read it? Stevie?' Then he coughed again.

'Sit down, Noah.' I opened the door. 'You won't help yourself, will you?'

'I'm so glad you're here,' he said then and kind of stumbled.

I grabbed his arm. 'Sit down, let's eat then we can talk,' I said, trying to bribe him to rest. He looked so frail.

Noah nodded weakly and let me lead him back to the sofa. I had never seen him like this. He looked so vulnerable. It made me want to cry all over again.

Once Noah was back on the sofa, I returned to the kitchen and plated up the pasta bake and carried over two trays to the sofa.

'It has all the good stuff in it,' I said. 'I hope you like it.'

I curled my legs up and tucked in as Noah put his on the coffee table and leaned over to eat it. For a moment, the only soundtrack was the rain still falling down outside soaking London while we stayed warm and dry in Noah's flat.

'So good,' Noah said, breaking the silence. 'I forgot what a good cook you are.'

He was eating at a frantic pace. He must have been so hungry.

'Do you live on takeaways and ready meals?'

'I did try to learn to cook but I just don't have the patience,' Noah replied. He leaned back, his plate already clean. 'And most of the time, I work so late I have to eat in the office anyway.'

'You never used to be such a workaholic,' I pointed out, putting my plate down too.

'I had better things to do back then.'

Noah looked at me and I felt that jolt again. I told myself it was just recognition of someone that I'd been so close to once but when he gave me that look, like he had before I'd kissed him in the alley, it was hard to make my body see it as past tense only. The spark felt live and real and... present tense.

'Did you read it?' he asked again.

I sighed, knowing I couldn't put him off any longer. 'Yes. Did you really regret leaving me like you said in the email?'

'Yes,' he whispered.

I looked away. 'I wish I had known that. I wish I'd read it then. But I don't think it's a good idea to talk about it any more, Noah. We are just hurting ourselves. It's all in the past, right? That's what we agreed.'

'Then I might not get a chance to talk to you again,' he said, coughing. 'Stevie, you being here... Liv was right, I don't deserve it. Leaving you like I did.'

'You already apologised,' I said, going to stand up. I really didn't want to keep digging up the grave of our relationship. It was too painful. If I had received that email, maybe things would have been different. But I hadn't. He stayed in New York and I'd had to move on without him. It felt too hard to keep talking about it.

Noah put a hand on my thigh and I stilled, hating how I responded to his touch. He moved it away as if maybe it had given him a jolt too.

'Please can I explain? You never got that email. I never got a chance.'

I sighed. 'What's the point?'

'I'm ill; you can't refuse,' he said with a hint of mischief in his eyes.

'Guilt trip, nice. Fine, but I'm closing my eyes. I can't look at you.' I curled my legs up under me, leaned against the back of the sofa and closed my eyes. I felt like someone was about to stick in a needle in my arm and I didn't want to watch it going in.

'I didn't tell you who my father was when we met,' Noah began. His voice was rough and croaky and he kept stopping to cough and have a sip of water, but he carried on and I listened. 'For years, I'd tried to make my own way out of his shadow. I wanted to work in publishing because I was good at it, not because he got me the job. He kept asking me to come to New York and work with him and it was hard to refuse, but then I met you and I knew I'd made the right decision to stay here.'

I shifted in my seat but didn't say anything.

Noah waited a beat then continued. 'I wanted to keep you mine, just mine. I was worried if my father got involved, you'd run a mile. Then, just when I knew I had to tell you, the secret being the only thing between us, Dad called me and told me my mum was ill. She had cancer.'

My eyes flew open. 'Noah,' I whispered.

'He was shouting down the phone. He told me that me being so far away and the rift between us had caused her so much stress it had made her ill. She was asking for me. He told me I had to come home, that I needed to stop being selfish and be there for her. Which, of course, I wanted to do. I wanted to be there for her. I felt so guilty. What if he was right and it was all my fault she was ill?'

I wanted to reach for him but I knew it was a bad idea. 'You can't give someone cancer. How is she? Is she okay?'

Noah shook his head. 'I was devastated, Stevie. I was in a mess. My head was all over the place. All I knew was I had to go and be there for her.'

'Why didn't you tell me? I would have told you to go,' I said.

'I know. And you would have waited for me. But I couldn't. I think I wanted you to hate me.'

'Why?' I asked, shocked.

'Because I hated myself for lying to you, for leaving my mum, for not being a good son, for putting my happiness first, for knowing I was going to hurt you and for knowing I had to leave you. For all of it. Leaving you like I did, I knew I didn't deserve your love. It's like what Liv said – I don't deserve you.'

20

Noah finished speaking but I didn't know what to say. He looked at me and I stared back, unsure how to even make sense of what he'd just said. He had just rewritten our last day together in five minutes but that day, he had broken my heart. How was I meant to feel now he was telling me it was all because he thought he didn't deserve to be with me? Part of me longed to believe him, but part of me—

'Bullshit.' This time, I jumped up from the sofa before he could stop me. 'You're really going with "it wasn't you, it was me"? You left me, Noah. You broke my heart. I've spent five years trying hard to get over you! You made me feel like I spent a year living in a dream. That I had been on my own in this. In our relationship. I loved you so much, but I thought you didn't love me. I was devastated when you left. And God, it's awful about your mum, I'm so sorry you had to go through that, but you should have told me. If it's true that you left me just to be with her, then you should have told me. It wasn't fair of you to let me feel the way I felt.' My voice cracked. 'I thought you didn't love me,' I repeated.

I sagged then, my chest heaving. I could feel the tears behind my eyes, and I really didn't want them to come out.

Noah looked up at me from the sofa. Suddenly, he seemed so small. 'I fucked up. I completely fucked up.'

'Yes, yes you did,' I said. 'I think I should go.'

'Please don't.'

'I'm sorry but this is too much.'

He nodded once, showing he understood. That was a relief because I was sure that if he begged me, I wouldn't be able to leave.

'You need to sleep anyway. Your father wants you in tomorrow. I have to be in work too. We need to rest. That's what we need.'

I nodded and hurried over to where my bag and jacket were.

'Stevie, there's more.'

I flinched as I realised he'd followed me and was right behind me. 'I don't think I can hear any more.'

'That's fair.'

Turning around, clutching my things, I looked at Noah. He was completely miserable. I never wanted anyone to feel that way but what was I supposed to do here?

'I need to think about what you've told me. But, Noah, whatever happened back then, however badly you handled it, it doesn't change the fact that you left me and we are over.' I shrugged. 'I'm not sure if going over it all helps either of us. I've had to move on from the future I saw with you, and you've moved on too.'

I started to walk to the door, desperate to get away from him and all those feelings I had that were bubbling back up under the thick layer of skin I'd had to grow without him.

'I get it, Stevie. I can't thank you enough for today. You are the kindest person. I just...' He walked past and held open the door for me. 'You need to know though – I never moved on.'

'What?' I stopped short.

'I never moved on,' he said again, this time in the strongest voice I'd heard him use all day.

Fuck. Me.

'There are more emails.'

'More?'

'I wrote you emails. Lots of them. It made me feel like you were still in my life even though you weren't.'

God, I wanted to see them but I also didn't think I should.

'If you've moved on then I understand. I'll... accept it. But if not, please read them.' He pulled his phone out of his dressing gown pocket. 'I'll send them to you. You can choose. I'll go to bed now. I'll see you at work. Thank you again.'

I made my feet pick themselves up and move for the door again.

'I mean it. Thank you, Stevie.'

I moved past him and stepped into the corridor. I looked back as he smiled and closed the door. I stared at it for a full minute before I put my jacket on, slung my bag across me and got into the lift.

I hadn't caught Noah's flu but my head felt like it was stuffed with straw. I felt like I was mush. Like I could melt into a puddle on the floor and people would just step over me. I felt like I'd lifted up out of my body and was far up in the clouds just watching everything happening from above.

I pulled out my phone and saw Noah had sent what looked like about twenty emails. All sent to me from him in New York. And he said it was up to me whether I read them or not. If I had moved on, he'd understand.

But he hadn't.

He hadn't moved on.

Noah had floored me completely. I had no idea what to think or feel or say or do. All I wanted was to crawl into my bed, pull the covers over me, and sleep. So I went home and that's what I did, deciding that processing what had happened today could wait until the morning.

Until then, I wanted to exist only in my dreams.

* * *

I woke up feeling like I'd run a marathon. I rolled over in my bed as my alarm beeped at me and I sighed. What a day yesterday. Everything flooded back as I sat up and stretched. My whole body and head ached but it was from emotional tiredness. I climbed out of bed and put my slippers on and padded into my kitchen. It was still dark out but I didn't turn on the lights, sure they would hurt my eyes. I shuffled to the coffee machine knowing I needed a big cup before I could even think about getting ready.

Leaning against the counter as the coffee machine whirred, I ran through everything Noah had said to me in his flat. Perhaps he had been mildly delirious from his flu or just taking the chance of us being alone together, but he had been more honest than I could ever have expected him to be. What he said changed that whole final encounter we'd had when he'd told me he was moving to New York, and that we were over.

I picked up my coffee cup and sipped from it, enjoying the warmth. It was a chilly morning and I felt discombobulated. How was I meant to feel about what he said? I wasn't sure, but I did believe him. I had seen the truth in his eyes. He really had believed that walking away from me was the right thing to do. I didn't understand, I didn't agree, but that's what he had thought. I didn't know yet if it made me feel better.

There was some relief that maybe it meant he had really loved me once, it hadn't been pretend or some kind of game, but in some ways, it hurt even more. Because of what we could have had if he'd just told me what was going on.

I felt sad for him and his family. His poor mum. And him for having to go through that. And anger towards his father for making Noah blame himself. I had no idea what had happened between them in the past five years but I could tell this wasn't a happy family and I hated that for Noah. There were so many emotions. My head and heart were full.

My phone loomed large in front of my eyes. It contained emails from Noah. Emails from the past five years.

I took a deep breath and picked it up off the counter, leaning against it. I found the next email he'd sent after that first message to me.

This one was sent the following month.

> Stevie, it's autumn in New York. And I can't stop thinking about you. When I go out of my apartment and I see the beautiful trees or when I order myself a coffee in Starbucks and I carry it into one of the bookshops I've discovered here... it all reminds me of you. You would love it here.
>
> I bought a book yesterday because I remembered you told me how much you loved it. It's such a sweet love story. It made me feel closer to you when I started reading it. I hope there's a happy ending. I need one right now.
>
> I see you in everything here.
>
> And wish you were here with me.

My eyes blurred again as I read Noah's words. It was everything I had once fantasised about him saying to me, but he hadn't and I'd shut down the hope in my heart that he'd regret leaving me. But he had. He had written everything I would have wanted him to. But I was only reading it now five years later.

> And don't get me started on what it's like at night. My apartment has a good view but it doesn't mean anything without you on the balcony to gaze at it with me. I went out there last night to watch

the city lights but I thought about that night in London. On my balcony. Do you remember it?

My face heated up. I knew the night he meant. Out on his balcony. It felt like only two of us were in the world that night. We hadn't worried about anyone seeing us from other flats. We had been swept up in that moment together. Kissing frantically, tearing at our clothes even though it was cold outside. Wanting. Needing to be closer. Noah had asked me what I wanted. When I told him, he'd turned me around and bent me over his balcony railing, and it was burned in my memory as the best sex of my life.

> I went straight inside. I hate how everything reminds me of you. How cold and lonely this place is without you. I wish I could talk to you. Hold you. Just be with you. But I know this is all my fault. This punishment is only what I deserve. I should feel like shit. I should feel terrible. I should feel only half a person without you. Because I hurt you.
>
> I told my mother about you today. In the hospital. She told me I should tell you I miss you. Life is too short. She knows that better than anyone. I know though it's too late. You don't want to hear from me. My last email bounced back. You've blocked my calls. I can't see your social media. I even called your old flat but they said you'd gone. Don't think for a minute that I blame you. I did this to us. I know that.
>
> I just wish I could undo it.
> I just wish you were here.
> Noah

The tears spilled down my face. That man could write an email. God. I was a broken mess after reading that. I thought he'd gone and forgotten all about me. But it had been the opposite. I'd been pining for him, and he'd been pining for me.

And now we were in the same city again. What the hell should we do now?

I checked the time. I was running late so I dashed into the shower, turning it up to the hottest setting to help ease the ache in my body and heart.

21

I listened to a playlist of girlboss anthems on my way in to work to build up the confidence to face both Noah and his father, and picked up an iced latte on the way, drinking the whole large cup before I entered my building. It was a grey, chilly day, fitting my mood as I headed into Turn the Pages.

The office floor was quiet and I saw Noah's office door was closed.

I headed to my desk and waved to Emily and Gita. 'Is Mr Matthews here?'

'Yep. And Noah,' Gita said. 'They both came in an hour ago and have been in there with the door shut. They asked for you to go in when you got here.'

'Yikes,' I said, slipping my blazer off and hanging it over the back of my desk chair. 'How was it yesterday?'

Emily grimaced. 'Not great. Mr Matthews made us all feel like we're doing everything wrong and I think he's been shouting at Noah. These doors are thick but not that thick.'

'He's kind of scary,' Gita admitted with a shiver. 'I've always got on with bosses but not him. I think he's just looking for an excuse to replace us all with people from New York. He said if I edit like I speak then we likely have severe grammar issues in all our books.'

'He didn't,' I said, my eyes widening.

'He told me that my designs were childlike,' Emily said. 'And all our covers need work if we're going to stand out in the market. Basically, I should go back to the drawing board on the next six books coming out.'

'Oh God, what's he going to say about *Bitten*?' I gulped. 'I suppose I'd better go in.'

'Good luck,' they said in unison.

I straightened my pleated dress, the fanciest item in my wardrobe as I thought I better look as smart as possible, and pushed my hair off my shoulders then headed for the office. My nerves increased with every step. A few other people called out 'good luck', which made me worry that they thought I needed luck. By the time I knocked on Noah's office door, any confidence I had tried to summon earlier had seeped out like air from a popped balloon.

'Come in,' Noah called out before I could turn around and decide against this.

I entered. Noah was at his desk and his father stood by the window. Mr Matthews was tall like Noah but he had salt and pepper hair and a trimmed beard. He wore a dark suit and had his hands behind his back. He regarded me with a disdainful look as I smiled brightly. The whole vibe was immediately off. I glanced at Noah, pleased to see he had more colour than yesterday, but he looked tense.

'This is Stevie, our new publicity executive. My father – John Matthews.'

'Pleased to meet you, Mr Matthews.'

He merely nodded. 'Take a seat and tell me how you're getting on with Ms Day's novel.'

I gratefully sank into the chair on the other side of Noah's desk, fearing my knees might have wobbled otherwise. Noah's father definitely had a headteacher vibe going on.

I straightened my shoulders and went through the plan for *Bitten*. 'So, I've sent out all the review copies and kickstarted the social media campaigns. This week, we start the paid-for advertising and then it's publication next week when we have her launch party.'

I looked up. Noah gave me a nod and we turned to his father.

'We need to cut the paid advertising by three quarters,' he said.

'Sorry, what do you mean?' I asked fearfully.

'I know you asked for extra budget,' he said, glancing at Noah. 'But after speaking to your team here and back in New York, I agree with the consensus that this isn't the book to spend extra on. Based on the sales and profits we made for Ms Day's last book, we have already spent enough.'

'But we have a plan to get the book on the bestseller list...' I began, looking at Noah in horror.

Mr Matthews held a hand up and my reply stuttered to a stop. 'There is no guarantee that she can garner new readers, and I'm not prepared to risk such a high marketing budget on the off-chance she might become popular again. She's been around too long in my opinion. We'd do better to focus on debuts. I want to move the money you allocated to the new thriller that's coming out in January.'

I narrowed my eyes. 'Because thrillers are worth more than romances?'

'They have more earning potential.'

'No! Romance made more for this company last year and—'

'Did you just say no?' Mr Matthews cut in, looking flabbergasted.

'Hang on,' Noah said hastily. 'We all agreed that Ms Day was worth focusing on as this book hits the current book trend perfectly and—'

'I disagree,' his father told him. 'New readers won't notice it and it will alienate her core readership as it's different to her backlist. In my opinion, it should never have been given the greenlight but we weren't involved then. We are now. Cut your plans and just get the book out and done with then move on to the thriller, which has a better chance of charting on the bestseller list. Thank you, Stevie.'

'But...' I looked desperately at Noah, who avoided my eyes. 'This plan can succeed. This book is brilliant. I read a lot of romances and it's the best one I've read all year, even over the past two years.'

'I'm not sure that says a lot, Stevie, does it?' Mr Matthews said coldly. 'We have to publish some romance but it has never been, or will be, our focus. We want to prioritise the best-written books we have.'

I gaped at him, my blood boiling. Was he serious right now?

'So, you're saying if a book has romance in it, it can't be well written? I can't believe you'd even think such a thing. You think romance is less than because it's written mainly and read mainly by women, I suppose?' I stood up. 'I didn't realise I was working for a misogynistic company.'

'Don't get hysterical,' Mr Matthews said coldly. 'I didn't say anything of the sort. In this instance, I believe the thriller has a better chance of selling more than the romance.'

I couldn't believe he told me I was hysterical. Had we been transported back to 1950?

'Noah, you can't agree with this decision?' I asked my very silent ex and current manager.

Mr Matthews's phone rang. 'I need to take this. Noah, get the next meeting set up.'

With a dismissive look in my direction, Mr Matthews left the room to answer his phone call.

Noah stood up. 'I know, I know. He's always been less than enthused about romances even though they make up so much of our profits. He's old school and—'

'No, that's not old school; that's so sexist, I can't even believe it,' I snapped. 'And you just sat there! You can't tell me that you agree with cutting our budget? That we should shift our focus to the thriller?'

Noah sighed. 'I don't agree entirely but I do see what he's saying. This is a risk based on Deborah's previous books. And this thriller is new. We have a good shot at getting attention for it.' He paused and gave me a reassuring smile. 'We can still do a good job for Deborah.'

'No. You're doing exactly what she's been complaining about. Not putting in any effort for her books. We promised her! We said we'd get the book on the bestseller list.' I walked to the door. 'I don't care what your father thinks – that's what I'm going to do. And, Noah, I know you don't agree with him, I just don't understand why you wouldn't tell him that.'

I stormed out, furious. The real Noah – the man I'd fallen in love with – would have stood up to his father, not just sat there.

Gita and Emily looked up as I marched back to my desk.

'I'm going to show that dinosaur what a bestselling publicity campaign looks like,' I told them as I sat down. 'Thank God he didn't turn out to be my father-in-law.'

'I'm loving the energy,' Emily said, clapping her hands. 'What happened?'

'He just dissed romance books,' I said, opening my emails, my fingertips flying on the keys. I was going to do everything I could to get free publicity for this book. I looked over my computer and saw Paul from sales trying to eavesdrop on us. 'And don't think I don't know who went running to the boss about *Bitten*,' I called over.

He shrugged but I saw the smug smile on his face as he turned away. Traitor.

'No one slags off romance books to me and gets away with it,' I declared. 'Right, I'm going to email an SOS to my friend Liv. She works in a library and loves romance books. I need her help.'

'I hate people hating on romance,' Gita said, rolling her eyes. 'What help do you need from me? We have no idea if we'll still have jobs in six months' time so why not stand up for something we believe in? If we're going to get one over on Mr Matthews after how he's treated us all since he's been here then I'm all in.'

'I know we weren't sure about *Bitten*,' Emily said, 'but the fact that Mr Matthews and Paul think we can't make it a hit really makes me want to prove them wrong.'

'Me too,' Gita agreed. I smiled at them both then saw Liv had sent a prompt email back to me.

> Of course I'm in to help DD's new book! What do you need?
> Proud to be a romance reader! Romance readers for life!

Liv was in. And I had a potentially mad idea but an idea nonetheless.

I turned back to Gita and Emily. 'Two questions – do you know a cheap printer? We hardly have any budget left but I'm going to use every last penny they've given me. And is there a way to email all staff without Noah, Paul or Mr Matthews seeing it?'

Gita and Emily both grinned back.

I'd never been so fired up. There was no way I was going to let Deborah Day down. *Bitten* was a brilliant book no matter what Mr Matthews thought, and I was going to prove it.

22

I didn't speak to Noah for two days. The first, he was holed up with his father in his office and I went home before they left the room. The second day, we all breathed a sigh of relief when Noah came in to work alone and Mr Matthews appeared to have gone back to New York, but Noah didn't come out of his office. I felt a huge gap had opened up between the two of us and I wasn't sure if we'd ever build a bridge to close it.

I didn't open any more of the emails Noah had sent me from New York. I was too angry with how he'd acted in the meeting with me and his father. I was curious about them but it felt like Noah was a different person now so it would only be a kick in the teeth to read them. Based on how he hadn't supported me, I guessed his illness had been a blip and now he was reverting to his pact of focusing on work. Not us.

And I would do the same.

So, I ploughed on with my idea to promote *Bitten* for as little money as possible and yes, you could say I was ignoring anything personal to focus on this. I couldn't solve what was happening or not happening between me and Noah but I was going to solve this work problem.

Avoiding the office, I went straight to Book Nook on Thursday to see Georgina. It was still so strange to think of it as Noah's bookshop. I walked in and the bell on the door jangled. Georgina turned from where she was shelving books to say hello to me. I was prepared this time for the rush of memories and forced myself to focus on the task in hand.

'Georgina, I've had a somewhat mad publicity idea that I'm hoping you'll want to come on board with,' I said, pulling out leaflets I wanted her to put out in the shop.

Georgina grinned. 'I love mad ideas.'

I told her about how the budget had been cut for *Bitten* and my plan to make it a bestseller anyway, and her eyes lit up.

'What do you think?'

'I love it. I hate how romance readers can be treated as second-class citizens. And that romance books can be seen as less than other genres,' she said. 'I will help any way I can.' She tipped her head to look at me. 'What does Noah think about this?'

'Well, he doesn't know my exact plan,' I admitted. 'His father was pretty against us focusing on *Bitten* so I didn't want to put him in the position of having to lie to Mr Matthews or anything. But they will both be happy when the profits roll in, right?'

Georgina put my leaflets out on the till desk. 'I can't see Noah being against publicising a romance novel; they are his favourite genre, aren't they? My dad told me he used to devour thrillers but then wanted to buy all the love stories he could get his hands on.'

I thought about the bookshelf I had seen in Noah's flat. 'He never used to read romances,' I agreed. 'When we were together, I was the romance junkie, not him.'

Georgina raised an eyebrow. 'Maybe you influenced him more than you knew then.'

'I suppose I did talk a lot about books with him.'

I could never help myself; if I read a good book, I could wax lyrical about it for days if you let me and Noah always liked to talk about books or come book shopping so maybe he had taken my book reviews more seriously than I'd thought.

'Well, more men should read romance,' I said.

'Preach,' Georgina agreed. 'Noah said you two met in here?'

'We did. It was like something out of a novel. I'd always had this fantasy of meeting someone in a bookshop,' I said, looking around. 'It felt like fate or something. But then Noah moved to New York without me. I suppose that's the problem with life, isn't it? It isn't a book. We don't get a happy ending.'

'You still might now Noah's back in London.'

I shook my head. 'Noah is very different now.'

'You think?' Georgina raised a pierced eyebrow. 'He seems the same to me. Maybe it's all the stress of work that you're picking up on. He finds his dad a nightmare to work for, I know. I used to get emails from him at the office in New York at like midnight. I don't know how he coped with it all.'

I thought about his emails to me and wondered if any of those had been sent at the same time.

'I kind of cut off contact when he left so I don't know about his life out there,' I admitted. I had always pictured Noah as living his best life in NYC. Like a male Carrie Bradshaw swanning around with cocktails and women hanging off his arm. I wasn't sure how to feel now I knew that wasn't the case. 'I blocked him everywhere, to be honest.'

'I understand. I'm not friends with any of my exes.'

'Did he tell you about his mum?' I asked.

She nodded.

'I had no idea. He left without telling me. I only know now. And I feel terrible that I wasn't there for him but he didn't let me.'

'I think it's been a rough time,' she said. 'His family seems complicated.'

'Yeah, I just met his dad,' I replied ruefully.

'All I know is when Noah told me you were working at his company, I'd never seen him so happy.'

I hated the way my heart soared when she said that.

I shook my head. 'I was furious.'

Georgina laughed. 'I don't blame you. But he's a good guy. He was there for my family when we had nowhere else to turn. So, I am a big fan.' She gestured to the leaflets. 'Noah would want to be part of this, I'm sure.'

I wasn't as certain. Not after the way he'd backed down so spectacularly with his father, but I thanked Georgina for her help and left the bookshop for my next meeting.

* * *

I walked from the Book Nook to the Starbucks opposite our office to meet with Ed Thomas, Deborah's agent. I spotted him at a table with his laptop. He'd instantly agreed to meet me here, saying he needed a caffeine fix so often he preferred working in coffee shops to working in his office. I sensed a kindred spirit.

'Thank you for meeting me,' I said as I sat down in the chair.

'I'm intrigued. You weren't making a lot of sense on the phone talking rallies and protests and t-shirts but I agreed when you said we can't let Debs down,' he replied with a grin.

'Well, I've had my budget cut for her publicity and marketing campaign,' I said. His face turned to thunder. 'I know, I know.'

I briefly explained how the big boss had come over from New York and chosen to give the money to a new thriller instead.

'I'm going to be honest, I didn't like the dismissive way he talked about romance books. I reached out to my librarian friend, who's just as much of a romance fan as me, and we came up with this idea. Everyone at Turn the Pages is on board so all we need is Deborah to agree to join us.'

I proceeded to tell Ed what we were planning.

He whistled. 'I like it. Bold but fun. A way to get people involved. But how will you keep the focus on *Bitten*?'

I pulled out my phone and showed him the t-shirt design Emily had knocked up for me.

Ed nodded. 'I like it. And I think Debs will too. But what will John Matthews say? And Noah? I don't want them pulling the book or something like that.'

'They can't, they'd lose too much money and once we have all this publicity, they wouldn't dare. Talk about bad press! Are you okay with it being a secret?'

'I'm all for getting one over John Matthews. I have a friend at the firm in New York and he's pretty terrible. I know things have been shit for them this past year but they are really making enemies. And Debs deserves this book to be a hit so I say we do it.'

I nodded. 'Great.' Then I thought about what he'd said. 'Things have been bad for Noah and his father?'

I was surprised that he knew about Noah's mother being ill.

'Yeah, it was a terrible time and everyone feels so sorry for them, of course, but John Matthews took it so hard, it's made him lack any empathy when it comes to dealing with people. Not the way to get the best out of your staff, in my book.' He saw my confused expression. 'You didn't know that John's wife died?'

I sucked in a breath. 'Noah lost his mum?'

Ed nodded. 'Just last year. Then they went hell for leather with this takeover. Throwing themselves into work was how they coped, I reckon.'

'Noah didn't tell me,' I said in a small voice. I suddenly felt terrible for attacking him after the meeting with his father.

'They don't like talking about it,' Ed said. 'Well, if nothing else, you're trying something different which is what Debs has been pushing for. I think she'll be on board.'

I was relieved. 'Good. I'll see you on Monday then.'

I stood up, my mind on what had happened to Noah. Why hadn't he told me about his mum?

'I know I made a joke about it when we first met but Stevie, if it's a success, you're going to leave Turn the Pages, aren't you? Come and work for me, Stevie. I like you. You're smart, passionate about books and not afraid to do something outside the box.'

'Let's see how this goes first,' I said, smiling. I was flattered, I couldn't lie, and things at work were definitely not easy.

As I left Starbucks, I thought again about the emails Noah had sent me in New York. Had he said anything about his mum in them?

I pulled out my phone and scrolled to the final email he'd forwarded to me and opened it up. It was dated a year ago. I began to read.

23

Stevie,

I don't know why I'm still writing to you. Maybe it's like a diary. It gives me comfort. It's been four years since I saw you and I thought I wouldn't write any more. I decided that I was finally over you and I was going to look to the future without us.

But yesterday, my mum died. It's been a horrible illness. I've watched the light leave her slowly and painfully. And I've fucking hated every minute of it. But being here and being with her, that's a decision I'll never regret. She needed me. And I needed her. We've had so much time together. I'll always be grateful for that. Even if she kept telling me I was working too much. Or that I was crazy to let you go. I know these things are true.

I feel relief that she's at peace now. But I'll miss her. And I feel... adrift. Like I lost my purpose, maybe? And so helpless. My father isn't coping but is pretending it's all business as usual. He feels unreachable. I know you'd tell me to talk to him. But we just don't have that relationship you have with your parents. I wish we did. I wish I could tell him how I feel and for him to tell me how he feels in return.

What I do know is my parents loved each other more than maybe I even realised. I saw it this last week they were together. And it's made me want that more than I ever have before. Stevie, this is my last email because writing to you when you can't read these letters or write back is making it even harder for me to think about finding that with someone else.

I hope you are happy. I hope you found love. I hope you're like a character in one of those romance books you loved, and which by the way I'm now hooked on too, and you got your happy ever after.

Goodbye Stevie.

I'm going to try to find mine.

'No.' The word flew out of my lips automatically.

I shook my head. No? What was I saying? What was I thinking?

My feet turned towards the office. I had to see Noah. I had to talk to him. That last email. I was gripped by the fear that Noah would find his happy ending with someone else. It was crazy to think that, wasn't it? But I couldn't help it. There had to be a reason that neither of us moved on. There had to be a reason that we'd met again.

A tall, dark-haired man in glasses walked past me, head down, the collar of his dark coat pulled up. I did a double take.

'Noah!' I called, pushing through people to get to him. He turned towards the river path and I caught up with him there. 'Wait!'

Breathlessly, I laid a hand on his arm.

'Stevie?' He looked for a moment pleased to see me but then his eyes turned hard. 'I was trying to find you but Emily said you were meeting with Ed Thomas. Were you having a job interview?'

'No, I wanted to tell Ed about my new publicity idea for *Bitten*.'

'And not me?' He looked hurt.

The Plot Twist

'I thought you'd feel obligated to tell your father. And he'd stop me.'

We stared at one another. Noah shook his head. 'I'm sorry, Stevie, you were right. I should have said more. You know I don't agree with him about romance books; they are important. They have been important to me. I want *Bitten* to do well, I really do.' He sighed. 'Things are really complicated with my father.'

'I understand. Noah, I read the last email you sent me.'

'Oh.'

I gestured to the bench nearby. 'Can we sit for a minute?'

I led the way and Noah trailed after me and we sat down together.

'I'm so sorry about your mother,' I said, reaching out to squeeze his arm. 'Why didn't you tell me?'

Noah looked at my hand. 'I didn't want you to feel sorry for me; you shouldn't after what I did...' He trailed off and looked out at the river.

'I feel so bad,' I said after a moment. 'I yelled at you the other day about you and your father...'

Noah turned to me. 'You were right to. I should have said more when we met with him. I want to say more to him. I disagree with him a lot but he's broken-hearted about my mum. We both are. And I think that he blames me still. For not being at home when she became ill. It's a mess.'

I saw a tear form in his eye. 'Noah,' I said, reaching for him again. There was a hesitancy on both sides but then I wrapped my arm around his shoulder, his settled on my waist and we were embracing. 'It must have been such a hard few years.'

'I wished you were with me so many times but then I felt guilty for even thinking it after the way I ended things,' he whispered into my ear. 'The only reason I went along with my dad and this takeover was so I'd be back in London again. The place I had been so happy in once.' He pulled back to look at me, his eyes glistening. 'I'm a mess, Stevie. I was ill all weekend then there was the hellish meeting with my father. I shouldn't be putting more on you. But I don't know. Seeing you again has turned everything upside down.'

'But you said in that last email that you were ready to move on,' I said quietly.

'I was trying to convince myself. I thought I needed to let you go. And then you came back into my life.' He reached out and brushed back my hair. 'I'll do better. I'll be better. I know that I'm not the man you fell in love with any more. I guess I've put up walls, pushed myself into work because of everything that happened with my family. I've been scared to open up to anyone because of how I ruined us. I wish I was like you. Look how I hurt you but you're still this bright spark.' He looked at me in wonder.

We were still wrapped around each other and my heart was thumping in my chest at his closeness. I watched his lips curve up just enough to show me his dimple. I couldn't stop myself. I touched it with my fingertips.

'I missed that.'

He smiled fully. 'Yeah?'

'Yeah.' I pulled away though. It was all too much. I looked down at my hands as I folded them in my lap. 'I can't believe you wrote me all those emails. I'm sorry I blocked you everywhere. I wish I had read them before now,' I said softly, my heart still pounding. 'Your words were beautiful.'

'Almost as soon as I got to New York, I knew I'd made a huge mistake. Everything was shit out there. My mum, work, my father... but nothing compared to the fact you weren't with me. And then as you know, I tried to contact you in every way I could think of, but I couldn't get through.'

'I didn't want to hurt even more. Being in touch with you seemed just too much to even consider.'

'I get it.' Noah turned back to me. Our legs were still touching. I wondered if he'd realised or not. 'You were right to do whatever you needed. I'll never forget the look on your face when I walked away.' He shuddered. 'It's haunted me for years.'

'I wished you had told me the truth about why you had to go. I could have helped.'

'I wished I had,' Noah said. 'I don't know how to say how sorry I am. When my mum died last year...' His voice caught and I found myself touching his hand again. He looked down at our hands. 'I was so lost. I *am* lost, Stevie. I want to be the man you loved again. No, I want to be better.'

'Noah...'

He took my hand in his and lifted his eyes to meet mine. 'Do you know how hard it is to be this close to you and not be able to kiss you?'

I looked at his lips and I knew what he meant. There was this cloud of longing enveloping us. But was it just the familiarity of what we'd once had or did it mean that spark had never died? God, I wanted it to be the second one but I was scared of that. So scared that Noah would hurt me again.

'I want to but...' I whispered.

Noah let go of me. 'Shit, Stevie. I shouldn't have said anything. I know I shouldn't say things like that to you. It's not fair after what I did.'

'I did kiss you first,' I said, trying to lighten the mood. 'A man buys a bookshop, you kiss them.'

'I can't stop thinking about it,' Noah admitted.

'You said it was a mistake,' I reminded him.

'I don't want to hurt you again. God, when you walked into my flat when I was ill, I thought for a crazy, flu-ed up moment you had come home. Isn't that mad?' He put his head in his hands. 'It's not the same without you there. After we met, it never was.'

How was he saying everything I wanted him to now? Five years too late. Or was it too late? My heart wanted it not to be but my head was telling my heart to shut the hell up.

'Noah,' I said, and he lifted his head to look at me. 'You're right. You are a mess. And you have fucked up. So, do something about it.'

'I will,' he vowed. 'And I'm going to start by helping you make Deborah Day's book a bestseller no matter what my father says.'

My whole body was attuned to his but I knew I wasn't ready to kiss him again. But maybe I would be soon. And maybe sounded pretty damn good right now.

'Don't worry, I have a plan. You sure you want in on it?'

'I've never been as sure of anything before,' Noah replied.

24

Friday was a hectic blur of me trying to organise everything I could for next week. My big idea was planned for Monday, and the launch for *Bitten* at Noah's bookshop was happening on Wednesday, Halloween night, so it would be a week of doing everything possible to get the word out about the special book. The bestseller list came out on Sunday but we'd know on Friday if we'd done enough to get the book on there.

I had an email from Noah's father asking for the publicity plan for the thriller he wanted us to focus on so I had to spend a couple of hours on that. It was most definitely not my best work but I said I would revise it after I'd read the book, so that bought me some more time and I ploughed on with my ideas for *Bitten*.

Friday afternoon, I called a meeting in the boardroom for all staff and Noah sat down while I stood at the front, which was pretty scary. I'd never been a public speaker but it helped that I was talking about books and one that I loved.

'I know that not everyone thinks *Bitten* has the potential to be a bestseller,' I began, glancing at Paul who had his arms folded. I turned to Emily and Gita, who gave me supportive looks and smiles. 'But I hope you'll get on board with my idea for Monday. I would love us to do it together as a team and make this work. We need to show New York that we can do great things with our books and we have a big chance next week to do that.' I told everyone the plan, trying not to rush.

Then my eyes fell on Noah. He had his hand propped on his chin as he listened to me. Every time I looked at him, it still felt incredible that he was there in front of me again. I was trying to focus on this campaign, on work, and not think about him, but each time our eyes met, it was becoming harder and harder.

I took a breath and continued. 'Deborah Day is on board and will be outside the office at 9 a.m. If you can please turn up a little earlier to grab a t-shirt, books to hand out or a sign, that would be great. And if you know anyone who would want to join in, bring them along. It really is the more the merrier! And thank you again to everyone who has helped us get ready. I am really excited to see what we can do with *Bitten* and I hope you are too!'

Emily and Gita cheered and a few others joined in and clapped. Paul still looked annoyed but he seemed to be the only one not willing to try this. And I couldn't care less what he thought after he'd told tales to Noah's father like we were back at school. I liked to support colleagues, not stab them in the back.

Noah stood up then and the room quickly fell silent.

'Thank you, Stevie. I know that the past couple of weeks have been a real transition period. It's been all hands-on deck and we have a huge mountain still to climb, but I've seen some incredible team work this week and that goes a long way. I'm excited to see what we can do with *Bitten*. Together.' There were a few exchanges of looks at this, frankly, motivating speech for him. I bit back a smile. He was trying to turn around the opinion of him but I think everyone was unsure whether to trust it or not. 'Okay, see you all on Monday!'

I gathered my things. 'I'm off to the library with Emily and Gita,' I said to Noah as the room emptied around us. 'Unless you need anything before I go?'

He shook his head. 'No, you've got everything covered. I can't believe how much you've managed to organise.' There was that damn dimple again.

'I really hope it will work,' I said, pulling my coat on. 'Don't stay too late – it's Friday,' I said as I headed for the door.

'I could say the same to you.'

'Well, without a hot date, I might as well work,' I said. I met his gaze. 'Um, I mean...'

Noah's eyes sent sparks across the room to me. 'If you ever want to change that and have a hot date, I know someone who's available,' he said with a grin.

Shaking my head, I pulled my bag on my shoulder but my body had very much taken his suggestion on board. I thought about the nights I'd been pressed against him in bed and I realised it had been far too long since I'd had any experience you could describe as 'hot'.

'Right then, well, I'll just head off then,' I babbled, tripping a little bit as I fled the scene. I heard Noah laugh under his breath and I smiled because it had been a long time since I'd heard that sound.

* * *

'I feel like I'm back at university when we used to protest about everything,' my mum said excitedly.

The evening had drawn in and we were at my old workplace. Liv had kept the library open for us and we were making placards for what I hoped was going to be a fabulous launch week for *Bitten*. Outside, night had fallen and there was a crisp October breeze blowing the orange leaves from the trees, scattering them everywhere like confetti. The moon was changing, promising a full one for Halloween next week.

'I wish I'd had a protest at my uni,' Liv said wistfully.

'This will make up for it,' I promised her.

'What did Deborah Day say about all of this?' Emily asked. She and Gita sat opposite us using their artistic skills, their placards putting the rest of ours to shame. Georgina was struggling, as was Liv, and I had to admit it was proving harder than I had first thought. My mum was coming up with the slogans for the placards, and she was a genius at it.

'Ed emailed me to say she thought I was crazy but, in her words, "Crazy women change history".' I grinned. 'She said she'll be there.'

Gita shook her head. 'She really likes you. She'd never have done this if I'd asked her.'

'Ed told her what Mr Matthews said about her book, and romances in general, so I think it's more about getting one over on him than liking me. But I'll take it.'

'I still can't believe someone can be so narrow minded about romance books,' Liv said, shaking her head. 'If he'd said that to my face, I think I would have thrown one at his head.'

I grinned. 'I did consider it but I need to keep my job. For now. This is a better way to get revenge.'

'Noah doesn't agree with his father, does he?' Liv asked.

'I can't see Noah loving romance books,' Gita said.

'You'd be surprised,' I told her, thinking about his bookshelf in his flat.

'He's always ordering romance books into the shop,' Georgina said.

Gita and Emily exchanged surprised looks. 'Well, maybe the boss has hidden depths then,' Emily said.

'But he didn't stop Mr Matthews cutting your budget,' Gita added.

'No. I think Mr Matthews is used to getting his own way so Noah didn't say much in the meeting. But he's on board with what we're doing and wants to help. He thinks this book can be more successful than his father does. Let's hope this does well otherwise Mr Matthews will think he's right and will probably replace us all with people from New York.' I saw their faces. 'But no pressure.'

Emily tutted. 'Yeah, right. I wish I could tell Mr Matthews to stuff his job.'

'Is he like Noah?' my mum asked curiously.

'No,' I said at the same time Emily and Gita said 'Yes'.

'Noah didn't back you up in that meeting, did he?' Emily challenged me.

'No,' I agreed. 'And I told him off about that. But things are more complicated than you know.' I wasn't sure it was my place to tell them about Noah's mother but then Georgina saved me.

'Noah and his dad lost Noah's mum recently. They took it really hard,' she said.

My mum looked at me. 'Is that why...?' She trailed off, but I knew what she meant.

I nodded. 'She was sick when he left for New York,' I said.

'Oh,' Mum replied. She had been furious like my dad had been that Noah had left me broken-hearted. They had both really liked him and thought we were a great match. My mum, in particular, had been confused as to why he had suddenly changed his mind about me, about us. She had told me she had been sure he loved me; she had seen it in his eyes. I told her she was mistaken like I was. Now though, I knew she had seen the truth.

'I'm so sorry for Noah; he must have been heartbroken,' Mum continued. Then she lowered her voice so only I could hear. 'Now it makes sense why he left like he did. I wish he had told you.'

I nodded. 'He has said sorry for that, but it's hard to forget how much he hurt me.' Noah's mother's illness and passing had changed my view of our past. I knew now Noah hadn't left me because he hadn't loved me. And that meant more than I think he knew.

'Well, of course, but it sounds like he realises he was wrong,' Mum said gently. She spoke louder then. 'Noah must have been through a lot.'

Liv nodded. 'I can't even imagine. I bet he really wants to make his father proud of him; that's why he's been so tough since he took over as your boss,' she said to me, Emily and Gita. 'Maybe he isn't like his father really.'

'He feels guilty too because he was here when his mum got ill,' I said. 'His father encouraged that guilt.'

'He really is terrible,' Gita said. 'My opinion of Noah is improving. I can't believe it.'

'Me neither,' Emily said. 'Maybe he isn't the worst boss in the world after all.'

'Or ex-boyfriend?' Georgina asked.

All eyes turned to me. I felt myself flush and my palms turned sweaty. I thought about Noah talking about a hot date earlier and how panicked that made me feel. But also how I hadn't been able to stop thinking about it.

'You are never supposed to get back with an ex,' I said, more to remind myself than them.

'There are no rules when it comes to love,' my mum said. 'I met your father two years before we became a couple. I thought he was the last man I'd ever marry.' She smiled. 'He changed my mind.'

'Oh.' Liv clutched at her heart. She was more of a hopeless romantic than even me. 'That's gorgeous. And what about me and Aiden. I hated him for years! Look at us now...'

I rolled my eyes. 'Yes, you all have your happy ever afters, thanks for rubbing it in. Can we talk about something other than my ex-boyfriend, please?'

Emily nudged my foot with hers under the table but before I could ask her what she was doing, she and Gita stared in shock at something behind me.

Or someone, I realised, when they spoke.

'Should I come back later?'

25

I spun around to see Noah had walked in through the library's double doors carrying a huge cardboard box and was now stood right behind me. Bloody hell. I coughed to cover my embarrassment and didn't dare meet anyone's eyes.

'What do you have there?' I asked, hoping my voice sounded normal, but I think it came out far higher pitched than usual.

Noah's eyes twinkled and he was smiling so I didn't have much hope that he hadn't heard what I said. He knew we'd been talking about him. Awesome.

'The printers called just after you left the office,' Noah said as he placed the box on the table. He was wearing his dark coat, the collar turned up to block the wind, his face flush from the weather. The library suddenly felt a few degrees warmer. It was strange to see him in here. This had been my sanctuary for so long and the place where I felt I had finally healed from him leaving me. But there he was, waiting for me to reply.

'Oh,' I said, shaking off my thoughts. 'What did they say?'

'The t-shirts were ready so I picked them up.' He tapped the box.

I leapt out of my seat. 'Oh my God!' I rushed over to it. 'Thank you.'

He twisted the box towards me. 'You do the honours.'

Everyone stopped what they were doing to watch as I ripped open the packaging and leaned over. I saw a flash of black. Picking up a t-shirt, I squealed.

'It's perfect!'

I held it up to show them. On the front was a picture of a stack of books with the words:

What happens if you mess with a romance reader?

I turned it around to show the back which had the cover of *Bitten* on it with the words:

They will give you a love bite.

Liv burst out laughing. 'It's bloody genius. Pun intended.'

'I love the biting wit,' Georgina added, which made us all laugh.

I tossed one to each of them. 'Wear with pride, ladies.'

'Hey,' Noah said as I pulled one out for myself. 'What about me?'

My mouth twitched. 'Okay.' I threw it at him and raised an eyebrow. 'If you actually wear it.'

He slipped off his coat and pulled it on over his shirt. 'I'm never taking it off.'

I grabbed my phone and I snapped a photo of him in it.

'For the publicity,' I said. 'Turn around so I can get the back.'

Noah did a deliberately slow turn and afterwards, dropped me a wink.

'Okay, let's start the social media campaign,' I said.

> Are you a romance reader who's been made fun of for loving love stories? Have you heard someone say romance books aren't worthwhile? Have you seen a selection of 'must-read' books that didn't include any romance novels? Are you a proud romance lover? You need one of these t-shirts in your life! Come to our offices at 9 a.m. on Monday and BITE BACK.

I shared the caption and picture of Noah to all the company's social media accounts and tagged Deborah Day.

The likes and shares started to roll in.

As I responded to people on social media, everyone at the table began chatting but one voice made me pause in my typing.

'It's lovely to see you again, Mrs Phillips.'

Looking up from my phone, I saw Noah go over to my mum at the end of the table. I tried not to listen but it was impossible.

'Hello, Noah. How are you finding it being back in London?'

'There have been a lot of changes but I'm slowly catching up with it,' Noah replied politely. 'The important things have stayed the same,' he added with warmth.

I glanced over and Noah caught my eye and smiled.

Surreal. This was so surreal.

'You okay?' Liv appeared beside me and whispered as she leaned into the box and took out a shirt.

'Sure.'

She looked sceptical. 'No more kisses in alleyways?'

'Shh,' I hissed, definitely blushing then. 'And no, that's not happening again.'

'Hmmm.' She looked unconvinced. 'I'm making Aiden wear this,' she said, putting a shirt in her bag. She leaned in to whisper again. 'Remember how when he first came to work here, I said I wasn't interested in him? But you can't lie to yourself.'

'We're not like you and Aiden,' I hissed back. But by the look she gave me, I wasn't convincing myself or her. I glanced back at Noah, who was still talking to my mother and she was smiling at what he was saying. Then I turned back to Liv. 'The difference is, you never were a couple before you got together. We have been and it didn't work out. Once *Bitten*, twice shy,' I said, pointing to my t-shirt.

'Stop with the puns,' Liv groaned. Then she rubbed my arm. 'I get it. Lord knows I get it. Relationships are bloody scary. But five years is a long time. Things change. People change. Timing is everything.'

Emily's voice cut into our conversation. 'What do you think?'

We stopped talking to look at her placard.

Proud to be a romance reader

'Amen,' I declared, holding out my palm. She gave me a high five across the table. I looked around. 'This could actually work,' I said in wonder.

'Of course it will,' Noah said, coming back over. 'I've asked the New York team to share your posts.'

'And I've asked Dan to pop along and he said he'd film some bits,' Liv said, waving her phone. Her brother was big on TikTok so that was really useful.

'I love Dan,' I said, beaming. 'Thank so much, guys; we could have given up on this book but I'm so glad we didn't.' My phone beeped and I looked to see Deborah Day had shared the picture of the t-shirt and told her followers where she would be on Monday, which caused a flurry of excitement on her social media. 'This is gaining traction. Okay, guys, thanks so much for your help but it's Friday night – go have fun and I'll see you on Monday!'

Liv went to find Aiden, who was working late in his office

waiting for her, while Gita and Emily persuaded Georgina to join them for a drink. But I needed an early night.

My mum got up. 'I'm going to catch my train home.' She leaned in and kissed my cheek. 'I wish I could be there but it's going to be great. So proud of you, darling.' She looked at Noah. 'Make sure she gets home safe. I always worry sick thinking of her alone in London.'

'Of course,' Noah promised before I could protest. 'Why don't we walk you to the train station first?'

It was all settled without me. Noah grabbed the t-shirt box so I trailed behind him and my mum as they chatted about a Netflix documentary they both had enjoyed, pulling on my coat and getting a strong sense of déjà-vu seeing them together.

As we left the university library and walked to the nearest Tube station, the autumn chill wrapped around us like a cold but cosy blanket. I had walked this way so many times before but never with my mum and Noah. It felt so strange but lovely too. The sky was clear and dotted with a thousand sparkling stars watched over by the silvery moon. There was something about the moon and stars. They were fearless like we should be. We were so small, so insignificant, in comparison, but our problems always seemed as huge as the universe. The moon and stars didn't worry. They were happy to just be.

'What are you thinking about?' Mum asked as she stopped outside the station to hug me. Noah hung back to let us say goodbye.

'The moon and stars,' I replied honestly as I held her tightly. You were never too old to not need a hug from your mother. Especially when everything felt in turmoil.

'A dreamer, just like your father.' She pulled back and smiled. 'I remember when I gave you your first romance book. I loved that it was something we loved together. One day, you'll find that happy ever after you've been looking for like I did. And maybe that's a person, maybe it's a job or a place or a home – or all of the above – but you will find it.'

'Thanks, Mum,' I said, grateful for so much more than she even knew.

She looked at Noah. 'It's nice to have you back, Noah. Just remember that we as parents may claim to want many things for our children but really we just want you to be your own person.'

With a wave, she disappeared into the station.

'She was always wise.'

I started at how close Noah suddenly was to me. 'Yeah, she is.'

Without looking at him, I set off walking again, this time towards my flat.

'Does your dad know what we are doing on Monday?' I asked.

'I haven't spoken to him since he went back to New York.' He put his hands into his coat pockets. 'We need some space. I need to think. Things haven't been the same between us over the past year. Since my mum... I guess I find it hard to talk to him, to tell him what I want to say.'

'I bet it's not easy,' I said. 'But I'm sure your dad would listen when you know what you want to say. I'm sure he wants you to be happy.'

'Even if he isn't?' Noah asked, looking across at me. 'You have a special way of looking at the world; you always have.'

'And what's that?' I asked, curious as to what he thought about me. Once, I thought I knew, but I'd been wrong.

'Like everything will work out okay.'

'Well, it's not like life can't be pretty crap, but there is always hope, right?'

'I'd like to think so.' Noah looked ahead. 'You live here?'

'Yes,' I said as we stopped outside the converted Islington townhouse. 'In the top flat. It's basically a shoe box but I love it.'

'You always said you loved these houses,' Noah said, looking up at it with a smile. 'We walked this way a couple of times and you said you'd love to live here one day. You did it.' He met my eyes in the pool of light from the lamppost above us. 'So many changes since I left,' he murmured. 'I missed out on so much.'

'I missed your life too,' I reminded him. 'I thought about it often.'

I remembered so many nights lying in bed at night looking up at the ceiling, wondering where he was or what he was doing.

Noah's eyes lit up. 'You did? Even after what an utter dick I was to you? I didn't deserve that.'

'No.' I smiled. 'You didn't but I couldn't help it.'

'Well, you know from my emails that I spent a ton of time thinking about you. Wishing I was still part of your life.' He looked up at my flat. 'Now I know where to picture you when I think about you.'

'You still think about me?' I asked, hating how happy that made me feel.

'Of course I do. If I thought about you a lot when I couldn't see you or snoop on your social media, how bad do you think it is now?'

'I'm sorry you couldn't snoop,' I said with a laugh. 'Here.' I took out my phone and unblocked him on my social media and showed him.

'This could be dangerous,' he said with a grin. Then he looked at me seriously. 'It kind of killed me not being able to see you or talk to you. Why do you think I was so, well, rude, when you walked into my office? I wanted to pretend that I didn't care I was seeing you again, like I thought you wouldn't care about seeing me. And I took it so far, you called me a dick.'

I laughed. 'Yeah, you really committed to that role. So, that guy at work isn't really you?'

'I don't want it to be,' Noah said. 'You called me out on it immediately and I could see how much I'd changed when I saw myself through your eyes.'

'You've been through a lot. If I'd known about your mum, I wouldn't have called you a dick,' I said.

It was cold out though I wasn't sure inviting Noah into my flat was a good idea. But my lips still remembered the kiss outside the bookshop and they wanted more. My body wanted more. It had been a long time since I'd had a man in my flat and my body missed being touched. But it was too complicated with Noah to give in to that.

'She would have cheered you on,' Noah said, then on seeing me shiver, he said, 'You should go in. We have a busy week ahead.'

I nodded and turned to go but on impulse, I looked back. 'What are you doing this weekend?'

'I could lie and say I have exciting plans but I'll probably end up working,' Noah said ruefully.

This was a bad idea but I didn't not want to see him for two days. And he was on his own so it would be nice to offer him company. Just company. Nothing untoward about that.

'I heard you say to my mum that the city had changed so how about I show you the new places I've discovered that I love?'

'A tour from a local?' Noah smiled. 'How can I say no?'

'Meet me here Sunday morning. Say 10 a.m.?'

'I'll bring coffee.'

Noah waited as I walked into my building and when I stole a glance back at him, he was still under the lamppost, lifting his hand in a wave to me. I closed the door and went up to my flat, telling myself we were just two old friends hanging out outside of work, but I was unable to stop myself from smiling.

26

On Saturday, I did all those things you put off all week – washing, tidying, cleaning, watering my plants – and then I did some pampering. I had a long soak in the bath, shaved my legs, washed my hair, and put on a face mask. When I got out of the bathroom, I glanced in the mirror and wondered if I was prepping for tomorrow's date with Noah. I shook my head. It wasn't a date, I wasn't doing it to look good for him; I wanted to feel good for me.

But I couldn't quite convince myself.

A few friends were going out for a drink but I needed a night in to try to relax and get a hold of my confusing thoughts related to my ex. I curled up with a pizza and a book on my sofa with a glass of wine. And it was bliss.

But Noah kept drifting through my thoughts. I wondered what he was doing but I resisted messaging him. I needed to keep up a barrier between us. I couldn't let myself get too invested. Not unless I was 100 per cent sure that he was too.

Fool me once, shame on you, but fool me twice, shame on me. My emotions were all over the place when it came to Noah. I had loved him once. I had thought he was the one. Then he had broken my heart. I'd been upset then angry but I hadn't met anyone who had made me feel the way he had. Now he was back and first, I was furious, pissed at him for not acknowledging what we had once been. But I knew he'd done that to protect himself. The same thing I'd done when I'd blocked him on my phone.

Now though, I knew that he'd tried to contact me. He'd sent me beautiful emails telling me he had missed me. And he'd been going through the awful months of being with his mum while she was ill and dealing with his father who had blamed him, made him feel guilty, put a hell of a lot of pressure on him, and then he'd lost his mum. I felt sorry for him. I knew he was devastated. And he and his father had a difficult relationship, which had made him this tough boss but had also made him unable to talk to his father about things. Then there was him telling me he thought he hadn't deserved my love. His father had made him feel that way. He hadn't wanted to tell me the real reason he was leaving. He hadn't wanted me to wait or miss him or love him.

But I had done those things anyway.

So, it was bloody complicated. I couldn't deny the fact I still fancied Noah like crazy. That smile. That dimple. The way he looked at me like I was the only thing he'd ever need. All of this had made me kiss him once already. And that kiss. God. It had been electric. And I remembered the way he'd touched me and held me and made love to me. It had been like nothing I'd had before or since. That connection. I was still looking for it. But what if I could have it again? With Noah?

I picked up my phone and started to read the rest of the emails he'd forwarded on. In them, he told me about his life in New York and how he was wondering about mine, but he always told me that he wished we were still together. He told me about his mother. Her good days and bad days. How hard he was working in New York but how he still felt he hadn't proved himself yet. That everyone thought he had the job only because of his father. And how demanding his father was with him. How they never talked about what his mother was going through. How one night he heard his father crying and wished he could do something. And how he longed to hold me but knew he never would again.

> I wasn't sure if you loved me as much as I loved you when we were together. I didn't dare hope that you did. But I should have told you what you meant to me. It kills me that maybe you didn't know. That me leaving you might have made you think I didn't love you.
>
> Because I did, Stevie. And I think I always will.

I finished his emails with that one. God, my heart. It swelled reading that. He really had loved me. He was right. I had wondered if it had all been a lie. Or a game he'd been playing with me. That he'd walked away without a second thought. But I knew differently. I knew he'd missed me. That he'd regretted leaving. And now I was so confused. He was making it too hard. I should hate my ex-boyfriend, right? Only I didn't.

Noah was making me want him again.

I fell asleep thinking about seeing him the next morning and how I longed for what we'd had. I knew we couldn't have that again. If we were ever going to move on from the past, it had to be something new. Something stronger. Something better. And I wasn't sure yet if that was possible.

But as I feel asleep, I knew I wanted to find out.

* * *

Noah was waiting outside when I stepped through the door to my building. It was the perfect autumn day for a lover of the season like me. The sun was out and the sky was blue and the air was beautifully crisp. The colours of the trees shone brighter under the gaze of sunlight and the fallen leaves crunched under my boots as I walked up to him. I'd put on leggings and a long cosy jumper with my wool coat to keep warm, and Noah was in jeans and his coat, his gloved hands holding two coffees.

'I went with the seasonal favourite,' Noah said, greeting me. He leaned in to kiss me on the cheek. I breathed in his musky scent, hoping he'd appreciate the Jo Malone perfume I'd sprayed liberally. 'Here.'

'Perfect,' I said, taking one of the coffees. I sipped it and smiled. 'I've turned you into a basic pumpkin spice latte bitch, I love it. So, let's go on my favourite walk; it's the day for it.'

Without thinking about it too much, I slipped an arm through Noah's and we set off together, sipping our coffees and walking through the leaves. We had met in winter and Noah had left me before Christmas so this would be only our second autumn together.

'My favourite time of the year.'

'Mine too,' Noah agreed. 'New York is the best in the fall. I hope we get to publish *Bitten* over there as they go nuts for Halloween. It would be a big hit, I'm sure of it.'

I nodded. 'Definitely. This way.' I steered him into the park. 'I want to show you my favourite tree.'

'You have a favourite tree?'

'Don't you?'

He shook his head. 'We're not all like you, Stevie.'

'I'm choosing to take that as a compliment. Just look.'

I stopped us in front of the tree and we both lifted our faces to look. It was huge, twisted and old, the roots stretching out into the ground, going on for who knew how long, and the bark reached high up into the sky. It reminded me of trees in fairy tales, like you could walk through it into another world. And this time of the year, it really came into its own. The leaves had turned the most vibrant of yellows and oranges; some even looked gold in parts as they floated down gently on the breeze like colourful snowflakes.

'I tried to find out what it is using a tree app but it doesn't recognise it. I'm choosing to see it as one of a kind. A magic tree. You can tell it your secrets or make a wish. It never judges. It always listens.'

I didn't add that I had walked to the tree every day after Noah left me. Sometimes crying. Sometimes kicking at the grass. Sometimes feeling lost. But this tree had always grounded me somehow.

'It's not a tree but there's somewhere in New York I used to go that made me feel like that. A spot in Central Park by the lake. I used to sit there sometimes just to think. To have a moment of peace. It was a place where problems felt far away, you know? I wrote a couple of your emails there.'

I looked at him and he smiled back. 'I wish I could see it.'

'I'll take you there one day.'

27

There was a silence between us after Noah said that. I longed to go with him to New York. For him to take me on a tour like I was doing today, but that felt like a dream I didn't dare even think about.

I swallowed hard and looked away. 'Maybe you shouldn't make promises like that, based on our past. Come on, next stop.'

I pulled Noah's coat sleeve and he followed me but by the frown on his face, I knew what I said had perturbed him. So, of course, I kept talking to diffuse the tension.

'So, about two years after you left, they opened this bookshop café a couple of miles away and I won't lie, I've become a permanent fixture there. It's so cute. When I met Liv, I took her there one weekend and it became our spot for when we wanted to hang out without drinking. We don't go as often now she's loved up with Aiden but I don't mind being there alone. I mean, you're not actually ever really alone in a bookshop, are you? Books are friends.'

Noah nodded. 'I've always thought so too. So, I should picture you in this place on weekends with a pile of new books and an iced latte?'

'I'm a cliché but I accept it.'

'If you're a cliché, so am I. Weekends in New York were spent pretty much the exact same way.'

I was curious about whether he had always been alone or not when doing those activities. I knew he'd been tagged as an 'eligible bachelor' but I still wondered about the women he met in New York and his dating life after me. We had tentatively ventured into dissecting our past relationship but neither of us had talked about other exes. I couldn't help hoping I had been the only woman he had loved but I couldn't ask him that. I couldn't admit I hadn't loved another man since him either.

We reached the bookshop café then.

'Oh, I can see you here.' Noah smiled as I took his arm and pulled him across the road. 'Let me guess, they do good cupcakes?'

'The best,' I confirmed as I opened the door. The smell of freshly baked cakes floated around the café area and in the back was the bookshop, complete with comfy beanbags on the floor and acoustic covers of pop classics playing softly in the background. If my personality was a place, it would likely be very close to this. We wandered through to the books and looked around.

'Not quite as good as our bookshop,' Noah whispered to me, leaning in close as I reached for a book to look at. I wondered if the hairs on his arm stood up like mine did.

'No,' I conceded. 'But you don't have cakes. Shall we get one to take to our next spot? I'm going to buy this book. It looks cute.'

Noah took it from me. 'I'll get it with the cakes.' He saw me about to protest. 'I have to as a thank you for the tour,' he said, darting away before I could stop him.

I smiled. He hadn't changed his generous nature or love of buying people presents. After the night we met, I quickly learnt Noah loved buying me things that made me smile or taking me to places I would love. It felt nice to repay those times with this little tour today.

Noah glanced back from the café queue and smiled. I gave him a little wave and then I slipped outside for some air. It was hard not to get a bit carried away when a handsome man bought you books and cake and smiled at you like that. I was only human.

'Okay. I got you the pinkest one they had,' Noah said, reappearing with a paper bag. 'And a chocolate one for me. Where shall we eat them?'

'Up there.' I pointed up to a building on the corner.

Noah raised an eyebrow and I took his hand and we hurried down the road to it. It was an office building but at weekends, they let the public up to their rooftop. Not many people knew about it so for London, it was like a hidden gem.

We got into the lift and went up. It was a small courtyard with tables and chairs. Before we sat down, we walked to the edge to lean against the barrier. We looked down at the city beneath us, which stretched out like a painting.

'Wow. What a view,' Noah said. 'How did you find this place?'

I pushed back my hair, which was billowing out in the breeze. It was cold but exhilarating. 'Actually, I had a date who brought me up here. It was the best thing he gave me.' I smiled. 'The best free viewpoint in London. Shall we sit?'

We sat down at a table and a server came over to take our orders so we both asked for another coffee. After the server brought them over and we were alone again, I turned to Noah. 'So, can I have my cupcake now?'

Noah passed me my cake and took his out of the bag. He watched me for a moment. 'I thought I'd come back and find you married.'

I choked a little bit on my cupcake. Attractive.

I took a sip of coffee. 'Why?'

'Who wouldn't want to be married to a woman like you?'

I studied him as he ate his cupcake. 'I'd take that more seriously from a man who hadn't dumped me.'

It was Noah's turn to choke then. 'I forgot how you speak your mind. It was always the thing I admired, and was scared of the most. I thought we'd already agreed I was a dick?'

I nodded. 'We did.' I bit into the cupcake. Sweet sugary goodness. 'Mmm.'

'The truth is,' Noah said, wrapping his hands around his coffee cup, 'you scared me when we met. Because I thought maybe I had found the woman I wanted to marry. And I knew I had this big secret stopping me from giving you all of me. I should have told you about my family. From the start.'

'Why didn't you? Your father wouldn't have liked me?'

I doubted Mr Matthews would like any woman Noah brought home, to be honest. But it did hurt to think that Noah hadn't thought I was good enough to introduce to his parents.

'I thought it would put you off me. That you'd think I was like him.' Noah sighed. 'I also knew how much you wanted to work in publishing and I was embarrassed that my dad was one of the leaders of the industry. I suppose I've been trying to prove myself since I left university.'

'I know how hard you work,' I said. 'I wish you'd been honest with me.'

Noah sighed. 'It was all my fault things didn't work out between us. I've been kicking myself ever since.'

I half-smiled. I tried to lighten our tone. 'So, what did you think when you realised I wasn't married?'

'I was incredibly relieved,' he replied.

'I saw an article about you being an eligible bachelor so I knew you weren't either,' I admitted. 'There wasn't anyone that made you consider it?' My heart sped up as I waited for his answer.

'I won't lie and say I've been a monk since I left,' Noah said. He reached across the table and brushed my hand so lightly it was like the breeze had touched me but still, I felt it everywhere. 'But there was never anything serious, no.' He took his hand off mine. 'Anyway, I'm jealous as hell about the man who brought you up here; it's pretty romantic.'

'It was,' I conceded. 'I dated him for a few months but… I don't know. It got to a point when it was either serious or not and I realised I wasn't one hundred per cent in. Like he was. Since then, it's been bad date after bad date and so I decided to give it a rest. Although seeing Liv loved up with Aiden has given me some hope it can work out.'

I looked out at the view and felt that wistful pinch I often felt when I thought about happy ever afters. I wished one day I would have one, I couldn't deny it.

There was a short silence. I could feel Noah watching me. Maybe he wasn't sure what to say. It wasn't like he could promise to be my happy ever after, was it? Even if there were these feelings, this pull, attraction, whatever you wanted to say, between us. He had still hurt me and there was a big mountain to climb for either of us to forget that.

'My mum, when she was really sick, told me that my father was her soulmate.' I looked at him and he nodded. 'Hard to believe, isn't it? But that's why I haven't rocked the boat. He really loved her. He's broken without her even if he won't admit it to anyone, even himself. I know Mum would be upset with how he's been treating people though.'

'Especially you,' I pointed out. 'Making you feel guilty about your mother wasn't fair of him, Noah.'

'Maybe not but he's right. I tried so hard to make it on my own, I pushed them away. I wasn't there when my mum needed me.'

'Yes, you were!' My forceful words startled him. 'You left to be with her as soon as you knew. You did all you could. And he's wrong to make you think otherwise.'

'Thank you, Stevie. I don't deserve that praise but I appreciate it.'

'Can I ask one thing?' I said tentatively. He gestured for me to go ahead. 'If things are that difficult between you and your father, why do you keep working for him? Why come over here to run the new business?'

'My mum made me promise before she died that I'd look after him. That I'd keep our family together. I had to say yes.'

I looked away, worried I might cry. 'Of course you did,' I whispered. I finally looked back at him. He was watching me carefully. 'She'd be proud of you.'

I reached out to brush back my hair, which was still blowing in the breeze.

Noah caught my hand in his when I moved. My breath hitched but the wind took it away so he didn't hear. 'I wish you could have met. I told her all about you and she told me I was a fool to walk away. She was never wrong.'

I stared at him. 'Noah, you're making me feel like...'

He pulled my hand, tugging me closer to him, stopping my sentence in its tracks. He leaned close to me and my heart picked up speed.

'I have to tell you these things, Stevie. I can't stop. I wasn't planning to. That first day, I told myself to act like your manager and that's it, that's all I'd ever be now. But as soon as you told me off, I knew I was in trouble.'

He reached out and tucked my hair off my face for me. He then brushed his fingertip over my lips.

I trembled. 'I was in trouble when you told me you'd bought our bookshop.'

'I pretended to myself I was just supporting a small business but

I couldn't let it go. Not when it brought us together. I hoped one day, you'd walk right back in there and I'd see you again.' He smiled. 'I didn't know we'd meet again at work.'

'Talk about a plot twist – you becoming my boss.'

I kept the inches between us, knowing that if one of us leaned even a centimetre closer, we'd kiss.

'Do you hate it?' Noah asked then.

'It's growing on me,' I admitted.

He leaned even closer but turned and spoke his next words into my ear. 'If I remember correctly, you quite enjoyed me bossing you around sometimes.'

I let out a puff of air and squeezed my thighs together under the table, my mind instantly flashing to nights with Noah, him telling me exactly what to do in his bedroom, and me melting under his touch…

'Any more coffees?'

We sprang apart as a member of staff appeared to take away our empty cups. I flushed deep red as Noah chuckled under his breath before telling the waiter that we were fine.

'We should go.' I jumped up from the table, knowing a minute longer and I'd be in his arms again. In fact, my whole body ached with wanting to press itself against him. But I knew this time, we wouldn't stop at kissing and that was a giant leap to take. One I wasn't ready for even if my body was screaming at me to do it. My body was not the boss of me though. 'One more stop on the tour.'

'Lead the way,' Noah replied, standing up, still smiling, that dimple looking like it was never going away now.

28

We arrived at my favourite Sunday lunch spot just as the rain started. The beautiful autumn morning changed in a minute, it seemed, as the sky grew black and we hurried into the pub, eager to get out of the drizzle. I loved this place. I'd first come here when I moved to Islington one day when I was desperate for a roast dinner. I'd never eaten anywhere but Maccy D's on my own, but I brought a book and ordered wine and a roast and I decided that if I was going to be single, there was no point in not doing the things I wanted to even if it meant having to do them alone.

I waved to the landlord and dived into my favourite booth close to the window, which offered a view of the city in the rain. They had lit the open fire so the pub felt perfectly cosy.

'I missed places like this in New York,' Noah said as he sat down. I draped my coat on the back of the chair and sat down, Noah doing the same across the table from me.

'Stevie!' Mel, one of the wait staff, came over with two menus. 'You just made it before the rain.' It was pouring down outside now.

'We were lucky. This is Noah,' I said as Mel handed him a menu.

'You want one?' Mel asked me, but I shook my head and she smiled. I always had the same thing. 'A bottle instead of a glass?'

'Go for it,' I said.

'I'll have whatever Stevie has,' Noah said, handing the menu back.

'Got it.' Mel dropped me a wink before walking away and I shook my head. I knew she'd grill me about this the next time I came in.

'You come here a lot?' Noah asked.

'I come here most Sundays in autumn and winter,' I said, looking around. 'It's so close to my flat and the roast dinners are amazing.'

'It's been a long time since I had a roast dinner,' Noah said.

'You couldn't find one in New York?' I asked.

'I hated to eat by myself; I always ordered deliveries. So, I can't wait to try the food here.'

I propped my hand under my chin. 'I know what you mean about not wanting to eat alone; I had to force myself to do it but now, I quite like it. I always bring my Kindle. And have a glass of wine.'

Noah smiled. 'Sounds enjoyable that way.' He glanced around the pub. 'I can see why you like it in here. It feels like a home from home. Thank you for showing me your favourite places today. I feel like I know the now you much better.'

'As opposed to the me from five years ago?' I asked, raising an eyebrow.

'You are different,' Noah said.

'In a good or a bad way?'

Mel returned with a bottle of red wine and poured us a glass each and said the roasts would be ready soon.

When we were alone again, Noah took a sip before answering. 'You're fearless now.'

I shook my head. 'No one is fearless. We're all scared of something. Of more than something. But I suppose I decided to do what I wanted to, what I had to, anyway. It all took time though. I've only just got my dream job.'

'Be honest – was it ruined when you realised I was there?' Noah pushed his shirt sleeves up to his elbows.

'I did wonder what I'd done for the universe to punish me,' I joked. Then I saw his anxious expression. I sighed and answered honestly. 'Noah, you broke my heart but I'm okay. I will be okay whatever happens. It's taken time to feel that way but here I am. If you are serious about...' I took a moment to get my words out because it was hard. I didn't want to get hurt again. Even if I knew I could get through it. Who would? But I also knew that some things were worth the risk. I wasn't sure yet if Noah was, and I think he knew that. '...missing me, I would need to be sure that this time, it would be different.'

'It would be forever?' Noah asked.

'Forever is a long time.' But I nodded. 'Something like that, I guess.'

I wanted to tell him I'd need a sign, but that sounded too cheesy for real life. I sometimes recited dialogue from romance books without realising it. I had probably read that idea somewhere.

Noah was thoughtful as he looked out at the rain, swirling the wine in his glass. I wanted to know what he was thinking, but who ever wanted to tell someone their actual thoughts?

Our beef roast dinners with all the trimmings arrived then and we tucked in, hungry from our walking around the city and the chill in the air. Noah declared it the best he'd ever eaten apart from his mother's and I said it was far better than my mother's, and we laughed so much, other diners glanced over curiously. I saw Mel and the landlord, John, look over at us several times and I knew they were wondering who Noah was. I'd never told them about him. Noah had been in the past when I walked in here. But somehow, he was sitting across from me here in the present. Whether he'd be here in the future though, I really wasn't sure.

After our roasts, we shared the sticky toffee pudding and had two coffees. We talked about *Bitten*, and New York, and my library job and meeting Liv, and of course we talked about books. I told Noah what I was currently reading and he said he was reading an enemies-to-lovers romance that I had on my list to read next.

'So, you're reading that and I saw you have a lot of love stories on your bookshelf in your flat. Did I turn you into an avid romance fan then?' I teased him.

He held his hands up. 'I admit it, you were always so enthusiastic that I read a couple of the ones you love and then I was hooked. My father was completely wrong. Books that make people happy are the best kind.'

'I agree.' We smiled at one another and I got the warm feeling you get when you connect with someone else. 'I'm so nervous for Monday,' I admitted then.

'Don't be. I have a feeling it's going to be awesome.'

'Did you just say awesome? Are you American now?'

Noah laughed. 'It rubs off on you, you can't help it.'

'You do have a slight New York twang to your accent. It's cute.'

'Cute? Can't it be sexy?'

I shook my head. 'Nope, sorry, that's reserved for only a few accents. I don't make the rules.'

'Actually, I think you always have.'

The day drew on and the afternoon soon turned dark outside the pub where it felt like time stood still. Finally, we looked at one another, knowing we couldn't delay leaving any longer. Noah walked me back to my flat, holding a large umbrella over us to block out the rain. It wasn't far from the pub and all too soon, we were back outside my building.

'Honestly, thank you for today. I guess I've been kind of isolated for a while now. You've reminded me...' Noah trailed off, looking down at me.

'I know what you mean,' I said when he looked confused as to how to finish his sentence. 'I'm glad we did this.' I reached up on tiptoes and kissed him on the cheek. 'See you at work, boss.'

I dropped him a wink then dashed out from under his umbrella and inside my building.

I glanced back before the door closed and Noah gave me a wave before turning and walking away through the rain.

Sighing, I leaned against the door for a second. I had wanted to kiss him goodbye properly. So badly. As I went up to my flat and let myself in, I told myself it was for the best that I hadn't. I pulled my phone out of my bag and opened up Google.

Is it ever a good idea to get back with your ex?

I scrolled through article after article, most of which were on the side that it was not a good idea; they were your ex for a reason.

Sighing, I went into the kitchen and made myself a cup of tea, deciding I'd get into my pjs and curl up with a book and relax ahead of the working week, which was going to be a huge one for Turn the Pages. And me. And Noah. This week wasn't the week to be lusting after him or stressing about his feelings for me.

29

When my alarm went off at 6 a.m., my phone started to light up with notifications. I grabbed my phone as I headed for the bathroom and smiled at the motivational messages from my mum and dad, from Liv, Aiden and Georgina. They all wished they could join in but they had to work. I wished they could be there as my body was humming with nervous energy. It felt like my new career in publishing hung in the balance.

I got ready in record time and left my flat to walk to work, hoping the fresh air would calm me down a little bit. There had been some excited buzz on social media after we announced what was happening this morning but I knew that might not translate into a successful event. It could go down like a damp squib and my mind flashed with potential consequences. Mr Matthews would definitely fire me and sweep in with a team from New York. Noah would be disappointed. Poor Deborah Day would leave Turn the Pages and hold me personally responsible for messing up her career. I'd never see Emily or Gita again. And finally, no one in publishing would hire me and I'd have to go back to the library with my tail between my legs and beg for my old job back.

But I was staying positive, obviously.

Thank God the weather was at least dry so that wouldn't put people off. When our office came into sight, butterflies swirled in my stomach. I went up to our floor and was grateful to see Emily and Gita, as well as a few others who had come in extra early. Noah was also there handing out t-shirts for everyone to put on. Our eyes met across the floor and he smiled.

'There she is.'

'Oh, thank God.' Emily and Gita rushed over when Noah nodded at me. They were both wearing their t-shirts and gripped the placards they'd made in the library.

'Is something wrong?' I asked them nervously.

'No, we just need to go to the loos and make sure we look good,' Emily said, taking my hand and pulling me along with them. I glanced over my shoulder at Noah who was grinning, so I assumed nothing bad was afoot. I was stumped as to what was causing the panic though as Emily and Gita practically dragged me into the toilets.

'Noah has done something,' Gita said, moving to the mirror and pulling out her lipstick. 'He won't tell us what. He was actually teasing us about it.' Her eyes met mine in the reflection. 'I don't know what you've done to that man.'

I hid my blush by fluffing up my hair. 'I have no idea what you mean.'

Emily snorted. 'Every time we said your name, his eyes lit up and he was very excited about a surprise he has planned.'

'I have no idea what that is,' I said truthfully.

'Someone asked him if he'd had a good weekend and I swear he blushed,' Emily said, scrutinising my face. 'And your cheeks look flushed. Did something happen between the two of you?'

'No!' I cried, but I knew instantly that sounded like I had something to hide. 'I suppose we did hang out yesterday. For a bit,' I said, trying to sound casual.

'Stevie, you can't hold out on us like that!' Gita scolded. 'So, has he got down on his knees and begged forgiveness for dumping you?'

'Ouch,' I said. 'Thanks for not sugar-coating that.'

I couldn't help but smile though.

'Kind of,' I continued. 'He wrote me emails. When we were broken up. And they're pretty romantic.'

'Oh God,' Emily said. 'Love letters? How can anyone resist love letters?'

Gita nodded. 'That's so sweet. Who would have thought Noah could be like that?'

'I'm still not sure I trust him yet though. And my head keeps telling me exes are not a good idea even if he is...' They both waited. '...gorgeous,' I finished with a sigh.

'He does have something about him,' Gita mused. 'If you ignore the bluntness. It's that smile, isn't it?'

'I was always a sucker for that dimple,' I admitted. 'But, he's my boss too; it's complicated.'

Emily put some more blusher on. 'Well, yeah, you guys would need to work out the logistics of it at work, him being your manager and all, but it's not like workplace romances don't happen all the time. HR aren't going to ban it. We're all grown-ups. But I get you being unsure based on the past.'

Gita nodded. 'I don't speak to any of my exes.'

'Nor me,' I agreed. 'Apart from Noah now.' I looked at them. 'Noah was *the* ex.'

'The one that got away?' Emily checked.

'The one who *walked* away,' I corrected her. 'What would you two do?'

'I'd need to be sure of his intentions,' Gita said, sounding like my grandmother. She was right though. Noah had told me he regretted the past but we hadn't talked about the future.

'You're right,' I said. I checked my reflection and spluttered as Emily sprayed us all with her perfume. 'I think you've used half the bottle,' I said, waving her off.

'You'll thank me when we find out what Noah's done,' she replied. 'Just see what happens, no need to rush into anything.'

That was easier said than done when it came to Noah, but I nodded, deciding not to mention that fact I'd already kissed him. That had been just a blip. Liv knew, but Liv knew what it was like to like someone you thought didn't feel the same. It had taken her and Aiden ten years to finally get together, after all.

'Okay, ladies.' Emily assessed us. 'We're ready to rock this, right?'

'We are ready to give it a go,' I said.

She tutted at me.

'We are ready to rock,' I amended. 'I can't pull that off, can I?'

Gita chuckled. 'No, but neither can I. Let's just get out there.'

* * *

I surveyed the scene in front of me in disbelief. We had all the remaining staff at Turn the Pages outside in their *Bitten* t-shirts holding signs with messages like 'romance books make me happy', 'love stories are the best stories', 'romance or bust', 'I like romance books and I cannot lie', and there was a table piled high with tote bags – because publishing loves a goddamn tote bag – with copies of *Bitten* in them and the 'Love Bites' t-shirt. I was worried we would be trying to hand out the bags to disinterested commuters rushing past our office on the way to their own ones but thanks to the social media buzz, people had actually turned up to get one. No forcing them into their hands needed.

'Well, well, well.'

I turned to see Deborah and Ed beside me. Deborah wore a black wool dress and gothic jewellery that gave me nineties vintage vibes and red lipstick the same colour as the lips on the *Bitten* cover.

'Oh my God, you look amazing!' I gushed. 'Isn't this such a good turnout?' I gestured to the crowd that had gathered to collect a tote bag, some of them filming for social media and most of them putting the t-shirt on immediately. 'Romance fans are the best.'

Deborah's mouth twitched at my enthusiasm. 'I have to admit this is bigger than I was expecting.'

I turned to Ed, who grinned.

'Okay, I'll give it to you Stevie; this is pretty amazing,' he conceded.

'Let me film you joining and picking up a tote bag and seeing what's inside then wearing the t-shirt,' I said to Deborah somewhat bossily; this was no time to be meek with her. This was our opportunity. And she seemed to realise it too and just nodded, although she did roll her eyes at Ed – but you can't have everything, can you?

I pulled out my phone and followed her to the crowd. Helpfully, Emily and Gita called out to everyone the author was here and there were even a few cheers as Deborah made her way to the table. She did what I asked and put her t-shirt on to enthusiastic applause from everyone, mostly my colleagues, but it made for a great video.

'Brilliant, I'm posting that everywhere!' I said, frantically jabbing at my phone. I was likely to get RSI but this was no time to worry about that.

'I'm here! I'm here!' Liv's older brother Dan arrived and I filmed him grabbing a tote bag for his TikTok. Then he told his followers that if they loved romance books, they had to get down here.

'You're amazing, thank you,' I said gratefully.

'Agreed,' he said, but he pulled me in for a hug. 'Anything for you, Stevie! I hope it helps.'

'Fingers crossed,' I said. I checked my phone and shared his video. It was already doing well. 'This is brilliant, Dan.'

'So, where is this Noah of yours?' Dan asked in a low voice.

I blushed and looked around. 'He was here a moment ago.'

'Oh my God,' Emily cried from behind us. When I turned, she pointed to the road in shock. When I saw what had caused her to have a meltdown, my mouth dropped open. A few vans had pulled up and reporters with cameras were filing out of them.

'Stevie,' Dan said in awe. 'Am I seeing things? Is that a BBC reporter?'

'No way,' I whispered, rooted to the spot.

'Yes, way,' a voice said in my ear.

I jumped as Noah briefly touched the small of my back and as usual, his touch was like an electric shock. 'What's going on?' I asked as I looked up into his twinkling eyes. He looked thoroughly pleased with himself.

'I may have given an anonymous tip to a few news stations,' he said softly. 'That there was a protest happening today.'

He nodded at our colleagues holding the romance placards, walking in a circle chanting 'respect for romance books.' He shrugged. 'I didn't mention what the protest was for.'

'Okay, I get what the fuss is about now,' Dan hissed at me before moving politely away from us.

In a complete lack of any decorum for the fact that this was a work situation and Noah was my boss, I threw myself at him and wrapped my arms around his neck.

'That is genius!'

Noah chuckled as his arms wrapped around my waist and he lifted me off the ground. 'I'm glad you approve. They might be pissed when they realise.'

I pulled back and we grinned stupidly at one another. 'As long as they mention the book, it's all good.'

'Put each other down,' Emily hissed at us. 'Someone has to go and talk to them,' she said, pointing at the reporters looking around, bemused at what they had walked into.

'Time for our close up,' I said.

Before Noah could protest, I wrapped my arm through his and pulled him along with me, beckoning to Deborah Day to join us with sharp eyes that even she couldn't ignore. The three of us faced the reporters.

'So glad you could join us,' I said cheerfully. 'Are we live?'

30

'Oh my God,' Emily said, erupting into giggles again at the scene she was watching on the TV. 'You actually said you were protesting the lack of respect given to romance books.'

We were all crowded in the boardroom with replays of the lunchtime news rolling on the large TV hanging on the wall. Someone had brought in wine and beer and there was a celebratory mood in the air even though we didn't yet know what this morning's event would do for *Bitten*. But the publicity we had got was priceless.

I took a bow. 'I mean, too right. Romance books should be respected! And look at how many people agreed.' I gestured to the crowd behind me and Noah on the TV as the BBC reporter interviewed us. The shares on social media had gone crazy. We had a few trolls coming out saying romance books were crap and a few mocking articles from the press diminishing something that was beloved by so many, but mostly everyone had jumped on board and were sharing their love for love stories.

On screen, I was telling the reporter that part of the reason romance was overlooked was because it was written and read mainly by women and when male books came out with a strong romance theme, they were generally called 'fiction', not 'romance'. Beside me, Noah was shaking his head and then told the reporter that he was a proud romance fan and always would be.

'I just got a message calling me a traitor to manhood,' Noah said, looking up from his phone. 'So, that's fun.'

'Have another drink.' One of the sales team pushed a paper cup into his hands. There had been an unofficial let's stop working mandate since the BBC news aired but Noah hadn't said anything. He was smiling more than he had for the past month.

'I remember being embarrassed taking romance books out of my local library,' Deborah said, suddenly by my elbow. 'And when I started writing, I told friends and family I was writing 'women's fiction' because I didn't want them to assume I was writing smut. But you know what? I love writing smut,' she said, a twinkle in her eye. I chuckled. 'I don't know what this will do for my book but I'm glad to have you on my team, Stevie,' she added.

I tried not to gape at her. 'The best team.' I held out my paper cup and, shaking her head at me, she tapped it with hers.

Ed joined us then. 'You actually pulled today off. I'm impressed, Stevie.'

'Thank you.'

'The proof will be in the pudding though,' he said.

'I know,' I agreed. This was all amazing but we couldn't know for sure if it was enough to make *Bitten* into a bestseller. I felt excited though. Possibility hung in the air. 'I really hope people will pick it up; I know they will fall in love with it if they do – just like I did.'

My phone rang and Deborah and Ed gestured for me to take it.

I stepped away and answered my mum's call. 'Did you see it?'

'Yes! I came home for lunch and me and your father both

watched it. My little girl on the actual news! And campaigning for romance books. You've made your mum very proud.'

I smiled. 'Well, you gave me the love of romance books so this is for you too.'

'Everyone I know is messaging me about it. And everyone is ordering *Bitten*. My book club are going to do it next month. And your aunt Pat has ordered copies for everyone at her bridge club.'

I chuckled. 'Well, thank everyone for their support. I'll be sure to tell Deborah.'

'You will?'

'No, Mum, she already thinks I'm slightly mad; I don't think she can take my family as well. I better go but I'll see you for dinner on Friday?'

'Keep us updated with how the book's doing!'

I promised I would and Mum hung up. It was followed by a message from Liv inviting me round tonight to watch the news segment again with her and Aiden.

Before I could reply, Gita and Emily drew me back into the group and we looked at the company's social media accounts, which were growing by hundreds of followers each hour as our romance 'protest' started to go viral. The *Bitten* hashtag was trending too.

Then Paul came over. 'Stevie, I am sorry for talking to Mr Matthews behind your back,' he said stiffly. 'It was uncalled for.'

I nodded. 'It's okay.'

He gestured to the TV. 'It's not the book I would have chosen for us to focus on, you know that, but you followed your gut. I have to respect that. I don't know if it will work but this is great publicity.'

'Thanks, Paul,' I replied. He gave me a formal nod then walked away. I watched him go, really hoping that this was going to work.

'What are you talking about?' Noah said angrily from behind me.

Turning around, I saw him storm out of the boardroom and head towards his office. He was on the phone to someone. My stomach sunk and I quickly followed him out.

'Yes, I know you did,' Noah said with an exasperated sigh as I watched him pace around his office from the doorway. 'But we didn't spend any more money. We saw an opportunity to create a social media campaign and—' Noah was forced to stop. I could hear how loud his father was speaking from where I stood. Anger rose up inside me. It was like he didn't want this book to be successful. 'How can you say it's embarrassing?' Noah turned then and saw me. He shook his head. 'I have to go, Dad, we'll talk later.'

'Mr Matthews is pissed?' I asked when Noah had put the phone down, walking into his office and closing the door behind me.

'You could say that,' he replied. 'He's just annoyed that we didn't do what he said and switch our focus to the thriller. I told him this is launch week, we might as well go for it, but he disagreed. Said us talking about how great romance books are isn't good for the company as we should be moving to more of a thriller and upmarket fiction market, not such commercial titles. He thinks that's where the trends are right now.'

'Or he just hates anything to do with love after losing your mum,' I said. I quickly moved forward and touched Noah's arm. 'I'm sorry, I didn't mean to be flippant about that.'

'It's okay,' Noah said. 'You might be right about there being a personal angle to him not wanting to focus on romance books. But I know that business wise, he's under a lot of pressure. He needs this company to show improvement within six months for the Board. It was a real gamble taking over Turn the Pages. But listen, don't let what he said take away from what we did today. This was a great idea.'

I shook my head. 'I just looked at Amazon. There's been a small shift but nothing crazy,' I said. I bit my lip. 'What if it doesn't do anything for *Bitten*?'

Noah took my hand in his. 'The official release day isn't until Thursday and we have the launch night on Wednesday. It's nowhere near over. We can still do it.'

'Will your father let us though?' I looked down at our hands. 'Thank you for joining in and calling the press, even though it has made things difficult with your dad.'

'What can he do?' Noah smiled and I gave him a weak one back because I was worried now. It felt like we'd poked the bear and I didn't think any bears would let you get away with that.

* * *

That evening, I curled up on the sofa in Aiden's flat.

'Dare I ask how things are with Noah?' Liv asked while Aiden made us drinks in the kitchen. The TV was on to replay the news segment and I had my phone in my lap, obsessively checking the charts on all the book retailers, hoping to see *Bitten* shoot up. It was yet to happen and I was starting to worry that Noah's father might be right after all.

'I'm not sure,' I admitted. 'He really helped with *Bitten* but his father is pissed off about it. I just hate that Noah thinks his father is right and that he's somehow to blame for what happened with his mother. I worry his father might tell him he has to go back to New York. And he'll leave me again.'

'But he regretted that so much,' Liv said, handing me a bowl of popcorn. 'He wouldn't do that again. Not after everything he told you in those emails.'

I'd told Liv all about them and I had read her a few lines from my favourite ones. She, like me, had swooned at Noah's words. But words were just words.

'I don't know if I can risk it.' I saw Liv's face. 'Don't give me that sad look! I wanted to focus on my career, right? Noah was a complete surprise. And it's not like I don't know what being without him feels like.'

'But you wish you could be *with* him?'

I shrugged helplessly.

Liv patted my knee. 'Don't stress. If it's meant to be, it will be. You found each other after five years. That has to mean something. And he totally got behind your love romance campaign. Even though his father hates it. He's on your team. And I think *Bitten* is going to be huge. It takes time to get the word out, that's all. Then his father will have to eat his words.'

'Here we go.' Aiden carried in drinks for us all. 'Can we watch Stevie on the TV now? I'll be honest, I thought if you were ever going to be on the news it would be because you're getting arrested for something.'

I rolled my eyes, knowing Aiden's favourite pastime was teasing Liv, and me by extension.

'For your murder?' I asked cheerfully, taking my wine from him. 'There's still time.'

Aiden grinned. 'I'll wear a bulletproof vest just in case.'

He played the news segment and the three of us lapsed into silence to listen. The report introduced the romance 'protest' outside our office and then interviewed Noah and me about what we were doing. After we spoke about our love for romance, the camera cut to the last shot of the segment, showing the cover of *Bitten* in all its glory.

'Okay, I have to admit,' Aiden said once our interview had finished, 'you won even me over about romance books.'

Liv nudged him. 'I've seen you cry at *The Notebook*, don't forget.' She beamed at me. 'You were amazing, Stevie. And Noah was very swoon-worthy telling the world how much he loves love stories. I bet his favourite trope is second-chance romance.'

I saw her suggestive smile. 'Subtle!' I tutted, but I couldn't help smile back because I wondered if he had thought of me when he read a book that used that trope. I knew I had thought of him when I had. 'I really don't know,' I said, then shook my head. 'But thank you both. I do think it went well and everyone has got behind it. We just need it to turn it into book sales now otherwise Mr Matthews is going to flip.' I leant back against Aiden's sofa with a sigh. *Bitten* officially came out on Thursday and then it would be in the shops. Until then, we needed all the pre-orders online that we could get. 'Dan just tagged me on TikTok,' I told Liv, showing her my phone. 'Your brother is the best.'

Dan had created a video montage of the romance protest with clips of my interview.

'He is,' she agreed. 'We all love a grand gesture around here.'

She looked fondly at Aiden and I tried to ignore the gut punch to my stomach. I really wanted someone to look at me like that.

My phone buzzed and I saw there was a message from Noah. My stomach flipped.

> I have to speak to the Board on Zoom tomorrow so go to the bookshop without me in the morning. And I'll meet you there as soon as I can.

Disappointment flowed through me at the business-like message.

'A message from Noah?' Liv asked, eagerly trying to see.

I showed Liv the message. 'So romantic,' I said sarcastically.

'Maybe grumpy is his default setting when he's stressed,' she suggested. 'It doesn't mean he's not buzzed about today or seeing you tomorrow.'

I took a gulp of wine. 'Aiden, why are men so hard to work out?'

'Stevie, he's a fool if he thinks he can do any better than you,' Aiden replied.

'Aww,' Liv said, smiling over at him like he'd just melted her heart.

'God, Aiden,' I tutted. 'Now I feel bad about wanting to murder you.'

'I forgive you,' Aiden said with a grin.

I went to reply to Noah but decided against it. That was very much a message from my boss. So, I'd be a good employee and do what he asked. And not obsess about the fact that my ex hadn't added any kisses to the message.

31

In the morning, I went straight to the bookshop to help Georgina get everything ready for Deborah Day's launch party. She didn't ask where Noah was and I was glad to not have to discuss him. Instead, we focused on preparing the back room. As it was Halloween, we wanted to create the perfect gothic vibe to suit *Bitten*. I had found some red velvet curtains in a charity shop so we hung them either side of the platform. Georgina had lined the room with chairs that we'd covered in black pillowcases and added red bows to the backs. I dotted LED candles around the room and on the stage. Then I piled the pumpkins I'd bought by the platform. I'd found a velvet chair for Deborah to sit on and Georgina had brought a crow statue from her flat to stand beside it.

I raised an eyebrow and she laughed. 'It was for a play at university and I can't part with it,' she explained. 'Even though sometimes I swear it's watching me.'

We put up a table at the back where we laid out all the alcohol, soft drinks, paper cups and nibbles we had bought. All the drinks were red-coloured. We hung up posters of the book all along the side and a copy on each chair. Then Georgina brought out a speaker from the back room, and we set up our gothic playlist that we'd made to play softly in the background. Then when Georgina turned off the ceiling light, we stood back to look at the room.

'Does it look enough like a room where a vampire might seduce you?' I asked, putting my hands on my hips to give it a critical look.

Georgina laughed. 'I'd say so.'

I snapped a picture and attached it to a message to Noah.

> How's this?

'Okay, well, looks like we're all set. I hope everyone we've invited turns up.'

'After you were all over the news, I don't think they'd miss it,' Georgina said, pulling her hair into a ponytail.

My phone vibrated and I looked at Noah's reply.

> Perfect. Go home and get ready and I'll meet you there at six.

'Looks like Noah's stuck in his meeting,' I said. 'He will be here at six.'

'And it starts at seven?'

I nodded. 'Right, well, I better get ready then and try not to stress about this going well.'

'It will be great, don't worry,' she said, walking back into the bookshop as a customer came in.

I looked at the room. It did fit *Bitten*. And Halloween. I hoped Deborah would be pleased. She'd been asked to do a few radio shows and podcasts since our romance protest and she was in her element sharing her love of romance with the world. I checked Amazon again. The book was finally climbing the charts. And with the official publication date tomorrow, I was hopeful it would keep climbing. But high enough to chart on the bestseller list? That was still unclear.

Giving Georgina a wave, I left the bookshop and headed back to my flat to get ready. Everyone in the office was leaving early to change too. I had asked everyone to dress for Halloween.

My spooky Halloween playlist got me in the mood, as did a few sips of red wine, and soon I was ready and looking at my reflection in my full-length mirror. With my blonde hair, I had been torn between Alice in Wonderland and what I had gone with, but I couldn't resist jumping on the social media trend. I wore a pink gingham dress and matching headband, my blonde hair down, with pink lipstick and pink high heels.

'Is this okay?' I asked Liv when I FaceTimed her.

'Stevie, you are Barbie! I love it! I wish I could be there.' Liv and Aiden had a university Halloween party to go to instead. 'I hope it goes brilliantly.'

'Thanks Liv. At least we get to toast to the book no matter what happens with it. It's weird I haven't seen Noah all day. He said he'd see me at the bookshop in half an hour.'

'Is he actually going to wear a costume? I can't picture it.'

'Nor me,' I admitted. 'Maybe as the boss he'll say it isn't professional, but it doesn't matter. Everyone else said they will be. Deborah is dressing up as a vampire, of course. Okay, I better jump in an Uber. Happy Halloween!'

'Have a witching-good time!'

'Don't be a basic witch.'

We grinned at one another and said goodbye and then I drained the rest of my red wine and headed out.

The night was dark with the promised bright full moon lighting up the London skyline. I'd always enjoyed Halloween and there was a spookiness to the cloudy night that made it perfect. The city was lit up and I passed people going trick-or-treating and lots of carved pumpkins in doorways.

My Uber dropped me at the edge of the alleyway and I stopped in awe to see the bookshop lit up so spectacularly. Georgina had been busy since I left her. There were pumpkins piled up outside with LED candles and the windows had been stripped and replaced with lit-up pumpkins, cobwebs and a pile of spooky books.

'What do you think?' a voice rang out in the darkness. Noah stepped into the light from the only lamppost down here. He was dressed in dark colours so I could hardly see him.

'You did this?' I asked, gesturing to the bookshop.

'With Georgina. I wanted to surprise you.'

'You did.' I smiled. 'It looks perfect.'

Noah stepped closer. Now I could see him better, I realised he *had* dressed up. In a tux. I raised an eyebrow.

'James Bond?' he said. 'Can I get away with that? It was all I had.'

I chuckled. 'I'll allow it. So, shall we go in?'

'One more surprise first.' He pulled out his phone and handed it to me. I saw he had an email from the buyer of the biggest bookshop chain in the country asking for a huge bulk order of *Bitten*. 'They saw your protest and customers have been asking for the book. We're rushing them an order in time for the weekend. They're going to stock it in all of their shops.'

'Noah!' For the second time, I threw my arms around him, making him stumble backwards with a laugh. He held me tightly and I didn't want it to end. 'Will it count for the bestseller lists?'

'I'm not sure, it depends when they get the stock out, but the visibility for the book will be great.' Noah pulled back and looked at me. His hands slipped to my hip, his touch warming through my pink dress. 'Am I allowed to say you look gorgeous tonight? Because you really do.'

'Why thank you,' I said with a pleased smile. I liked us like this. Light and not weighed down by our past.

'Now I wish I'd come as Ken,' he said.

I shook my head. 'No, you're definitely more Bond than Ken,' I said, itching to run my fingers through his tousled hair but keeping them down by my side.

'I'm sorry I haven't seen you today until now. My New York Zooms were mind-numbing; I just wanted to get here and do this. And then see you.' His thumb stroked my hip and I couldn't help wishing he would pull me closer. I think he saw something of that on my face because he smiled enough to show his dimple in the light from the shop and leaned in closer. 'I'm supposed to be focusing on work but you are much more enjoyable to focus on.'

God, he really did have a way with words. 'You won't say that when the launch party starts and we have to network our butts off and make this book a success.'

'Network our butts off?' He laughed. 'I have never tried that, I must say. Okay, I'll let you go. But just know, I don't want to.' His arms left my body, leaving me several degrees cooler. 'Shall we?' He gestured to the shop.

I exhaled a little bit shakily. 'We shall,' I said and led the way inside, all the time thinking that being Noah's sole focus was something I would really enjoy.

Inside, the bookshop was full of pumpkins and LED candles and the effect was mesmerising. We walked together to the back room where Georgina was pouring out wine and blackberry juice, the music from our playlist lending a suitably spooky atmosphere to the night. She was dressed as Daphne from Scooby Doo and looked amazing. I glanced at Noah but he greeted her with no more enthusiasm than usual and relief washed over me. Because even if I was unsure about us, the thought of him being interested in someone else brought out a jealous streak I didn't want to have.

Emily appeared in the doorway with Gita. 'Let's get this party started!'

'Oh, I love it,' I said, beaming at them. They were dressed as Rachel and Monica from *Friends*. 'Genius,' I said, because I could definitely see their personalities as those characters.

'God, I hate how good your figure looks in that dress,' Emily said, smiling at me. 'Where's the wine?'

The room soon filled up with the rest of my colleagues and then in came the booksellers, book reviewers, romance authors and press we'd invited. Everyone had taken the request to dress up seriously and the room was full of witches, skeletons, ghosts and TV characters. Everyone was excited to have their copy of *Bitten* and I was pleased to see people taking photos and posting them on social media.

As 7 p.m. approached, I turned around to see Deborah and Ed walk in. Deborah looked magnificent as a vampire with a long black dress, cloak and red lipstick. She smiled, showing off her fake fangs. Ed had also come as a vampire and they made a striking pair.

'You guys! I love your costumes. You could be the couple in *Bitten*,' I said, clapping my hands. 'After he turns Rebecca,' I added in a low voice so not to spoil the ending for anyone nearby.

'I don't know how Debs got me to do this,' Ed said. 'You look lovely, Stevie,' he added, leaning in to kiss my cheek.

'Ed.' Noah appeared by my side and nodded at the agent, before turning his attention to Deborah. 'Lovely to welcome you to your launch,' he said. 'We're really happy with the buzz around the book so far. Did you get my email about the bookshop order?'

'I did,' she said. 'I've had so many requests to do things this week. It's like a shock to the press that people not only love romances but want to shout it from the rooftops. Thanks to Stevie here, they know now.'

I curtseyed, holding out my dress. 'I knew being an avid reader would come in handy one day. Shall we get you ready on stage?'

'I'm a bit nervous,' she said softly as we walked to the platform. 'I haven't had a launch party for ten years.'

'We are going to celebrate in style then,' I promised. 'It'll be a breeze. Just read the chapter you picked then I'll field questions and then we can have more wine.'

'I like the sound of more wine,' she said as we stepped up on the platform. She glanced at me. 'Did I sense something between you and Noah? He gave Ed daggers when he said how lovely you look tonight.'

'Well, I don't know. It's complicated, I guess,' I hedged, not sure what to say. I looked over and saw Noah watching us. He gave me a smile, which made me blush as I turned back to see Deborah looking at me.

'Hmm. Isn't it always?' She looked over my shoulder and gave Ed a wave, which made his face light up.

I raised an eyebrow. 'You and Ed?' I asked, unable to hide my surprise. I mean, there was, what, twenty years between them? Not that I should have judged, I knew.

'Shh,' she said hastily. 'It's complicated.'

'I'm kind of sick of that,' I admitted as I handed her the book with her chapter marked with a Post-it. 'I would love things to be easy for once.'

'I think it's us that makes it complicated. Ed has told me how he feels; I just find it hard to believe. I'm too old to play games. And I don't want to hold him back.'

'If he loves you then that could never happen,' I said. I glanced at Noah. 'I'm scared too. We used to date, me and Noah. I only just met him again after five years. He has told me he made a mistake in letting me go but hasn't said what he wants now. And I don't want to get hurt again.'

Deborah sat on her chair and nodded. 'That's understandable. I think the only way to know is to ask him, right? Once you know what he wants, you can decide if it's worth the risk. But let me know how you decide because I'm stuck.'

We smiled at one another. 'And I thought romance authors had all the answers!'

Deborah sighed. 'I think that's why I write about love – because it is a complete mystery to me.'

32

Deborah did brilliantly. The whole room fell silent as she read from *Bitten*. I stood at the back with Noah watching everyone's rapt gazes as she read the scene where the leading lady was seduced by the vampire for the first time. You thought for a moment he might have been there to kill her but you realise they had fallen in love. You could hear a pin drop as she described their first kiss. I rubbed my arms as I got goosebumps. I loved this book so much and this was such a sexy scene.

'She's brilliant,' Noah leaned in and whispered to me. 'The team missed a trick not getting her to do more events like this.'

'The whole room is in the palm of her hand,' I whispered back. 'I envy the way she has us all hooked. I could never do that.'

'If you only knew how I see you,' Noah said, his hand on the small of my back to steady us as he leaned in even closer.

My heart thumped beneath my dress. 'How do you see me?' I asked softly as Deborah reached the moment the vampire kissed the heroine and they both realised their lives were irrevocably changed.

'I can't take my eyes off of you,' Noah replied. 'You are beautiful and sweet and kind and enthusiastic, and so sure of what you want. You did this here tonight. Everyone had given up on Deborah but you knew this was a special book and you fought for it. You fight for what you believe in. And you bring everyone right along with you. And that smile of yours. I feel like I want to do anything I can to make you smile.'

I swallowed hard and the room began to clap Deborah. We leaned away from one another, staring into each other's eyes as we joined in. I wondered if Noah could hear my heart beating because it was so loud. That was how he saw me? God. I really was in trouble, wasn't I?

'And now Stevie is going to join me on stage,' Deborah said.

The whole room turned to where she pointed and I tore my eyes from Noah and walked on unsteady legs up to join her for the Q&A.

'Before we start with the questions, I want to thank Stevie. If you don't know, Stevie is publicity executive at my publisher, Turn the Pages, and she only joined the company this month but she did all this, can you believe? Not only this party but the romance rally on Monday too. Stevie is passionate about romance novels and she's reignited my love for the genre and for writing in it. Books that bring people comfort and joy have always been my favourite to read and write. I'm so happy that I can do this as my job and work with people equally enthusiastic. That hasn't always been the case,' Deborah said, turning from me to the room. 'But if Stevie is the future of publishing then we are in very good hands, I think.'

I was blushing from head to toe as people clapped me. I met Noah's eyes through the crowd and I couldn't miss the look of pride on his face.

'I don't know what to say,' I said when the room quietened down. 'Deborah's book is brilliant. It's my absolute pleasure to help get it into the hands of readers who I know will love it as much as I did. So, does anyone have a question for Deborah?'

After the Q&A, everyone grabbed more food and drink. Georgina turned the music up and it really did feel like a party then. Noah was surrounded by people all through the night, and I couldn't get over to him, being pulled by Emily and Gita to introduce me to people and then walking around with Deborah so everyone got a chance to chat to her. It was a busy night and before I knew it, it was 9 p.m. and people started leaving.

'Well, Stevie, you pulled it off,' Ed said as he and Deborah came to say goodbye. 'We might consider re-signing with you guys again after all.'

'But let me guess, we'd need to offer a lot more money,' I said with a laugh.

'Debs is worth it,' he said, giving her an adoring look. 'Let's see what the bestseller list says first,' he added, making the nerves return to the pit of my stomach. So much was riding on this book for all of us.

'Even if this doesn't work, I've had more fun with this book than I have for a long time,' Deborah said. She actually gave me a hug then. 'Enjoy yourself tonight; you deserve it,' she said, close to my ear.

'You too,' I said back.

I waved to the two of them and smiled to see Deborah take Ed's hand once they were outside the bookshop. They were why I loved love so much. How two people could connect in a way no one understood but them.

'Shall we go to the pub?' Emily asked, appearing behind me with Gita and the rest of the team.

I could see Noah was talking to Georgina.

'Let me sort some things out and I'll see you there,' I told them and waved as they stumbled across the cobbles towards the pub over the road. 'That was amazing, Georgina,' I said, walking back into the now empty bookshop.

'It was so fun,' she agreed. She looked at me and Noah. 'No need to help me clear up. I'll come in early tomorrow and do it. No arguments,' she said, giving us a stern look. 'You should go and celebrate.'

'Thank you,' Noah said.

I rushed over to hug her. 'This place is so special,' I said.

'It is,' she agreed, smiling as I let her go. 'Have a good night!'

We walked out and Georgina locked the door behind us. The alley was quiet now. Once the bookshop lights went out, all we had to guide us was the moon and one street light.

'That went well, right?' I said. 'I think everyone loved the reading and Deborah was amazing. So, shall we join the others at the pub or do you—' My voice was nervous but I hoped it didn't show.

'Stevie.' Noah reached out for my hand and pulled me to a stop. 'Yesterday, spending the day with you like that, I just... It made me happy. You make me happy. And I hate that I ever made you unhappy. I want to fix it so badly it hurts,' he said with such fierceness, it took my breath away. 'I want to make you happy. That's all I want now. Is there any way you might let me try?'

My head was still saying this was a bad idea but his words tugged my heart so hard that I pulled him closer with our entwined hands.

'I am still scared,' I admitted, looking up at his brown eyes shining behind his glasses in the moonlight. 'But being with you made me happy too.'

Noah wrapped his arms around me then. 'I'll take any crumbs you give me,' he said. 'We can move at a glacial pace. If you don't want me to kiss you yet—'

'Kiss me,' I interrupted. I couldn't hold any longer. My body remembered the hot kiss we'd had right here in this alleyway and it wanted more. I needed more.

Noah looked at me. 'Are you sure?'

'Yes,' I whispered.

Our lips met again and that same urgency pumped through us. Something seemed to crackle in the air as Noah held me tightly and I wrapped myself around him so easily, it was like my body was created to fit right against his. His mouth searched mine and I didn't know what answers he found but he let out a contended murmur and pulled me closer. When his tongue touched mine, I moaned and my hands moved to his hair where they had longed to be.

'Up against the wall,' Noah broke our kiss to half-growl at me.

I backed up instantly, my body sparked alight by his words. He'd always had that power. I loved it when he told me what to do. And he knew it.

'Arms up,' he purred into my ear as my back touched the wall. His arm came around my waist and when I lifted my arms, he kissed me hungrily. Then he moved his mouth to the neckline of my dress, brushing kisses against the top of my breast that just poked out of the material. I closed my eyes and felt my legs start trembling.

His hands moved to my chest and my nipples hardened as he touched me through the thin material that separated our skin.

I longed for there to be nothing in between us.

'More,' I gasped. 'I need more.'

'You can have anything you want,' he breathed. 'Will you part your legs for me?'

I moved them instantly on his command, my whole body full of anticipation.

He moved one hand to my thigh. 'Stevie, please tell me you want this as much as I do,' he said as his fingertips stroked slowly higher up my leg.

I trembled again and almost brought my hands down but he told me to keep them up so I did.

I looked into his hungry, dark eyes. 'Feel how much I want this,' I gasped out.

Noah's breath hitched then. He looked into my eyes as his hand moved under my dress and up my thigh. I was hardly breathing as his hand found my lacey knickers, making me gasp again.

'Hmmm,' he said contently as he rubbed me over the top of my underwear with his thumb. Then he moved the fabric out of the way and slipped one finger inside me.

'Noah,' I said then as he eased another finger in, helping finally to soothe some of the ache between my legs. The ache that had been there, if I was honest, since I saw him again. 'I need...' I said, trailing off with a groan.

'I know, I need it too,' he replied, leaning down to kiss me.

I writhed against his fingers and I couldn't stop myself. My arms dropped to his shoulders, pulling him closer.

'Noah, this isn't enough,' I said, my back arching off the wall.

'What do you need, Stevie? I told you. I'll do whatever you want.'

'Will you take me home? To yours...'

Noah paused and our eyes met. 'You really want that?'

'I want that,' I said, moaning as his fingers moved again inside me. 'I want you.'

'I've wanted to hear you say that for so long.'

Noah moved away from me and my body protested, but I knew it would be soon sated. He adjusted my clothing and I peeled myself off the wall. He was smiling and leaned down to kiss me. It was slow and lingering and when he pulled back, he kept his hand on my waist. 'This feels like a dream,' he said, using his other hand to brush my hair from my face.

I smiled. 'It's real. I promise. Let's go home.'

The look on his face when I said that made my heart leap. He took my hand and we left the alleyway to flag down a taxi. My heart was still beating hard and fast and everything felt confusing and crazy, but every fibre of me wanted Noah. I wanted to leap. To take the risk. Because I wanted to be in his arms too much to hold back any more.

So, I shut off my brain and any worries about tomorrow because I wanted to enjoy this moment. If it was only ever a moment then so be it. We'd make it a fucking excellent one.

33

We were silent on the ride to Noah's flat. I sent a message to Emily to say I wouldn't be coming to the pub and I'd see her tomorrow.

> If you're with who I think you're with, have fun! ;)

Smiling in the dark of the taxi, I put my phone away and looked across at Noah, silhouetted by the headlights of passing cars. He had a smile on his face and he reached across and squeezed my hand. It was like he was reassuring me and I anchored myself to his touch.

Soon we reached his place and got in the lift together. 'I'd kiss you now but there are cameras,' he said when the doors slid shut. We looked at one another and anticipation built up under my skin. I wondered if this would feel familiar or brand new. 'What are you thinking?' he murmured as I continued to watch him.

'You'll find out,' I said.

Noah groaned. 'This is the slowest lift ever.'

I laughed as we finally reached the top floor. The doors opened and Noah took my hand and let us into his flat. It was dark and silent but when he shut the door, mood lighting switched on to light the way.

I raised an eyebrow. 'Is this bring a woman home mode?'

'This is don't trip over anything if you're drunk mode but it works for this too,' Noah said, sliding a hand around my waist and pulling me towards him. I reached up to touch his cheek and he caught my hand in his. 'I can't believe I get to hold you again,' he whispered, leaning down to brush his lips against mine. A shiver ran down my body.

I reached up to kiss him and he pulled me closer, wrapping his arms around me as I planted my hands on his chest.

He pulled back for a moment and took off his glasses, putting them on the console table behind us, and then he scooped me up off the floor, making me giggle. I wrapped my arms around his shoulders as our lips met again. Noah's tongue pressed against mine and I let out a murmur. Like the kiss outside the bookshop, we kissed with hunger. It was like a need. Like our bodies had craved this for five years and couldn't hold back now they were being given a free reign.

'I need you in my bedroom,' Noah said breathlessly, his voice low and desperate like the craving I felt. I nodded eagerly and he carried me into his room, where he planted me softly onto my feet. Then he gently kissed my cheek then my nose then my forehead then my other cheek then down my neck and my collarbone. I gasped. The sweet, soft kisses were so tender, my heart lurched inside my chest. 'I've thought about this a lot,' he whispered into my ear.

'For how long?' I asked, pleasure surging through me.

'Arms up,' he said. I did as he asked, wondering if he was going to ignore my question. He stepped forward and pulled my pink dress slowly up. 'Honestly?' he said softly as he lifted the fabric over my head. 'Since you told me I was a dick.'

I giggled as the dress came off and Noah threw it on his bed. 'I can slag you off more if it turns you on.'

Noah's eyes moved over me in my pink underwear set, taking me in from head to toe. 'It reminded me how amazing you are...' He stepped forward and I trembled at the hungry look in his eyes. 'And made me want to kiss you and make you forget that I had been a dick. I wanted you to want me again because I really did want you. So much. Sometimes it was hard to think straight at work.'

He dropped down to his knees then and picked up my foot. I leaned on his shoulder as he undid my heels one by one and slipped them off.

'It has been quite distracting having you there,' I admitted as he stroked my ankle.

Noah looked up at me as he tossed my heels aside. 'Good. Because yes, it's been bad at work, but I can't even tell you how bad it's been here at night.' He gestured to his bed behind us.

I was finding it hard to breathe properly. I gripped Noah's shoulder for balance.

'What have you been thinking about in your bed?' I gasped out.

Noah kissed me behind my knee and then stroked my leg as he stood up slowly, brushing my inner thighs, causing me to let out a little moan.

'Getting you to make that sound was one of my thoughts,' he said, his voice husky, his hands moving to my hips. 'As was what you tasted like now. How you would feel if I touched you like this.' His hand moved across my belly button and round to my bum, caressing it. 'And how badly I wanted to make you come.'

I sucked in a breath. 'I'm surprised you got any sleep,' I managed to say as he moved his hands up my back to my bra and unclipped it.

'It was agony, Stevie, agony.'

He stepped back. His dark eyes smouldered at me. I bit my lip in anticipation at what he was going to say or do next.

Noah clocked the movement. 'Take your bra off,' he said, his eyes dipping to my chest. I pulled the bra off me and stood there in front of him in just my pink thong, breathing hard as he looked at me reverently. 'Jesus Christ,' he said, coming back to me and reaching down to kiss one breast and then the other then he flicked his tongue over my nipple. I shivered again.

'This is unfair,' I said. 'You're still fully dressed.'

'I need you naked first.' Noah stepped back again. 'Take that thong off, Stevie. I want to see all of you. I've waited a long time.'

Noah's commands were turning me on more than I remembered. It was like my body had been asleep with the other men I'd been with and now it was wide awake just waiting for him to tell it what to do, knowing how good it was going to feel. I stepped out of my thong and kicked it off. I was a little bit nervous for a second, fully naked in front of him in the dim light of his bedroom, until he spoke again.

'Fuck. You are so gorgeous. You are sexy as hell,' he said, making me feel instantly better. Noah pulled me into his arms and kissed me. His mouth moved back to my breasts and as he licked my nipple, his hand moved down my body. 'Legs,' he said, lifting off me for a moment, watching my face as I stood astride and his hand hovered between them. 'Guide me,' he said.

I moved my hand over his and moved him to where I wanted him. No, *needed* him. We both gasped as he touched me. Noah's eyes never left mine as I moved his hand exactly where it felt good. Then I took his fingers and guided them to me, groaning when they slipped inside.

'Noah, please, can you get naked now?' I begged.

'I need you to come first,' he said, his mouth returning to my breast. My head rolled back as he kissed me there, his fingers inside me. My hand clutched his wrist as my legs began to tremble. Noah's free hand gripped my waist steady as he touched and kissed me. It felt incredible. It felt new. I wasn't sure it had ever been this good before.

I moaned and Noah murmured contently.

'Please,' I gasped out. I wasn't sure what I was asking but Noah rubbed this thumb across me, and that did it. I slumped against him with a long moan.

'Oh,' I said, surprised at the sudden and delicious release that rocked through me. My whole body was tingling as Noah lowered me on to his bed. I lay back on his pillows, my back flat, as I let out a shaky breath. That had been hot. No other word to describe it.

When I could see straight, I turned my head to watch Noah shed his clothes, his eyes never leaving me.

'Now what are you going to do to me?' I asked as he stood naked by the bed. God, his body was better than I remembered it. Tall and lean but with delicious, defined abs and strong arms and that thin trail of hair pulling my eyes down to where he was very ready for me.

'Do you see what you've done to me?' he asked as he climbed on to the bed, propping himself over me.

I smiled. 'Good. Because I need you to come as hard as I just did,' I breathed, reaching up to kiss him.

'That won't be a problem. I can barely keep it together,' he whispered, reaching under my bum to lift me so I could prop my legs up. 'Shall I get a condom?'

'I mean, I'm on the pill and I've always used one with everyone since you...'

'Me too.' He moved between my legs and our bodies slid together. 'But I can still get one.'

I shook my head. 'I want you to come inside me.'

'Stevie, are you trying to make this last only a second?' Noah groaned. 'Are you ready for me?'

'Yes,' I said, biting my lip with anticipation.

'You want this, don't you?' he asked, searching my eyes for certainty.

'I want it more than anything,' I said. 'Please, Noah. I need you now.'

He smiled. 'I need you too.'

He brushed my hair back against the pillow and gave me a kiss, sliding his tongue against mine as he slowly entered me, finally easing the ache between my legs that had been there since I first saw him again. Everything was wiped out. The other men I'd been with. Even our past. It was all gone as Noah moved deep inside me and I squeezed my legs around him.

Noah looked down at me from his propped elbows and I moved my arms up to clutch the pillow. 'You feel perfect. You are perfect. We are perfect together,' he said, punctuating each word with a thrust deeper inside me.

I moved against him and we both groaned at the friction.

'It's too good,' I agreed, clutching the pillow harder as Noah moved above me. I could feel the pleasure building in me already. I looked at him. 'Tell me I'm yours,' I gasped.

'I thought I was the one making demands,' Noah said, flashing that dimple as he looked at me with such fondness, my breath was taken away. 'Stevie, you are mine. All mine. And I'm yours. I have always been yours. And you...' He moved faster and deeper inside me, making me moan even louder. 'Will always be mine.'

His words sent me over the edge and I cried out his name as he gasped. We looked at each other as we reached our finish together. Then Noah leaned down to cover my moans with his mouth, kissing me over and over as he thrusted into me until he couldn't move any more.

When he flopped down beside me, I turned to face him and as we tried to get our breath back, we watched each other face to face.

'Will you stay tonight, please?' he asked.

'Yes,' I said.

And our five years apart seemed to dissolve, like the final grains of sand in an hourglass.

34

An hour later, we were in the living room. Noah carried over the pizza we'd just had delivered while I poured us both a glass of red wine. I was wearing one of his dressing gowns and he was in a t-shirt and jogging bottoms.

'You're smiling,' Noah said when he placed the pizza box down and handed me a plate.

'I was just thinking this is all very cosy,' I said, curling my legs up on the sofa. The fire in the living room was lit and as Noah opened the box, the smell of pizza mingled with the fireside fragrance in the room. The sex had been amazing but this was bringing me very close to that same feeling of bliss.

I took out a slice of pizza and put it on my plate as Noah joined me on the sofa.

'You look very cosy in my dressing gown,' he agreed, reaching out to stroke the material that covered my thigh. 'I like it.' He watched as I took a bite of pizza then put a slice on his plate. 'I missed evenings like this with you.'

'Don't get serious on me,' I said as I chewed. I didn't want to come down from this high.

'I promise I won't,' he replied, flashing me his dimple. He saw my phone light up on the coffee table. 'You're popular tonight.'

'There's a reason you shouldn't introduce friends to one another,' I said with a sigh. 'Emily told Liv she thought I'd gone home with you and now they are all in a WhatsApp group demanding to know what's going on.' I grabbed my phone and showed him the messages coming through. 'I don't have to tell them anything. I mean, is it even allowed?' I pointed between us. 'You are my boss,' I said, biting back a laugh.

Noah rolled his eyes. 'So you keep reminding me. We might need to give HR a heads up but only if...' He trailed off and didn't finish his sentence.

I looked at my phone and not at him. Only if what? We actually became a couple again? I was dying to know if that's what he wanted but I needed him to ask me.

'You better tell them something, I think they're starting to worry,' Noah said then, frowning at the messages now turning into capital letters with a lot of exclamation points and question marks.

I nodded and quickly typed.

> Guys, chill please! I'm fine! Yes, I'm with Noah. And no, I'm not telling you nosey gossips anything.

And then I added...

> Unless you buy me something nice and tell me I'm pretty ;)

'You're very pretty,' Noah murmured in my ear when he saw what I'd written. 'Actually, you're beautiful. Inside and out.'

I felt myself flush at his words. 'Flattery will get you everywhere,' I said lightly, putting my phone down. I wasn't sure why I suddenly felt nervous. We'd been so caught up in lust that I'd pushed all my worries aside and gone with what my body wanted. But now my heart was longing to know what Noah thought.

I carried on eating my pizza and gave myself an internal stern talking to. Yes, I still wanted Noah. Yes, I still had feelings for him. But I wasn't still in love with him. That would take time to come again. Because of how hurt I'd been when he left, I needed this to move slowly. I wouldn't give my heart away to him again unless I was 100 per cent sure what he'd said when we were in bed was actually true. That I was his, and he was mine. But things said right before orgasm weren't admissible in a court of law, I knew that.

Noah was watching me. I could tell he was wondering what I was thinking and I kind of liked the fact he didn't know.

'You are still staying, right?' he said eventually.

'Yes, but I better leave early to get ready for work. It's bad enough I'll have to do the walk of shame in my Barbie outfit; I'm not rocking up to work in it. HR would definitely have a field day then.'

'You can borrow something from me to go home in.' He held out his arm and I leaned against him. I liked how strong his chest felt. I could lean against him with all my weight and he'd hold me steady.

We finished our pizza in a comfortable silence. Noah put his plate down then kissed me on the top of my head, before coming back to the same position beside me.

'It's official publication day tomorrow for *Bitten*. How are you feeling about it?'

I put my plate down too and snuggled against him. 'Nervous. I hope we did enough to make some dent on the charts. I hope Deborah will stay with us. And I hope the company won't be so quick to dismiss a romance again.'

Noah rubbed my arm. 'The world would be a better place if everyone read romance,' he said into my hair, giving me goosebumps. 'Okay, I have to ask... Did you read my emails? The one where I went into a bookshop and bought that love story that reminded me of you? That is your fault.' He pointed to his bookshelf and the pastel books there. 'And the fact I bought a bookshop.'

I laughed against him. 'I can't believe you did that. Yes, I read your emails. I've read them all now. I really am so sorry about your mum, Noah. I wish I had met her. I bet she was so proud of you.'

'I don't know about that. My father isn't.'

'I don't believe that.' I sat up and touched his chin so he would look at me. 'He made you CEO. He must believe in you. And he loves you. You're his son. And your mum loved you. And they made you together. You're part of them both. That must give him comfort.'

Noah reached out and took my hand in his. 'You always see the best in everyone. How can you say all that when I let you believe I didn't love you? That's what made me the craziest about it all. That maybe you didn't know how head over heels I was for you back then.'

'I know it now,' I said softly. 'You had a lot to deal with. And you regretted it as soon as you left. And tried to make it right. I'm sorry I didn't let you.'

'You have nothing to apologise for. You were right to shut me out. That's what I deserved. I still don't...' He let go of my hand. 'I still don't deserve you, Stevie. I'm trying hard to make it up to you but I don't think I ever will.'

I leaned in and kissed him. 'It's okay. I'm okay. I was okay. And I will be okay.'

He searched my eyes. 'You'll be okay if what?'

I looked down at my lap. 'If you leave again.'

He let out a growl in the back of his throat. I looked up in surprise and he pulled me onto his lap, my legs draped across him, his hands around my waist.

'I will never, ever leave you again unless you tell me to,' Noah said, his voice still fierce. He pushed back my hair from my face and put his fingers under my chin, tilting my face up to his. 'I swear it, Stevie.'

I wanted to beg him not to make promises he couldn't keep but when I looked into his eyes, I saw the sincerity in them. I swallowed hard.

'Stevie, do you hear me? Do you understand? Say you believe me. Unless you tell me to, I won't leave you again. I promise.'

He had barely finished his sentence when I pressed my lips against his. He murmured as I slid closer, my arms wrapping round him as our mouths met to seal the vow he just made. My body hummed with happiness. He wasn't going to leave. I could relax. I could let him in again. That's what I wanted. It wasn't going to be easy, I knew that, but when his arms were around me, it felt like the right thing to do. The only thing I could do. I melted into him and when he reached for the dressing gown cord and pulled it away, letting the gown open fully, my body naked in front of him again, I gasped out 'yes.'

Noah kissed down my neck and across my collarbone and lifted me so my legs were astride him. I reached for the waistband of his joggers and he broke away from me to pull them down.

As I lifted myself on top of him, Noah whispered my name reverently.

'Slowly,' he said, watching me as I moved up and down on his lap, his hands sliding to my hips then up to my breast then into my hair. 'Lean back.'

We both gasped when I did, Noah filling me deeply.

'Say it again,' I said.

He didn't need to ask what.

'I won't leave you, Stevie,' he said. 'Ever again.' He reached for me, touching me as I moved slowly, enjoying how we seemed to fit together perfectly.

Our eyes locked and I knew any second now, we'd both collapse over the edge again. I let bliss wash over me as Noah repeated his vow over and over again. When our release came, I clung to him and he held me tightly, shuddering beneath me, and I felt the part of me that had been holding back, holding Noah at arm's length, snap into two parts.

35

I woke up with a start.

Groaning, I rolled over and opened my eyes to see Noah fast asleep beside me. I smiled at how handsome he looked. It was still dark, the clock telling me it was only 7 a.m. But then I frowned. I could hear banging. It must have been what woke me up.

Noah opened his eyes. 'What is that noise? I was having a delicious dream,' he said, smiling sleepily. 'About you,' he added, wrapping an arm over me on top of the duvet.

'Oh yeah, what was it about?' I asked, leaning in to kiss him, but then the banging happened again. I pulled back. 'Is someone at your door?'

'Fuck. Who the hell is it at this time?'

With a groan, he got out of bed. He was only in his pants and I watched without shame as he grabbed the dressing gown I'd been wearing all evening.

'Don't you go anywhere,' he said before walking out. 'I'm coming, Jesus!'

Smiling, I rolled onto my back and looked up at the ceiling. I'd had a deep, restful sleep after we'd gone to bed, cuddling up like we didn't want to be apart even in our sleep. Now, last night replayed like a movie montage in my brain. Noah's kisses and touches. The deliciousness of it all. How good it had felt being with him again. How exhausted but contented my body felt. The ache in my legs was welcome. And then Noah's words flooded back. The way he'd promised not to leave me. The words I'd longed to hear finally leaving his lips. This wasn't just about regretting what happened in the past. Noah saw a future for us.

And now, so could I.

'What are you doing here?'

I frowned as Noah's voice floated towards the bedroom. Then I heard a second voice. I jumped out of bed and crept towards the half-open bedroom door. Leaning against it, I listened.

'Did you think you could do all that and I wouldn't notice?'

My heart sunk into my stomach.

I knew that voice and it wasn't a welcome one. It was Mr John Matthews. Noah's father was in his flat. At 7 a.m.

And I was naked!

With a yelp, I pulled on my underwear and bra and rushed to Noah's wardrobe and grabbed a shirt. I glanced in the mirror. I looked like I'd had a lot of sex. I rushed into the bathroom and splashed water on my face and then pulled my hair into the emergency scrunchie I always had in my handbag. Then I went back to the door and listened, my pulse racing.

'How could you go against my wishes like that?' Mr Matthews was barking at his son. 'You were on the bloody news! Promoting a book I told you I didn't want us to promote. It was an embarrassment!'

Anger flowed through my veins. This man was doing my head in.

I pushed the door open and marched into the living room. Mr

Matthews was pacing while Noah stood off to the side, his hands on his hips.

'*Bitten* is not an embarrassment,' I said, my voice cutting through the tense atmosphere like a knife. Both men turned to me in shock. Mr Matthews looked horrified and Noah was surprised but then he took in my outfit and I swore he smiled a little bit. On me, his shirt looked more like a white dress.

I stood up straighter in a vain attempt to make myself as tall as them. 'It's a really good book and we had a great idea to promote it without any additional budget, like you requested.'

Mr Matthews gave me a look of complete disdain before turning to his son. 'So, you did all this to impress a woman? A member of your staff? What were you thinking?'

'I was thinking that you were wrong,' Noah replied, matching his father's angry words.

There was a stunned silence.

'Excuse me?' Mr Matthews said.

'You are wrong,' Noah repeated. '*Bitten* was worth promoting and Stevie had a great idea to do just that so yes, we went for it, with very little money spent. And it got great buzz. We had the press there. It went viral on social media. We had orders in from the biggest bookshop chain here because of it. Stevie did the best campaign she could with the budget you gave her. I don't know why you're angry. Any publicity is good for the company. Any more copies we sell of this book means more profit for us.'

'I told you I wanted us to focus on the thriller,' Mr Matthews said through gritted teeth. 'You went against my instructions. I waited because you said that you thought the team here could step up but all I see is insubordination and failed attempts. How well is *Bitten* doing? I'm not seeing any great pre-order figures. I was right that it was the wrong book to focus on. And now I'll have to clear up the mess you made.'

'What does that mean?' Noah asked, glancing at me then back at his father worriedly.

'I'm bringing in the New York team. I want you to let everyone at Turn the Pages go. Including your girlfriend.' Venom dripped from Mr Matthews's voice as he looked at me.

Noah stepped forward. 'If you do that, I'm leaving. I'll never work for you again.'

They stared at one another. 'Don't be ridiculous,' Mr Matthews said after a moment. He stalked past us towards the door. 'Get dressed and meet me at the office within the hour to make arrangements. And you...' He looked over his shoulder at me. 'Don't bother coming in.' Then he swept out and slammed the door shut behind him.

Noah's ragged breaths were the only sound for a full minute as we both stared at the slammed door.

'I'm done,' Noah said eventually. 'I'm done with him, Stevie. How can I not be? He's going to sack everyone. After all we've done. After how hard I've been trying. He just doesn't care. Fuck!'

He threw his arms up in the air.

My heart felt like it was stuck in my throat. All that work. All that effort. Was it really for nothing? I felt awful. Was I about to be the reason everyone lost their jobs?

'There must be something we can do,' I whispered, trying to cling to some hope that together we could fix this.

Noah shook his head. 'I think we might have done too much already.'

36

We slipped into a stressed silence. I could hear the London traffic outside. But it all felt very far away. Noah felt very far away.

I forced my feet into action, walking over to Noah and laying a hand on his shoulder as he sank down onto the sofa.

'Can you talk to him?'

'What's the point? You saw just now; he doesn't want to listen. He hasn't been the same since Mum...' He swallowed hard. 'Stevie, how can I get through to him? He never wants to talk about her, about us, about things. And I know that what he just said isn't about *Bitten* or what we did; it's about him blaming me for what happened to my mother.'

'I just don't understand how he could possibly blame you for that. As soon as you knew she was ill, you went to New York to be there for them both.' I bit my lip, hating to see Noah so upset and lost. I was used to my easy relationship with my own parents. They were always there if I needed them. I knew I had their support. It must be awful to not have that certainty. Then I had an idea. 'Your emails!'

Noah looked at me as I sat down beside him. 'What do you mean?'

'Your emails were beautiful, the ones you sent to me. You spoke so honestly and poured out your heart in them. Why don't you write to your father?'

'I couldn't. We don't talk about our feelings like that.'

'Exactly,' I said, touching his hand. 'And that's what needs to change. Put work aside for a moment; you need to fix what's broken between you, otherwise you'll lose each other forever. And if it doesn't work then at least you will know you tried. Your mum wouldn't want this rift to get bigger, would she? She would tell you to try to reach your father, right?'

Noah nodded. 'She would hate for us to be this estranged. Do you really think he would read it?'

'All you can do is try.'

Noah reached for me and pulled me to meet his lips, giving me the sweetest kiss. 'You are amazing.'

'I don't know about that; your father is blaming me for ruining the company. While you write the email, I'll post everywhere that it's publication day for *Bitten* and I'll get ready for work. Even if I'm banned from the office.'

I shuddered at the thought. Noah gave me one more kiss then opened his laptop and I hurried into his room to have a shower and try to make myself look presentable – not that I hadn't been home all night.

Once I was ready, wearing Noah's shirt tied at the waist with one of his belts to look like a dress, my hair in a sleek ponytail and all the makeup I had in my handbag helping a little bit, I made us both a coffee. Noah was concentrating on his email so I went back to the kitchen, leaned against the counter and jumped on social media to share the publication day news.

Then I checked Amazon. The book was higher in the charts but nowhere near the top 100 yet. The book would be in bookshops today and all those sales would count towards the official bestseller list but Amazon was a good indication of how well it was doing so far, and it wasn't great. I sighed at my phone as if it was the one with the problem.

And then it rang.

I smiled to see it was Liv. Talking to her always made me feel better.

'Morning!'

'We have so much to talk about,' she said, sounding like she was walking.

'Where are you?'

'Walking to the library but Jamal is coming in later so I can come and see you and celebrate.'

'Celebrate what?' I asked, wondering if she meant *Bitten*'s release day or me staying at Noah's last night. The high from all of that had been put out swiftly by his father.

'You haven't seen? I thought you'd be on TikTok as its publication day. Go on there now,' Liv said impatiently.

'Yes, bossy boots.' I rolled my eyes, put her on speakerphone then opened up the app. 'What am I looking for? Oh.' I didn't need to search because I'd been tagged in it by Dan, Liv, Deborah and basically anyone who knew me. I opened the video. It was by a huge book influencer. Her account had millions of followers and not only had she shared a video of her holding a copy of *Bitten*, but she was raving about it.

'Any author who organises a rally supporting romance books gets a thumbs up from me but then Deborah Day goes and writes the best romance I've read so far this year. Yeah, I said it. *Bitten* is the book you all need to read. But Marcus is my book boyfriend, okay? Keep your hands off him, guys!'

'Oh my God,' I said, re-watching it immediately. It had thousands of views, comments, likes and shares. My breath caught in my throat. 'This is it. This is what we needed.'

'I told you we had to celebrate,' Liv said. 'The book will be huge now, I know it! Okay, call me and tell me where to meet you at lunch time. And don't think I haven't forgotten to grill you about what happened with you and Noah last night...'

I grinned. 'I'd expect nothing less.'

We hung up and, my heart pounding, I shared the video on all the company's accounts. Then I walked through to see Noah.

'How is it going?' I gestured to his laptop.

'Will you read it before I send it to him? While I get ready for work?'

'Of course.' I wished I could fix this for him. As he got up, I looked at the screen and read Noah's email.

Dad,

I have no idea how to reach you any more so I'm trying it in writing. This idea came from Stevie. The woman you were just incredibly rude to in my flat. The woman that I love. I wrote emails to her in New York. She was the woman I left when you told me that Mum was ill. I broke up with her because you told me that my mum being ill was my fault and you blaming me made me feel like I didn't deserve her. I'm not sure I deserve her even now but she's made me realise that you blaming me for my mum was your way of trying to make sense of it.

And maybe it was because you actually blamed yourself, because if I was too focused on work then I learnt it from you. All my life, you wanted me to come out of your shadow and prove myself like you did with your own father and that pushed me to the UK. Pushed me to work in London and try to make my own way with my own name. I didn't want to work for the family business because I didn't think I'd ever feel good enough. I suppose

I've never felt good enough. So when you told me that everything was my fault, I accepted it. I believed it. I left Stevie because I thought she should be with someone better.

My mum never blamed me. She hated to see us at loggerheads. She begged me to stay working with you after she was gone. Said you needed me. And I promised her, but what you said just now means I can't keep that promise. You are punishing everyone around you for her death. And that's not fair, and it isn't right. My mum accepted me for who I am and loved me. She was happy I came home but she knew I'd left my heart in London. She told me that she had always loved you and I should try to find someone I loved as much. But when she died, I felt too guilty to do that. And then when you pushed me to take over Turn the Pages, Stevie was suddenly back in my life. And I sent her the emails I'd written in New York so she would know I never stopped loving her. Only now do I feel like I might deserve her. That I want to try to deserve her.

Seeing you disrespect Stevie this morning has made me realise I've kept quiet too long. That I haven't tried to talk to you because I've been too scared to hear what you would say. I didn't want you to tell me it was my fault my mum died because part of me believed it was. But I can see now it wasn't. Cancer sucks. It fucking sucks. She didn't deserve to be taken from us like that. But I sure as hell know she would hate to see us like this. She loved you and she loved me. So why we can't love each other?

If you still blame me then I will walk away because I can't deal with this any more. I can't do any more than I'm doing to earn your approval or love. I'm tired, Dad. I miss Mum so much. It hurts every day and this thing between us is just making it even worse.

I want us to have a relationship but I can't keep banging my

head against the wall. I can't keep blaming myself or hating myself. I really hope one day you might be able to stop too.
   Noah.

Tears were streaming down my face at Noah's words. At how desperate he was for his dad to forgive him and love him. That he didn't think he deserved to be loved but he wanted to try to be enough.

I got up and found him in his room getting dressed and our eyes met in his mirror.

'That email... Noah.'

'You're crying. Shit.' He turned and came over to me, taking my hands in his. 'Why are you crying?'

'Of course you deserve love, Noah. I love you.'

His breath hitched as he reached out to wipe a tear from my cheek. 'You don't need to say that, Stevie. I just wanted to tell my father that you're important. And I'm glad you know it too. That's enough.'

'I love you, Noah.'

He looked into my eyes and his lips curved into a smile. 'You do? Really? Even after everything I put you through?'

'Honestly, I'm not sure I ever really stopped.'

Noah pulled me closer. 'I never stopped loving you. You were with me every second in New York. You always had my heart. I love you so much and I will never hurt you again.' He kissed me gently. 'Please stop crying though,' he added, wiping another tear. 'I hate myself for every tear I made you shed.'

I gazed at him through my tears. 'Your words are so honest and beautiful. That's why I'm crying. Send that email, Noah. If your father doesn't respond to that then you should walk away from him. You deserve better.'

Noah grabbed his phone from the bed.

'Done,' he said as he typed. 'So, now what? I don't want to go in to work and hear him tell the board we need to sack everyone. And I definitely don't want to go anywhere without you.'

'Let's set up a portable work station in Starbucks. Liv said we should celebrate *Bitten* and I think she's right. Look.' I held up my phone for him to see, a smile taking over the tears. 'We finally have good news.'

Noah whistled as he watched the video. 'So many TikTok viral books have started from that account.'

I checked my phone again. 'It's already climbing on Amazon. A lot.'

Noah looked. 'Bloody hell, Stevie, that's amazing.'

'We could actually do this.'

'I never doubted it.'

'Yeah, right,' I said with a laugh.

'Well, I never doubted you.' He reached for me and gave me a tight hug. 'Let's get everyone to Starbucks to celebrate. It doesn't matter what my dad does; we need to mark this occasion. Our first book together and it's going to be a hit.'

'Okay.' I pulled back. 'I'll message everyone. You're right. No matter what happens next, we pulled it off.'

We grinned stupidly at one another. We should have been terrified at what Mr Matthews was threatening but somehow, it felt like things might be okay because now we had each other. And this time, I really hoped it would be for keeps.

37

As the morning drew on, Starbucks became filled up with Turn the Pages employees. Everyone we messaged bypassed the office and joined us for pumpkin spiced lattes that Noah put on the company card with great relish. Deborah and Ed joined us too, both hardly able to believe that social media was full of excited posts about *Bitten* or that the chart position kept on climbing each time we refreshed the page. It was now inside the Kindle top ten.

'This hasn't happened to me for like fifteen years,' Deborah said as she sat down. 'It's hard to take in. I kind of felt like my career was over. Suddenly, it feels like it's beginning again.'

'The second time around feels even sweeter,' I said, glancing at Noah as he talked to Paul, pushing his shirt sleeves up. He felt my gaze and dropped me a wink.

'It sure does.' Deborah caught our look and leaned in closer. 'Does that mean you found your own second chance?'

'I think so,' I said, unable to stop smiling goofily. 'What about you?' I nodded at Ed, who was a few feet away.

'I've agreed to a celebratory holiday together in a couple of weeks. Life really likes to throw curve balls, doesn't it?'

Ed seemed to sense us talking about him and he drifted over. 'You two look like you're plotting something.'

'I don't think even I could have come with all of this,' Deborah said, gesturing to the crowd of us around the table. 'Talk about a plot twist.'

I smiled, knowing that I had thought the same thing myself when I met Noah again.

'Life is stranger than fiction, I guess,' I said, sipping my latte.

Ed leaned in. 'So, Stevie, what about you jumping ship and coming to work with me?' He saw me glance at Noah again and sigh. 'I already know the answer, don't I?'

'You don't know if I got the book on the bestseller list yet,' I reminded him.

'Yes, don't jinx it,' Deborah said anxiously.

'I'm going to try my very best not to jinx anything, don't worry,' he said, giving her a fond look.

I saw her cheeks flush and I hid a smile behind my coffee cup.

Emily came to sit down on the other side of me. 'I should have supported your idea to push *Bitten* from the start,' she said. 'You knew the market and that readers would love it. I told Noah he better promote you after this.'

'Thank you but I don't think his father would support that,' I said darkly. Everyone was a little confused why we weren't in the office but Noah hadn't said anything yet. We wanted to toast to how well everyone had done on this book before dropping the bombshell, but I didn't want to lie to Emily. 'Mr Matthews wasn't happy when we saw him earlier.' I had told them he'd arrived from New York without us knowing he was coming, but not why he was here.

'Has he heard about the TikTok though?'

'No,' I said. 'I hope it's enough for him. He's a hard man to please. We might still need those new CVs.'

'He's an idiot if he doesn't start rolling out romances after this,'

Emily declared. 'And if he doesn't sack Paul,' she added with twinkling eyes.

Paul heard his name and ducked away from Noah to come over. 'Congratulations to you all,' he said a little stiffly, but he seemed genuine. He turned to me. 'You proved me wrong, Stevie. I won't get in the way of any other of your campaigns.'

I smiled. 'Can I get that in writing?'

'Don't push your luck.' But he smiled back.

'I know I can get very enthusiastic about things,' I said. 'I think you all thought it was a bit much someone new coming in and trying to push a book that none of you thought was a good idea. It's water under the bridge.'

Paul reached out his hand and I shook it firmly, knowing we'd get past our issues. He walked away to another group of colleagues.

Emily leaned over me to look at Deborah, who had watched our exchange with interest. 'I am sorry that we didn't get behind your book from the beginning like we should have done,' she said with a stark honesty that I admired.

'I lost my temper,' Deborah admitted. 'I get that probably didn't help my cause. All's well that ends well.'

'You think you might stay on with us?' Emily asked with a cheeky smile.

Deborah glanced at her agent. 'We'll see.'

'Noah.'

I turned as the group around me fell quiet and saw Mr Matthews stride to the back of the coffee shop.

'Can we speak outside?' He seemed oblivious to the hush he had created as he waited for Noah's response.

Noah nodded. 'Of course.'

He put his drink down and looked at me. I gave him a reassuring smile and he seemed to study for me for a second before turning and following his father out.

'God, Mr Matthews is intimidating,' Emily said. 'Even the fact we call him that and not his first name in this day and age.'

'I hope Noah will be okay,' I said, biting my lip as they disappeared from sight.

Emily nudged my shoulder with hers. 'Are you ready to spill the beans about you and him?' she asked in a stage whisper.

'Can we not tell the whole company?' I said, shaking my head. I sighed as Gita appeared. 'Can you just smell gossip?'

'Yep,' Gita said proudly. 'And everyone knows you two ditched us at the pub for quality time together so your secret isn't really a secret any more, just FYI.'

'HR is talking about arranging a meeting,' Emily added.

I groaned. 'Great.' But they couldn't stop my smile. 'Okay, fine. Yes, last night was pretty incredible. And Noah still loves me. And I love him.'

Emily squealed and threw her arms around me as Gita clapped. 'We knew it. As soon as you came into the office.'

'No, you didn't. You said Noah was a grump.'

'Well, yeah, but a handsome one,' Emily said. 'And we saw the way he looked at you even when he was being grumpy.'

My phone lit up with a message from Liv asking where to meet me now she had cover at work so I told her where to come. She needed to be here. I messaged Georgina too to see if she could take a break from the bookshop and join the celebrations as they'd both been a big part of the promoting.

> Can you sneak away for a minute?

When I saw Noah's message, I excused myself and walked through the coffee shop and outside. I saw him waiting for me and I followed him to the river where we'd had more than one serious chat since our reunion.

We leaned against the railings. A golden leaf floated down from the tree that arched over the river and I watched it drop onto the water's surface and float on by. Autumn always reminded me that life was full of new beginnings. Like the one me and Noah were getting.

I covered his hand on the railing with my own. 'What happened?' I asked. 'Are you okay?'

Noah took a deep breath and faced me. 'He read my email. And he told me I was wrong. That he didn't blame me. He told me that when he said that, he was just angry and upset that Mum was ill. He needed me with them but didn't express it in the right way. He didn't think I still thought he felt that way. He feels guilty for...' Noah choked a bit and I squeezed his hand. 'Working all the time and not being at home as much as he could have been. The lost time he and Mum can never get back.' Noah sighed. 'He isn't good at talking about his feelings and that was hard for him to say, I could see it. He said he hasn't called New York. Yet. That he'll see what the bestseller list says first. But he did say he wants to meet you. Properly this time.'

'Wow.' I took that all in. 'I'm glad he's opened up. That you both have. It sounds like there's been a lot of missed communication. I hope you can fix that now. I really do.'

'Writing to him was the best idea. Thank you for suggesting it.' He picked up my hand and kissed it. 'For believing in me.'

'Reading your words while we were apart has meant so much to me. I like knowing what you're thinking and feeling. Finally,' I added with a wry smile. 'I'll meet him properly. I have perhaps a crazy suggestion for it.'

Noah's eyes twinkled. 'I like your crazy suggestions. Promise you'll keep them coming?'

I smiled. 'That's one thing you can count on me for.'

38

'It's been A MONTH,' I said to Liv later as we walked side-by-side through crunchy fallen leaves in the park by my Islington flat. It was kind of crazy to think we'd met in this very park when I was on my way for my first day at Turn the Pages at the start of October. It was now November and so much had changed.

'You can say that again,' Liv said. 'I thought you starting a new career would change a lot of things but never this much.' She slipped her arm through mine. 'I'm so proud of you. Not only did you get your dream job but you smashed it.'

'We don't know where it will be on the bestseller list,' I reminded her, but I smiled. 'I feel like I'm finally doing what I was meant to do. I know you know what I mean.'

She nodded. 'I just need to get a book deal and I'll feel the same.'

'You will, your agent is so enthusiastic about your book. And I love it. And my taste is never wrong, I say humbly.' We both giggled. 'I don't know what will happen next. Noah's dad is thinking it all through. I really don't want to leave though; not when I feel like things are only just getting started at Turn the Pages.'

'And with Noah too,' Liv said. She saw me smile at the sound of his name. 'I'm so happy you guys are getting your second chance.'

'Me too,' I confessed. 'But I'm still nervous; I can't help it. I didn't see us ending last time. What if I'm making the same mistake again?'

'Do you feel like you are?'

I shook my head. 'No. We are older and wiser. We have had our time apart and both hated it. Noah has been through a lot. He's different now. I know how he feels this time around. And reading those emails he sent me when we weren't together – they are so honest and vulnerable. I feel like he finally let me in. And I love him the more for it.'

'They sound amazing,' she said with a sigh. 'It's just so romantic. I'm rooting for you two. I remember you telling me it felt like he was the one who got away, and now you know that he felt the same way about you. It was fated.'

'You're more of a hopeless romantic than me,' I said with a laugh. 'But look at us now. We found our leading men, and so close together too.' I gestured to the trees. 'I always said autumn was magic. New beginnings and change in the air.'

'I hope what comes next is even better.' We turned towards my flat. 'So, how are you feeling about tomorrow? I love how you go all in on life, Stevie. I need to be more like you.'

'Wait and see if it's a disaster first,' I said. 'If me and Noah are for keeps this time around, and I really hope we are,' I said as we walked down my road, a scattering of orange leaves lining our path, 'then there's no point in waiting. Noah kept me from his family last time and that put a huge wedge between us. He wants to heal things with his father and I want to help, but I also want my parents there. They knew me and Noah before, and how it ended; I want them to be part of it now. And to make sure I'm not doing a completely crazy thing in giving him my heart again.'

'Mr Matthews sounds scary but your parents will put him in his place if he is horrible to you again,' Liv said. 'And it seems like Noah has decided things need to change or he will walk away. That's so brave. And I bet you've given him that courage.'

'Looking back, Noah gave me the courage to change my life. It's weird to say that when I felt so broken-hearted when he left me.' I let us into my building and we went up to my flat. 'But I was content to let life happen to me; now I want to make things happen.'

'I get that. Him leaving shook up your picture of the future and you decided to do what you wanted to do because you already knew what it was like to lose something so it was easier to go after what you wanted. You felt less fear. I think Noah is the same. Seeing you again has made him see what's wrong in his life and he's trying to make it better, and be better for you.'

'Coffee?' I asked, going to the kitchen.

'Always.' She leaned against the counter as I made us two iced coffees. 'So, how will you feel working with Noah from now on? I'm not sure I could take orders from Aiden if I'm honest.'

I hid my blush thinking about taking orders from Noah in the bedroom. 'Yeah, we do need to talk about that,' I agreed. I had been trying to convince myself Noah was just my boss but now that was over, I had to navigate how it would work if he was my boyfriend and my manager too. Not that he'd said the word 'boyfriend' yet. We hadn't had the future talk. 'One issue at a time. First, Noah's father is meeting not just me but my parents tomorrow,' I said, handing her a glass and taking one for myself.

That had been my idea. A way to help Noah and his father heal and also for my parents to see Noah again. It was potentially crazy but like Liv said, I saw no point in holding back this time around. Things had gone wrong when Noah had kept things from me and I hadn't pursued my dreams; now we wanted to be honest and open and support each other.

'I'm really nervous about it,' I admitted.

'It'll go well. No one can be grumpy with you around,' Liv said encouragingly.

Noah had said something similar and I liked that was how they both saw me. I had my tough days like we all did but Liv was right. My heartbreak over Noah had made me determined to be positive and focus on what was good because otherwise I would have turned bitter and cynical and that wasn't me.

I held out my iced coffee. 'Here's to curing grumpiness, our careers being successful and our love lives being like the ones in our favourite books,' I said, and with a grin, Liv clinked hers against mine.

* * *

I woke up with a jump when my alarm went off. It was dark and rainy when I climbed out of bed and nerves settled in my stomach as I got ready for work. Not only was I going to see Noah and his father in the office, and see them with my parents later, but today was bestseller list day. Mr Matthews might be opening up to his son but I knew his business face would very much be on still and he didn't need any excuse to replace us with people from New York. I got the feeling that was his preferred option so *Bitten*'s sales needed to be strong enough to change his mind.

As I walked to work, I passed by a bookshop and peered in the window. I was happy to see a stack of *Bitten* copies in there. It was still doing brilliantly on Amazon, rising every time I checked, and I was getting emails all the time from people asking for reading copies or wanting to interview Deborah, but the proof was always in the pudding. Just because in our book world it seemed to be popular, it didn't mean the sales would translate. But I bloody hoped that they would.

Crossing my fingers while I stood in the lift, I tried to take a few breaths. I straightened the headband in my hair as the doors opened and I walked through to the office.

'We are so glad to see you,' Emily called as I walked over. Gita was by our desks. 'Are you as nervous as us?'

She didn't need to explain why she was nervous. I hung my jacket over the back of my chair. 'I am terrified,' I confirmed. 'Have you seen Noah?'

'He's in his office with his father,' Gita said. 'They looked a little tense if you ask me.'

'They always look tense though,' Emily reminded her.

'We are all tense today,' I said, hoping Noah and his father had been able to talk about their relationship and not just work things. 'Let's just focus on our next campaigns and wait for the bestseller list to come in.'

I glanced over but I couldn't see into Noah's office. I hadn't heard from him since we'd left Starbucks. I knew he was focusing on talking to his father, and we'd be spending the evening together, but I wished I could see him. It would help my nerves. I sat down at my desk knowing it was going to be hard to do any work while we waited to find out how *Bitten* had done.

As the rest of our colleagues came in, I could see everyone was feeling the same way. We all glanced at each other as we tried to work and the office was as quiet as the first day when everyone had found out about the takeover. We were all on tenterhooks. And Noah's office remained shut, he and his father out of sight. But they were never out of my mind.

39

'Stevie, can you come in, please?'

I looked up from my desk as Noah stepped out of his office. Eyes swivelled to me as if our colleagues were watching a tennis match. I got up, smoothing down my trouser suit.

'Is this it?' Emily stage-whispered to me.

I looked at the time. It was early afternoon. I swallowed hard. 'I think it might be.'

People murmured 'good luck' as I walked towards the office. I paused by Gita's desk. 'Do you want to come?'

She was Deborah's editor and was desperate to know the chart position too. She had looked after her a lot longer than me and it felt strange that I would be the one to get the news.

But Gita shook her head. 'It's right that it's you, Stevie. Just put us out of our misery soon.'

I nodded and carried on my walk. This somehow felt even harder than that first walk to Noah's office when I thought my first day here might be my last. I was invested now. I loved this job, I liked my colleagues and our authors and my work with Deborah had quickly become a passion project that I really didn't want to have to walk away from. I'd been so sure we could make something of Deborah's book, and we'd achieved more than I knew they had done for years but I didn't know how much more. And I knew Noah's dad wasn't happy with our focus on *Bitten*, especially after he told us to drop it. I had no idea what he thought of Noah wanting to be with me but I was certain that, as a member of his staff, I might well be his least favourite.

So, it wasn't a fun walk to find out the results of our campaign. Crossing my fingers, I went into the office. Noah was standing by the window, a reflection of that first day I saw him here, while his father was behind Noah's desk, arms on the polished wood. Both men's faces were impossible to read as they watched me as I walked in. Noah must have learnt that from his father. I could feel my palms start to get sweaty as I closed the door behind me.

Mr Matthews gestured to the chair opposite him so I sank into it, grateful I wouldn't have to keep my weight on my shaky legs.

'We have just been sent the bestseller list for this weekend,' Mr Matthews said without preamble. My eyes flicked to Noah, who was watching me, then back to his father. I wondered if I was still breathing or not. 'Son? You want to do the honours?' he said, turning to Noah and surprising us both.

Noah looked startled for a moment then cleared his throat. 'Uh, yes. Yes. We printed it out for you. For everyone.' Noah walked over and moved his hand from behind his back to hold out a piece of paper to me. His brown eyes locked onto my blue ones. 'Stevie,' he said, his voice low as he passed the paper over.

I looked down at it hesitantly. Then I exhaled and held it up, my eyes scanning the page. I did a double take. Then I looked up at Noah. He was smiling. That dimple looking the dimpliest I'd ever seen. Even though I knew that probably wasn't even a word.

I jumped up. 'Oh my God. Is this real?' I pointed to the page again, my heart soaring.

'It's real,' Noah confirmed.

I looked from him to his father who, bloody hell, was smiling too.

'It's real. It's real! Number three!!!' I shrieked and, throwing the paper in the air, I launched myself at Noah. He wrapped his arms around me and lifted me off the floor, spinning me with a laugh as I kept repeating 'Number three, number three!' When he put me down, I was breathless. 'Oh my God, I can't believe it. Noah!'

'I know.' He was beaming at me. 'You did it, Stevie.'

'*We* did it,' I corrected him again, because I definitely couldn't have done this alone. I looked at Mr Matthews, who was watching us, a little bit shocked. I realised that I was probably behaving very unprofessionally in his eyes, but how could I be chill? 'Sorry,' I said.

'What for?' Mr Matthews stood up. 'Well done. Both of you. Stevie...' He held out his hand slowly.

'Oh, thank you,' I said, shaking it firmly. I wasn't going to let Mr Matthews think that I had a limp handshake. 'Can I tell everyone?'

'Of course,' Noah said. 'We'll finish up here then we can head to the restaurant. Right?' He looked to his father.

'Looking forward to it,' Mr Matthews said.

'Great. Great,' I said, backing away and grabbing the printed bestseller list from where I'd dropped it before he could change his mind and not be happy about this. No word about what would happen at the company now but I was going to just enjoy the win. I looked at Noah again before I left and he winked at me. I grinned back and hurried out, still feeling like I might be in the middle of a dream. I walked out and tried to stop myself from smiling.

Everyone stopped what they were doing as I walked right to the middle of the office, keeping my head down because I knew if I met anyone's eyes, I'd start grinning all along again. The room fell silent.

I held up the paper. 'I have the list,' I said dully.

Several people stood up. Gita was right by me. 'Shit, Stevie, how bad is it?' she asked worriedly.

I looked at her then around the room. My eyes fell on Paul and Aaliyah, Lewis, Emily, who was biting her lip, and the receptionist, who had hurried in when she saw me. They all waited with bated breath until I was ready to put them out of their misery.

I waved the paper again and broke into a huge smile. '*Bitten* is number three. We are number three on the bestseller list!'

There was a short silence where the news sunk in and then pandemonium broke out. People cheered and clapped. There were actual whoops. And I was rushed at by a blur of people. I was hugged, clapped on the back, and when Gita and Emily found me, they hugged me so tightly, I staggered and almost fell over. When I whimpered, they finally let go.

'You bloody superstar,' Emily said, beaming at me.

'How the hell did you turn our most difficult midlist author into a number three bestseller social media darling?' Gita added.

I couldn't stop laughing. 'The power of romance books, guys.' I turned around and saw Mr Matthews and Noah had come out of the office. I pulled out my phone. 'Hang on,' I said, shushing everyone, and then I phoned Ed and put it on speakerphone. 'Ed? Please tell me you're with Deborah.'

'I am,' he said. 'Tell us, Stevie.'

I gave a dramatic pause, everyone smiling around me. 'Okay, I'm so sorry, guys, we tried our best but unfortunately, we only managed number three.'

There was a pause. 'Say that again,' Ed said.

'I said we're number three. *Bitten* will be number three on the *Sunday Times* bestseller list!'

There was a scream. 'Do not joke, Stevie,' I heard Deborah cry in the background.

'Are you fucking serious?' Ed said at the same time.

'Number three, bitches,' I said. Then I saw Mr Matthews raise his eyebrows. 'Anyway...' I coughed and looked at Emily and Gita who were practically wetting themselves.

'You bloody genius,' Ed said. 'Deborah can't speak. I've never actually witnessed this before. She's frozen. Debs?'

'You did it, Deborah,' I said. 'Well done. And you, Ed. We'll be in touch with a five-book offer,' I added with a grin.

'Hell, yes,' Gita mouthed to me.

'I don't know how you pulled this off, Phillips,' Ed said then. 'If I was wearing a hat, I'd take it off. I better go and make sure Debs is breathing. Champagne next week? I'll be in touch.' He hung up.

'Great job, everyone,' Noah said, stepping forward. 'That's the best sales figures for any book all year. And Paul tells me retailers are calling for more copies now they've seen the buzz it's getting so I'm hoping we could climb even higher next week.'

I looked at Paul, who shook his head at me. 'I'll never live this down, will I?' he said.

'I don't hold grudges, Paul, but I do feel pretty smug right now, I won't lie. You're going to get *Bitten* into every shop that sells books now, right?'

'I owe you that,' he agreed.

Noah's hand grazed the small of my back then, making me shiver. I hoped no one but Noah noticed. 'Dad has gone to talk to the board in New York. He said he'll meet us at the restaurant.'

'Okay,' I said, hoping that the chart position would be enough to give us time to prove ourselves here to him and the board. 'And you two?'

Noah smiled. 'Getting there.' He looked around. 'I don't think anyone is going to do any work now, are they?'

'Probably not,' I agreed. I raised an eyebrow. 'And you're not shocked or telling everyone to calm down. Have you become a soft boss now? Grumpy Noah has left the building for good?' I asked him teasingly.

'I'll still crack the whip when it's needed,' he replied in a low voice that made me bite my lip. He grinned. 'I'm blaming all of this on you,' he said, nodding to everyone's excitement.

I smiled. 'I'll happily take the blame.'

It was great to finally feel like we were all a team. I just hoped Mr Matthews let us stay that way.

40

My mum and dad got the train into the city for dinner. I booked us my favourite table at the pub. A familiar setting was needed to try to put us at ease as much as possible. I thought perhaps Mr Matthews preferred a posher dining experience but Noah said it would be fine; he would appreciate the pub's cosy vibes. I really hoped he was right.

I got ready in an agitated state. I really wanted this to go well. I wanted Noah and his father to heal their rift, for Mr Matthews to not be my scary big boss any more but to get to know him as Noah's father, and I really wanted my parents to accept Noah was back in our lives. And I realised that was a hell of a lot of pressure to put on one meal.

I put on my favourite jeans with a black silky blouse, my heels for confidence and my pearl hairband with matching jewellery, and then my parents knocked at the door. 'I'm so glad you're here,' I said, letting them in to my flat.

'You look lovely,' Mum said, giving me a kiss. 'And a little bit nervous,' she added in a low voice.

'I am,' I admitted. I hugged my dad, who was wearing such a smart shirt and trousers, I was worried for a moment I might cry. 'But you guys are helping. You both look great,' I said, admiring my mum's black dress too.

'Not that Noah's father deserves us making the effort,' Dad grunted.

'Love,' Mum warned him. 'What did we say on the train down? We are civilised, polite, open-minded people.'

Dad snorted. 'I will be if they are. If not, then I make no promises. Noah has a lot of making up to do to Stevie and his father sounds like a *Mad Men* throwback.'

Then I laughed, surprising them both. I wrapped one of my arms through each of them. 'You two are my favourite couple. If Noah and me are anything like you ten years from now, I will consider myself the luckiest woman.'

'Oh God, Stevie,' Mum said, letting out a sob and dabbing her eyes.

'We're only the best because we have the best daughter in the world,' Dad declared. He looked at me. 'Seriously, love, you're sure about Noah, aren't you?'

I adjusted my expression to match the seriousness of his. 'Dad, I won't lie and say I'm not still nervous about the future, but I love Noah. I never stopped and nor did he. I think sometimes it's just meant to be but the timing is wrong. We had to be apart so we could find each other now. I know what I want and so does he.'

Dad nodded. 'Okay then. If that's the case then everything will work out, so there is no need to be nervous. If Noah's father can't see his son has landed so hard on his feet there was an earthquake, then I have no time for the man.'

'Well said,' my mum agreed.

'Come on, let's go before you two inflate my ego any further,' I replied. They really were my biggest cheerleaders and I'd never take that for granted. We left my flat and walked to the pub. The moon shone down from the cloudless sky. It was dry but with a sharp chill in the air. London on a Friday was lively and we passed restaurants and bars lit up with lights and merriment and when we walked into my pub, I smiled at the roaring fire and loud chatter inside. It was a welcoming place and with my parents by my side, I hoped that tonight would go well.

I waved to Meg and led my parents to the table I'd reserved for us. They sat beside me, ignoring the shake of my head as they did so. It now looked like we'd be interrogating Noah and his dad but I couldn't name three less intimidating people on the planet than us.

Noah and his father arrived just after we'd sat down and when our eyes met, Noah's face lit up. When he reached me, he leaned in to give me a soft kiss.

'Hi,' I said as his musky aftershave washed over me.

Noah flashed his dimple. 'You look lovely.' With his hand on the small of my back, he moved so his dad could get to the table. 'Dad, these are Stevie's parents – Sean and Sarah.'

I watched Mr Matthews shake their hands and then Noah walked round to kiss my mum on the cheek and shake my father's hand. He said something to him that I couldn't hear and then he and his father sat down opposite us. We ordered first and then made small talk about the weather until our drinks arrived and then Noah leaned on the table and cleared his throat, making us all look at him expectantly.

'It's really lovely to see you both again,' he said to my parents. 'I have a confession to make – I almost knocked on your door once. About three years ago.'

'You did?' Mum asked, confused.

'You never told me that,' I said in surprise.

'I don't know if Stevie told you but after I moved to New York, I tried to contact her but I wasn't able to.'

'I blocked him everywhere,' I said with a shrug.

'I don't blame her for that at all,' Noah said. His leg touched mine under the table. 'I felt like we'd never cross paths again. Three years ago, I had to come to London for a conference and I drove to your house. It was the only way I could think that I might be able to get in touch with Stevie. I sat outside for an hour wondering whether to knock on your door or not.

'I wanted to ask you to tell Stevie I wanted to speak to her but I was worried you'd just shut the door in my face. Then I was worried you wouldn't. And I had no idea if Stevie wanted to see me again or not and I was too scared to find out. I knew I'd made a huge mistake. I just didn't know how to make it right. I know that you might not ever be ready to trust me again but I will keep trying to earn it. Stevie has miraculously given me a second chance and I won't mess it up this time.'

'Well,' my mum said, looking at him then me. 'That's all we want. For Stevie to be happy and be with someone who loves and respects her and treats her how she should be treated.' She looked at Noah then his father. 'We were so sorry to hear about the loss of your mother and wife.'

John Matthews shifted in his seat. 'Thank you.' He looked at me. 'Noah's mother told me he'd left someone behind when he moved to be with us. She hoped he'd find you again.'

'She told you that?' Noah was the surprised one then.

'She did,' his father confirmed. 'My wife was everything to me and when she was sick, I didn't handle it well. I handled her, uh, passing even worse.'

'When you lose someone that special, you don't get to choose how you grieve,' my mum said gently.

'I think I'm part of the reason Noah stayed away for so long,' Mr Matthews said to me. 'I'm sorry for that. I think we have a lot of talking to do but I want to tell you, Stevie, I'm sorry for how I spoke to you at work and at Noah's place. Noah is extremely fond of you and I would like us to get to know each other,' he said. It was a little stiff but I could hear the sincerity in his words.

'I'd like that too,' I said. 'Listen, life is short. You guys know that better than anyone. We could all beat ourselves up about our past mistakes or we could just draw a line and start again.'

'Well said, love,' my mum said. She looked at my dad. 'Sean?'

My dad looked at Noah, then me, then back at Noah. He sighed. 'We can start again, but know this: if you hurt my daughter again, I will hunt you down.'

Bless my dad. He was about as scary as a koala but Noah nodded solemnly. 'As you should.'

'And...' Dad looked at Mr Matthews. 'I assume there'll be no more talk of firing Stevie after she turned a book that your company had given up on into a number three bestseller.'

I could feel myself turn red. 'Dad!' I regretted telling my parents what had happened.

But Mr Matthews also nodded. 'I spoke far too hastily. My board was putting a lot of pressure on us with this takeover but I let them do it. I threw myself into work after my wife... and I focused on the bottom line so much, I lost sight of the values I'd built my company on. Supporting authors. Buying the best stories even if they are tough to market. And encouraging creativity and innovation. I have told the board that the UK team are staying in place and we will review after six months. And I have moved some budget around for you, Stevie, because I think we can push the book to number one, don't you?'

'I like your ambition,' I agreed. Noah rubbed my leg under the table with his and I smiled across at him. 'I hope we can buy even more romance books now.'

'I bet you do.'

Was that a little twinkle in Mr Matthews's eyes?

Our food arrived then and I let out a breath in relief that we'd cleared the air between everyone and that now we could start again.

41

After dessert and coffee, my parents had to get the last train back to Surrey, and Noah's father hailed a taxi to take him to his hotel, inviting me and Noah to have brunch with him there tomorrow, which we agreed to.

Noah took my hand as we walked back to my flat in silence, both of us absorbing the evening.

'How do you feel?' I asked Noah eventually.

'Like maybe we have turned a corner?' Noah said hesitantly. 'I guess I understand my dad more now.' He sighed. 'After my mum died, I really wondered what had brought my parents together. I couldn't fathom how my mother fell in love with my dad, you know?'

I nodded. I hadn't known Noah's mother but his father did sound very different to the picture he painted of her.

'They seemed so different and my dad worked so much, I assumed that was because things weren't great between them,' Noah continued. 'But when I went to New York after she became ill, I sometimes saw these sweet moments between them when they thought I wasn't around.'

'He seemed to have really loved her,' I agreed after hearing how he had spoken about her at dinner.

'Dad told me he lost sight of what really mattered and he was furious with himself for doing that and only realising when it was too late. He said he didn't blame me for Mum being ill or for me trying to make my own way; he said he blamed himself for pushing me away and for not remembering that my mum was the love of his life.'

'I'm glad you're opening up to one another now,' I said. 'I'm sure your mum knew how much he loved her.'

'She did but he still thinks he let her down. He said reading my email made him see he'd become someone so different to the man who had married my mum and started the publishing company years ago.'

'I think your mum would be really proud of you both,' I said.

Noah lifted our hands and kissed the back of mine. 'I'm so glad I told her about you. She knew before I did, it seems, that we were meant to be. I wish I'd gone to your parents that day and asked them to tell you I wanted to see you.'

I shook my head. 'I wasn't ready to hear that then. I needed to know what I wanted from life before I was ready. I spent a long time learning about myself after you left, and I'm glad. Being single for so long sometimes made me feel lonely or got me down or made me worry I'd never find someone, but I wouldn't change it now for the world. I didn't love myself when you left me, I didn't know what I wanted apart from you, and I was sometimes ashamed of the things I loved or wanted.'

'Stevie...'

'I'm not now,' I assured him. 'I know who I am. I love what I love. And as you saw with *Bitten*, I'll fight for them all.'

He chuckled in agreement.

'But maybe if we'd stayed together, I wouldn't have that. And you… I know I said you're different now and I made you feel like that was a bad thing but you're different in a good way too.'

We reached my building then.

'Do you want to come in?' I asked as we stopped outside.

He smiled and squeezed my hand. 'I'd love to. I want to see your home, Stevie.'

I let us in and we walked up to my door. I unlocked it and stood back, letting Noah walk inside before following him and closing the world out.

'You were so desperate to succeed when we met, so focused on your career,' I said, picking up our outside conversation as he looked around my flat, 'and – I realised later on – so focused on proving yourself to your father. You were so worried about what people thought of you because you didn't want to be seen as benefitting from nepotism but it meant you did what you thought you should, not what you wanted. And yes, I told you off for being grumpy because I didn't know what you'd been through when we were apart, but I also thought you were trying even harder to protect yourself from what people thought, and to prove yourself worthy of your job. And I didn't like that. But it was all a front.'

'Yeah?' Noah turned to look at me.

'Your emails.' I stepped over to him. 'So open and honest and vulnerable. Something you never were when we were together. You didn't think you deserved love before but now I think you know you do, and you want it and you want to give that love right back. You know life is short and regrets are long. And that's made you want to go after everything you want no matter what people think of you. Am I right?'

'Fuck, Stevie.' Noah took my hand. 'You've guessed, haven't you?'

'I'd love to hear it from you though.'

Noah nodded. 'Shall we sit?' He kept my hand in his as we sat down on my sofa. 'And by the way, this place is so you; I love it. Apart from the lack of space for all your books.'

I sighed. 'I know, right?' I said softly. I leaned back against the sofa and tucked my legs under me. I kept my hands in his as Noah twisted to face me, crossing one leg over the other. 'Tell me,' I whispered encouragingly.

'You're right about all of it. I've spent far too long trying to make sure people didn't think I was riding on the coattails of my father, being ashamed of my family's success and money, trying to not be an entitled twat. But that made me push my family away, hiding behind my mother's maiden name in another country. When Mum became ill, I knew I'd focused on the wrong things. I'd hidden who I really was from the woman I loved...' He smiled and I knew he meant me. 'Because I was ashamed of who I was. These five years without you, I've learnt about who I am and what I want but I've still been too scared to embrace it. Seeing you again has meant everything. I don't want to waste another minute. I want to be who I am, to do what I want to do and be with who I want to be with. When my mum was near the end, she asked me to stay and look after my dad, to keep working for the company and be there for my dad because she knew he wouldn't cope.'

Noah took a breath and I stroked the top of his hand with my fingertips.

'That's what I've done for a year even though I've been miserable. And so has he. Until I saw you again. And it felt like this fog lifted and I could see again clearly what I wanted for my life. You. And to have my dad as my family only, and not as my boss.'

I'd had a feeling about that. Noah wasn't happy working for his father. I wasn't sure he'd ever been. But he'd felt guilty. He'd done what he thought was his duty, what his mother wanted, what he should do. Not what he wanted to.

'I could see you weren't happy,' I said softly.

'I know you could. Calling me a dick was an indicator.'

'Now I feel really bad!'

'You never have to feel bad,' he said quickly. 'It was a wake-up call. You shone a torch on me and I wanted to think you were wrong but I knew you weren't. I think me getting sick with that flu was a turning point. It forced me to rest and start thinking, when for the past year since my mum died, I hadn't let myself think. I thought about what I wanted again. And you. And when you turned up to help me, I knew that I couldn't go back to my old life. I didn't want to. The way you were at work, so passionate, I knew it was your dream but I couldn't say the same for myself. I love books. I always have, always will. But publishing, working for my father, it isn't my future.'

'Have you told him?'

Noah nodded. 'I told him what my mum said, what I promised her...' He swallowed hard. I could only imagine how hard it was to talk about his mother. 'He asked me if I was really sure that was what she had asked of me.'

'It wasn't?'

'I suppose I read between the lines too much. What she had said was, "You'll always be there for your father when I'm gone, won't you? You'll be there for each other. Promise me."'

I squeezed his hand. 'You thought she meant to stay working with him.'

'I think my brain just went there after feeling guilty for not being in New York before she got sick, for turning my back on the family business, but it never was. It's my father's company. And working together hasn't been good for our relationship. She wanted us to be there for one another but we haven't been. All we've done is talk about work. So, I want that to stop. For us to be father and son again, and not work together.' Noah paused. 'And I thought about what, apart from seeing you again, has made me happy in recent times. And it was buying the Book Nook.'

I smiled. 'It's a special place. I love that you bought it.'

'Georgina handed in her notice last week.'

'Ah.' I understood then.

'She's moving to be with her girlfriend in Manchester. I've decided to take over running the bookshop. Maybe even try to have a chain of them one day. What do you think?'

'I think if that's what you want then that's amazing. You'll be brilliant at whatever you do. But most importantly, I want you to be happy. Will that make you happy?'

'It'll probably make me less money...' Noah grinned. 'But yes. I want to get excited about discovering books again. I want to recommended books to people. I want to have authors in the shop. I want to be the first to promote the next great novel. I want to give someone what will be their favourite book. I want to create a must-visit place for anyone coming to London who loves books.'

'I know you will.'

'And I want you to stay at Turn the Pages and one day, run the place.'

I laughed. 'I don't know about that but I'll stay,' I said. 'I'm starting to really love it. But are you sure this isn't all because you don't want to be my boss any more?' I asked with a smile.

'I'd be anything you want me to be but I'm hoping instead of your boss, I can be your boyfriend instead?'

42

'Did you just ask me to be your girlfriend?' I asked with a grin. I climbed onto his lap, hanging my legs over his. His hands brushed my thigh.

'I did,' Noah said, smiling, but then he looked at me earnestly. 'I want to make sure that you know I'm serious. That this time around, I'm all in. I see my future with you, if you'll have me.'

He was saying everything I wanted him to say, but there was still a tiny speck of doubt deep in my heart. I was only human, after all, and I hadn't forgotten how hard I'd fallen before and how tough it had been when he left.

'I want that too,' I said.

'I will gain your trust again,' Noah said fiercely, reading my hesitation without me saying anything. 'I will love you like you deserve. Like you always deserved.'

'I know you will,' I whispered, touching his lips with my fingertips. 'This is only the beginning for us.'

It had been a whirlwind the past few weeks meeting Noah again and connecting with him. It was on a whole other level to what we had in the past. Our connection was so much deeper now. I knew we were different people and this would be a different relationship to the one we'd had before.

'Exactly. I love you, Stevie. And we will take this at your pace. I want you to be ready before we do anything more.'

'Like?' I asked him playfully, moving so my legs were astride his lap.

Noah smiled. 'Like you living with me. You moving into my flat or I can come here.'

'I don't think we'd fit,' I said with a laugh.

He reached up to tuck my hair over my shoulder. 'I always saw us in my flat but I know you love living here. I wouldn't care as long as I woke up with you every morning and went to sleep beside you every night.' He leaned in to drop a kiss on the side of my neck.

I loved my flat but Noah's had always felt like home. I suddenly saw us there together and God, I wanted it so badly. Islington had been the place I'd found myself, but I was ready to go home.

'I'll build you a bookcase for your books,' he said softly. 'As big as you want.'

My breath hitched as his lips moved to my collarbone. 'A bookcase? Tell me more.'

Noah laughed. 'I should have known books were the way to get you to commit.' He lifted his head and put his hand on my cheek. 'My bookworm girlfriend.'

He pulled me closer and our lips met. I sighed against him as we kissed, scooting even closer. Noah shivered beneath me as I moved.

I pulled back. 'You haven't had the full flat tour yet.' I climbed off him, earning a protesting noise from Noah. I held my hand out. 'Come on.'

He took my hand and I led him into my bedroom.

'You kept it,' he said, his eyes falling onto the plushie that sat on the windowsill.

It was a bookworm – a squishy green worm with glasses, holding a book. Noah had bought it for me from a bookshop we'd gone to together, both of us giggling at how cute and silly it was. Noah came over to me and tilted my chin up.

'You kept it,' he said again in wonder. 'Even after what I did?'

'It was my one reminder of the good times,' I said softly. 'I had to keep something. So I knew I hadn't imagined it all. That I hadn't imagined you.'

'I thought that so often walking around New York,' Noah said. 'That maybe I'd made you up in my mind or something, but you're more wonderful than I could ever have imagined.'

'Noah,' I groaned. What was it with this man and his words? I pulled him in for a long, lingering kiss before kneeling on the bed. I reached up on my knees to unbutton his shirt and push it off his shoulders. 'Just to check...' I said, looking up at him. 'How many bookcases am I allowed if I do move in?'

Noah leaned down to undo my buttons too.

'Hmmm... I'll have to think about that,' he said, slipping my blouse off and onto the floor on top of his discarded shirt. I reached for the belt on his trousers and undid it. 'Right now, you can fill the flat with bookcases.'

I then reached for my trousers zip. Noah watched as I pulled them off. He took in my black lace matching underwear set.

'So much better than I ever imagined,' he said again. 'Lie down, Stevie.'

I backed up and lay down on the pillow as Noah shed his trousers too.

'I might need that in writing. About the bookcases,' I said, my eyes closing as Noah dropped kisses along my collarbone.

'You can have whatever you want in writing or otherwise,' he said, undoing my bra and letting it fall off me. 'You are so sexy, Stevie. I am a very, very lucky man.'

His hand cupped my breast as he leaned down to draw my nipple into his mouth.

'Yes, yes you are,' I replied, wrapping my leg around him, pulling him closer, wriggling against him to create the friction I was craving. 'You're also being far too slow,' I complained as he moved to my other breast.

Noah lifted himself off me and raised an eyebrow. 'I think I need to go even slower than this. Make sure you are really ready...'

'I'm ready,' I protested as he returned to kiss down the centre of my breasts towards my belly button. I fisted the sheets in my hand as his lips moved lower. 'But you're right, you better be sure,' I said, arching my back as Noah's lips brushed the edge of my lace underwear.

Noah laughed against me and then he slowly slid my knickers down my legs. I lifted my bum and he pulled them off, tossing them onto the floor. Settling between my legs, his arms hooked under my knees as he continued his kiss, lower and lower, until he brushed his tongue against me and I gasped with pleasure. I gripped the sheets harder and as he'd promised, he took his time, leaving me breathless.

'Noah,' I breathed as my legs trembled. 'I... oh my God, yes... wow,' I mumbled incoherently as his tongue did things to me I hadn't known I needed. I cried out seconds later and my legs fell down onto the bed as he sat up. 'Okay, going slow can be good,' I said, my whole body trembling from how good that had been. 'But I need you inside me now.'

'Hmmm... I could make you wait longer...' He leaned down to touch my face. I shook my head beneath him. His lips curved into a smile, showing me that delicious dimple. I reached out to touch it with my finger. 'So lucky,' he repeated as he slid his underwear off and lay down beside me. 'Come here,' he said, his voice husky.

'Oh, hang on, I just need to do something...' Smiling, I reached for my phone on the bedside table.

'If you tell me you're texting someone right now, I might die.'

'I thought you said slower was better,' I said, typing onto my phone, my back to him.

'That's before I was this hard,' he replied.

I bit back a giggle. I sent the email then put my phone down and turned back to face him.

'Okay, check your inbox,' I said. 'Does that sound like an innuendo?' I grinned at him.

Noah shook his head but reached for his trousers, pulling his phone out of the pocket.

I smiled as I watched him read the email I had just sent him, his eyes lighting up.

> Yes, I want to move in with you. And yes, I'll have a giant bookcase please. I never stopped loving you. And I never will xxx

He threw his phone down and pulled me towards him, wrapping his arms around me, holding me close on top of the covers.

'Stevie, I'm yours for however long you want me,' he said, kissing me gently. 'I'll call someone to build you the bookcase of your dreams, starting tomorrow.' He pulled back. 'And Annie Leon to beg forgiveness for making her redundant and to see if she wants to run sales and marketing. I hated every minute of letting the former staff go. Asking her back might make up for that a tiny bit. I should have pushed back to my father long before now.'

'That's a great idea,' I said. 'But can we stop talking? Tell me what to do.'

His dimple flashed. 'Roll on to your side,' he said, his voice full of need.

I turned over as he settled behind me. He wrapped his arms

around my waist and asked me to move my leg forwards. When I did, he slipped inside me.

'Oh,' I said as I felt his thrust through my whole body.

'Push back,' he said into my ear softly. He held me tightly as he moved and I pushed back against him. 'Jesus, just like that, darling.'

My heart lifted. Noah hadn't called me 'darling' since we broke up.

'This is so good,' I managed to gasp as we moved faster together.

'It can be better.' Noah's arm came around my body and when he touched me exactly where I needed him, I moaned loudly. 'God, your moans drive me crazy.'

'Noah, it's too good,' I cried. I moved my hand on top of his and entwined my fingers with his as a delicious burst of pleasure rolled through me. 'Oh wow.'

Noah turned my head so we were looking at one another.

'Fuck,' he said as our eyes met and he came inside me.

I pulled his lips to mine, marvelling at how we'd made our way back to each other. My hesitation, that tiny remaining slither of doubt, disappeared as we kissed breathlessly. My body went limp against his and he held me tightly.

Outside my window, the last of the autumn leaves were falling. My heart took the final leap and I let myself fall for Noah again.

But this time, it was sweeter and harder.

This time, I knew how much he loved me.

How he'd always loved me.

This time, we were for keeps.

EPILOGUE
AUTUMN THE FOLLOWING YEAR

I walked through London enjoying the kaleidoscope of colours on the trees above me. There was a beautiful breeze ruffling through my hair, causing the leaves to float down around me. My hands were warm though as I was clutching a pumpkin spiced latte.

I headed towards Noah's bookshop with a spring in my step. It had been the happiest year I could remember. Noah and I had grown closer than ever and I now lived in his riverside penthouse, and he had done what he had promised – a whole wall of the flat was covered by a floor-to-ceiling bookshelf filled with my favourite books. It was what all bookworms' dreams were made of.

But it wasn't just Noah that was making me happy; Turn the Pages had gone from strength to strength and I now headed up a new publicity team. I loved my job so much. It was strange at first working there without Noah but I knew he'd made the right decision when I saw how much he loved running the bookshop. And my friends and family were doing brilliantly – Liv had landed a book deal for her novel and I couldn't wait to be beside her for the journey to publication.

My phone vibrated and I checked it, seeing I had a new email.

From Noah.

Surprised, I stopped by the river to look at it, wondering why he'd email me when I was about to see him at the Book Nook.

Stevie,

It's been a long time since I wrote to you. I had no idea when I wrote that first email from New York that I would see you again, let alone spend the best year of my life with you. When it bounced back and I realised you'd cut off any way to contact you, I kept writing because you were the one who made sense of everything. I knew if I kept talking to you, somehow everything would work out okay. I lost so much but losing it all made me realise what I wanted from life. I knew that my parents had something special. And yours too. And I wanted that. I wanted to be in a relationship that had a strong foundation so we would know that, no matter what life threw at us, we could make it through together. I walked away from that once thinking that I didn't deserve it. And I regretted it so much but now I think I did the right thing.

We both grew so much in those five years apart. We discovered what we wanted. We became the people we are now. And being apart from you once has made me know I never want to do that ever again.

This year has been wonderful. You've helped me in more ways than you'll ever know. And I hope you know that I would do anything for you. I love you more than anything in this world. You are my past, present and future.

I was thinking today about the first time I went into a bookshop in New York. I picked up a book you loved and reading it helped me feel close to you even though we were miles apart. It made me fall in love with love stories like I'd fallen in love with you. I didn't tell you what that book was but I've found a first edition of it and I have it at the bookshop for you.

I can't wait to see you.

All my love always,

Noah.

Damn Noah and his beautiful emails.

I sniffed and wiped the mascara from where it rolled down my cheek with my tears. I probably looked like a panda now but I ploughed on to the bookshop, desperate to get my hands on my man and kiss him. I entered the alleyway. It was still such a cute cobbled street tucked away from the hustle and bustle of the city as if it had stepped into its own world and time. I looked up at the bookshop with a smile on my face. The place where our love story had started all those years ago. We had broken apart but Noah was right – we'd come back together so much stronger for it.

Opening the door and setting off the bell, I found the place empty except for Noah, who was behind the desk smiling up at me, flashing that dimple, his sleeves rolled up, glasses perched on his nose. My Noah.

'Where's this first edition then?' I asked him with a smile.

'Right here.' He beckoned me over.

'Oh my God,' I said slowly as I saw the book on the counter. '*Second Chances* by Deborah Day,' I said, touching the cover reverently. I looked up at him. 'I had no idea this was the book you meant.'

'I've been looking for a first edition ever since I saw you again so I could tell you. This book meant so much to me because of how much it meant to you.'

'It was my first romance book. My gateway book. My mum gave it to me. How did you find it?'

'Deborah found it,' he said. 'I asked her at the book launch if she knew where I could get one but it had had such a small printing that she wasn't sure but said she would help. It's taken a year for us to get our hands on it. And guess where the person lived who I bought it from?'

'New York,' I said, laughing.

'Yep. The irony!' Noah grinned. 'Open it up. Deborah signed it for you.'

'She's so sweet. I can't wait for her and Ed's wedding next month. Proof that love conquers—'

The words died on my lips as I opened the book. Deborah had signed it but underneath, Noah had written something else. Just like he'd done on that night we met and he'd asked me out for dinner.

But this time the question was a rather more permanent one.

Will you marry me?

Eyes shining, I lifted my gaze from the book and into Noah's chocolate-brown eyes.

'Is this question for me?'

Noah hurried around the counter and took my hand in his. 'I have wanted to ask you since the first time we kissed in this alleyway but I wanted to make sure we were on the same page. And to have this book to propose to you with. What do you think?'

He pulled a box out of his pocket and got down on one knee. He opened it up and a sparkling ring dazzled me.

'I told you that this was forever for me but is it forever for you too? Will you marry me, Stevie Phillips?'

I wondered if a face could crack from smiling too wide because mine actually hurt from beaming down at Noah.

'Hell, yes!' I grabbed the ring and slipped it on. 'It's gorgeous, Noah.'

'Just like you.' He got up and held me against the counter. 'Will you forgive me for being the dick who let you go?'

'As long as you never do it again,' I replied and pulled him in for a kiss. I had long forgiven him for leaving me because he was right – we'd had to become the people we were meant to be first. And now we were rock solid. I had no doubts about that. Noah was my past, present and future too.

'One more surprise...' He passed me a sheet of paper.

I scanned it, my eyes widening.

'Tickets to New York?' I looked at him. 'Four tickets?'

'You, me and your parents – Dad wants us to come for Christmas. What do you think?'

'I think I can't wait for you to show me around the city.'

Noah grinned and wrapped his arms around me. 'Good because I can't wait either. And we better bring an extra suitcase for all the books we're going to buy.'

'Perfect.'

He brushed his lips against mine and I shivered. I looked up at him when we pulled apart.

'From meet-cute to happy ever after,' I said with a wide smile.

'I like the sound of that,' Noah replied.

It turned out happy endings aren't just for romance books after all.

ACKNOWLEDGEMENTS

As soon as I finished writing *The Love Interest*, I knew that Stevie needed her own book. I loved her and Liv's friendship and the fact they are both hopeless romantics dreaming of a happy ending just like the ones in the books they love. I have worked in publishing and a bookshop myself so I had a lot of fun setting this book in both a publishing company and a bookshop. I really enjoyed creating a character determined to support romance novels – I hope you root for Stevie as much as I did while I was writing her story.

Thank you so much to my lovely agent Hannah Ferguson and the fabulous team at Hardman and Swainson for supporting me and my books! Thank you to my amazing editor Emily Yau – I'm so happy we got to do this again with *The Plot Twist*. This is for all the Emilys who work in publishing haha! A huge thank you to the incredible Boldwood team for all your hard work. Special thanks to Niamh Wallace, Nia Beynon, Isabelle Flynn, Claire Fenby, my copy editor Emily Reader, my proofreader Jennifer Davies and Alexandra Allden for the lovely cover. And Geri Allen for reading the audiobook. Thank you all for being nothing like Mr Matthews in this book ;)

Thank you and love always to my family and friends and my fellow authors who are always so supportive and kind. This was the last book I finished with my cat Harry by my side – thanks for being the best writing assistant, Harry. I'll miss you forever.

As always, I can't thank anyone reading this enough for

choosing to pick up one of my books. I dedicated this to romance readers – I love reading romance too and I'm so lucky that I get to write happy ever afters. I hope you enjoy this one xx

PLAYLIST FOR THE PLOT TWIST

Butterflies – Kacey Musgraves
I Wish You Would (Taylor's Version) – Taylor Swift
Plot Twist – Sigrid
Lost the Breakup – Maisie Peters
Something in the Orange – Zach Bryan
I Should Hate You – Gracie Abrams
bad idea right? – Olivia Rodrigo
The Best I Ever Had – Limi
I Can See You (Taylor's Version) – Taylor Swift
Ruin – USHER, Pheelz
I Remember Everything – Zach Bryan feat. Kacey Musgraves
I Hate This – Tenilla Arts
Wishful Drinking – Ingrid Andress, Sam Hunt
Loved By You – Chelsea Cutler
Can't Get Enough – Jennifer Lopez
We Belong Together – Mariah Carey
Plot Twist – The Shires
I Hope You Know – Sofia Carson

Your Bones – Chelsea Cutler
This Time Around – Jennifer Lopez
This Love (Taylor's Version) – Taylor Swift

ABOUT THE AUTHOR

Victoria Walters is the author of both cosy crime and romantic novels, including the bestselling Glendale Hall series. She has been chosen for WHSmith Fresh Talent, shortlisted for two RNA novels and was picked as an Amazon Rising Star.

Sign up to Victoria Walters' mailing list for news, competitions and updates on future books.

Visit Victoria's website: www.victoria-writes.com

Follow Victoria on social media:

- instagram.com/vickyjwalters
- facebook.com/VictoriaWaltersAuthor
- x.com/Vicky_Walters
- bookbub.com/authors/victoria-walters
- youtube.com/@vickyjwalters

ALSO BY VICTORIA WALTERS

The Love Interest

The Plot Twist

LOVE NOTES
LOVE IN EVERY CHAPTER

WHERE ALL YOUR ROMANCE
DREAMS COME TRUE!

THE HOME OF BESTSELLING
ROMANCE AND WOMEN'S
FICTION

WARNING:
MAY CONTAIN SPICE

SIGN UP TO OUR
NEWSLETTER

https://bit.ly/Lovenotesnews

Boldwood

Boldwood Books is an award-winning fiction publishing company seeking out the best stories from around the world.

Find out more at www.boldwoodbooks.com

Join our reader community for brilliant books, competitions and offers!

**Follow us
@BoldwoodBooks
@TheBoldBookClub**

Sign up to our weekly deals newsletter

https://bit.ly/BoldwoodBNewsletter

Made in the USA
Middletown, DE
17 June 2024